DIE LIKE AN EAGLE

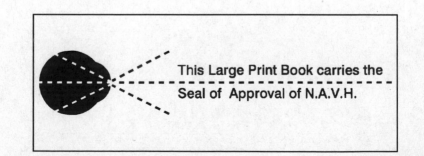

This Large Print Book carries the
Seal of Approval of N.A.V.H.

A MEG LANGSLOW MYSTERY

DIE LIKE AN EAGLE

DONNA ANDREWS

THORNDIKE PRESS
A part of Gale, Cengage Learning

GALE
CENGAGE Learning·

Farmington Hills, Mich • San Francisco • New York • Waterville, Maine
Meriden, Conn • Mason, Ohio • Chicago

GALE
CENGAGE Learning®

LIBRARY OF CONGRESS CATALOGING-IN-PUBLICATION DATA

Names: Andrews, Donna, author.
Title: Die like an eagle : a Meg Langslow mystery / by Donna Andrews.
Description: Large print edition. | Waterville, Maine : Thorndike Press, 2016. | Series: Thorndike Press large print mystery
Identifiers: LCCN 2016024576 | ISBN 9781410491671 (hardcover) | ISBN 1410491676 (hardcover)
Subjects: LCSH: Langslow, Meg (Fictitious character)--Fiction. | Women detectives--Fiction. | Murder--Investigation--Fiction. | Large type books. | GSAFD: Mystery fiction | Humorous fiction.
Classification: LCC PS3551.N4165 D54 2016b | DDC 813/.54--dc23
LC record available at https://lccn.loc.gov/2016024576

Published in 2016 by arrangement with St. Martin's Press, LLC

Printed in the United States of America
1 2 3 4 5 6 7 20 19 18 17 16

ACKNOWLEDGMENTS

I continue to be grateful for all the great folks at St. Martin's/Minotaur, including (but not limited to) Hector DeJean, Melissa Hastings, Paul Hoch, Andrew Martin, Sarah Melnyk, Talia Sherer, Emma Stein, and especially my editor, Pete Wolverton. And thanks again to David Rotstein and the art department for another beautiful cover.

More thanks to my agent, Ellen Geiger, and the staff at the Frances Goldin Literary Agency for handling the boring (to me) practical stuff so I can focus on writing.

Many thanks to the friends — writers and readers alike — who brainstorm and critique with me, give me good ideas, or help keep me sane while I'm writing: Stuart, Elke, Aidan and Liam Andrews, Chris Cowan, Ellen Crosby, Kathy Deligianis, Suzanne Frisbee, John Gilstrap, Barb Goffman, David Niemi, Alan Orloff, Art Taylor, Robin Templeton, and Dina Willner. Thanks for all kinds of moral support and practical help to my blog sisters and brother at the Femmes Fatales: Dana Cameron, Charlaine Harris, Dean James, Toni L.P. Kelner, Catriona McPherson, Kris Neri, Hank Phillipi Ryan, Mary Saums, Marcia Talley, and Elaine Viets. And thanks to all the TeaBuds for years of friendship.

And of course, Meg's adventures would not continue without the support of many readers — thank you yet again!

Die Like an Eagle was inspired by my nephews' many years of participation in youth baseball and basketball. They've learned so much about sportsmanship, teamwork, and the importance of hard work — if I'd known how good sports was at character-building, I wouldn't have neglected it in my own youth. The boys have also had many wonderful coaches and teammates over the years, nearly all of them much too nice to inspire any of the events in this book. In particular, I'd like to thank the Coker, Dornbusch, Griese, Hodinko, Jones, Kim, Kortum, Kupcis, Kramp, Neach, and Pierce families, who have come together to create a warm and supportive baseball family for the kids. Go Force!

CHAPTER 1

"Strike!"

"No fair! I wasn't ready!"

I glanced over at the field to see what was going on. My husband, Michael, in his role as assistant coach of the Caerphilly Eagles, was putting one of his players through batting practice. Probably seven-year-old Mason. They all looked alike with their baseball hats or batting helmets pulled low over their faces, but Mason was a good friend of Josh and Jamie, our twins, and I was pretty sure I recognized the voice.

"Mason, I asked if you were ready before I threw it," Michael said. "You said you were ready."

"But I wasn't really ready," Mason said. "Not *ready* ready. I was getting ready to be ready."

"In the game, you have to be ready when the umpire says 'Play ball,' " Michael said. "Are you ready now?"

Mason nodded.

"Ready ready?"

Mason nodded, and hunched his body fiercely as if to indicate his complete readiness to slam the ball.

Michael tossed another ball gently across the base. Mason swung mightily and caught the ball with the end of his bat, sending it gently dribbling into foul territory.

"Foul ball!" Michael called. "Better!"

"Good contact!" I shouted.

Several of the half-dozen fathers sitting with me on the bleachers glanced over in apparent surprise. Didn't they realize how important it was to encourage the kids when they achieved a breakthrough, like actually fouling the ball instead of striking out swinging or, worse, looking?

Evidently not. The cluster of fathers fixed their gaze back on the outfield, where Chuck Davis, the head coach, was drilling the rest of the team on throwing and catching. If I tried, I could probably have figured out which father belonged to which kid, by watching who winced when one of the kids missed a particularly easy catch. Or made a more-than-usually-bad throw.

I observed the action in the outfield for a few moments, noting that Josh and Jamie were definitely above average in the throw-

8

ing and catching department. Not surprising, since Michael loved baseball and had been playing catch with the boys since they were two or three.

"Wish Waterston would go out there and work on their form," one of the fathers muttered. "Let Davis handle the batting practice."

"Davis can't get the damned ball across the plate," another father muttered back.

"Well, yeah," the first father said.

"Damn," another father exclaimed, as Chuck himself missed a pretty easy catch. "Has that man ever played baseball?"

"I doubt it," another said, shaking his head.

I was losing patience with this particular collection of fathers. This was the third time I'd been to practice, and every time the same bunch were sitting there, glowering at the field while Michael and Chuck wrangled the dozen unruly little Eagles. If they had time to sit there in the bleachers, kibbitzing, why not help out?

And speaking of helping out . . .

I glanced down at my list and dialed another number. After four rings I got an answering machine. I was getting a lot of those today. Had I picked a busy time to call? Or were all the mothers of our players using their caller ID to dodge me?

"Hi," I said, after the beep. "This is Meg Langslow, the Team Mom for the Eagles. I'm still looking for some volunteers to help run the Snack Shack tomorrow on Opening Day. If you can help out, please let me know." I added my cell number and my e-mail address and hung up.

I glanced over at the posse of fathers. All of them had already either given me an excuse why neither they nor their wives could do Snack Shack duty tomorrow or said that they'd have to talk to their wives before committing.

"I give up." I shoved the list back into my purse and dialed one of my speed-dial numbers.

"Meg, dear," Mother said. "How is the boys' practice going?"

"Practice is going fine," I said. "My efforts to recruit volunteers, not so fine. I know we have at least a dozen family members coming to see tomorrow's first game. Do you think you could recruit a couple of them to help out in the Snack Shack?"

"Of course, dear," Mother said. "Nine to eleven, right? Leave it to me."

I hung up feeling very relieved, and pulled out the five-by-eight-inch three-ring binder that held my notebook-that-tells-me-when-to-breathe, as I called my giant to-do list. I flipped to the task section and pondered for a moment, my pen hovering over the item "Recruit Snack Shack volunteers." Technically, it was merely delegated, not done. But I'd delegated it to Mother. Her ability to draft people for volunteer work was legendary. And she'd be pulling from our family members, not the feckless parents of the boys' teammates. So I crossed the item out and added a new item for this evening: "Call Mother to see who she recruited for the Snack Shack."

I snapped the notebook closed, shoved it into my purse, and looked back at the field, feeling significantly less stressed. I took a deep breath and reminded myself to appreciate the day. The sun was warm, the sky was blue and cloudless — perfect baseball weather.

"Damn."

One of the fathers was standing up, staring at the outfield, fists clenched. Out in the field, Chuck appeared to be comforting a player who'd been hit in the eye with a ball. Michael was loping out to help.

"He should be fine," one of the other fathers said. The standing father nodded slightly, but his face was tense.

"I'm sure he'll be fine," I said. "At this

age, none of the kids can throw that hard. But your son would probably feel better if you went out to be with him."

"I can't," the standing father said.

"I'm sure Chuck and Michael wouldn't mind," I said. "For that matter, I doubt if they'd mind if any of you wanted to help out with practices. The kids have a lot to learn, and it's hard for two coaches to do it all."

"We can't," another father said. The others all shook their heads, and their faces wore looks of shock and horror.

"Especially not with him standing right there," another added. He pointed to center field, where a pudgy man in a too-tight brown t-shirt, a blue windbreaker, and a Yankees baseball cap was leaning over the fence, watching the action on the field.

"Who's that?" I asked.

"Biff," one said.

"Who's Biff?" I asked. Until lately, the only Biff I knew was a character in *Death of a Salesman* — Michael's Introduction to Acting students were always doing scenes from it.

"Biff Brown," one of them said. "The head of the league."

"And coach of one of the other coach-pitch teams," another said. "The Caerphilly Stoats."

"And he also coaches the Caerphilly Yankees at the majors level," the first one said. "You know, the eleven-to twelve-year-olds."

Out on the field, Michael had picked up the crying player and was carrying him in our direction. The kid's father began scrambling down from the bleachers.

"There's a Summerball rule that no one but official team staff can be on the field," another father said.

"During games," I said. The men began shaking their heads, which annoyed me, because I was pretty sure I was right. At Michael's request, I'd read the official Summerball Youth Baseball League rule book cover to cover, to make sure we weren't blindsided by any differences between that and the Little League rules he'd grown up with. In fact, I'd read the rules multiple times, along with the Little League rules and the official Major League Baseball rules — they'd been helping me cope with a bad stretch of insomnia.

"Local rule," one of the fathers explained.

"No one mentioned that there were special local rules," I said. "Where can I get a copy?"

"Oh, none of them are actually written

down anywhere," one of the fathers said. "Biff just sends them out whenever he decides he needs them."

Michael had reached the gate that separated the field from the bleachers and was holding the injured player while his waiting dad examined the affected eye. I grabbed my tote bag and hurried to meet them.

"I've got my first aid kit if it's needed," I said.

"Doesn't look too bad," the dad said.

"I think he'll be all right," Michael said. "Getting hit by a baseball's pretty painful, but it goes away fast. Right, Chase?"

The kid nodded. He was still sniffling a little, but looked as if he was feeling better. Michael set him on his feet beside his father.

"If he feels well enough to keep on practicing, that's great," Michael said. "And if he doesn't, just be sure to have him here by eight thirty tomorrow morning so we can do a little warm-up before the game."

"Okay," the father said.

"I'm fine," Chase said. "Can I go back to practice?"

Michael and Chase's father peered at his eye for a little while longer, and Michael performed the league-mandated tests to make sure Chase wasn't showing signs of concussion. They finally gave in to the boy's assurances that he was fine and wanted to practice. The fathers and I watched with approval as Michael and Chase walked back to the outfield together. Michael, at six foot four, dwarfed Chase, even though he was leaning down to demonstrate some fine point in the use of a baseball glove. Perhaps the trick of holding it so missed balls hit the chest rather than the face. It was a cute scene, so I pulled out my phone and took a few photos.

Then I turned back to the posse of fathers.

"Okay, let me get this straight," I said. "This Biff person makes up rules as he goes along and just expects people to follow them."

"That's the way he was when he ran the local Little League," one of the fathers said. "I don't expect him to do it any differently now that he's running Summerball."

"He's the reason we're in Summerball instead of Little League," another father said. "Biff used to run the local Little League, but last year we all got fed up and formed a Summerball league."

"And the Little League just imploded because almost no one tried out," another said. "Just Biff's kids and his cronies' kids. For the fall season, pretty much everyone else came over to Summerball. Lemuel

Shiffley ran the league, and everything was great. Then Lem got sick."

I nodded. Lem's nephew, Caerphilly Mayor Randall Shiffley, was both a good friend and my current boss, so I knew all about Lem's recent cancer diagnosis and his still very uncertain prognosis.

"We were trying to give Lem some time to figure out if he wanted to go on with running the league," a father said. "We figured maybe one of us could fill in for him till he got better, but we didn't want to push it if he wasn't ready to delegate. And suddenly Summerball National informs us that Biff is our new league president."

"The jerk got the job on the strength of his years of experience running the local Little League," another said. "Talk about irony."

"We thought you and Michael must be cronies of his," another father said. "But I guess you're just newcomers, like poor Chuck."

They all laughed, and shook their heads.

"Looks as if Michael and I should be talking to you guys," I said. "To help us stay out of trouble."

"You have no idea," one said. "By the way, I'm Evan Thornton. My son's Zack. Number twelve."

"Luis Espinoza," said another. "Mine's Manny; number nine."

The other fathers introduced themselves in the same fashion with both their names and their kids' names and uniform numbers.

"Meg Langslow — Waterston," I added. "I go by my maiden name professionally, so if I absentmindedly don't answer one of the kids who calls me Mrs. Waterston, just yell 'Meg!' "

They laughed at that. They probably thought I was kidding. There were still times when I'd hear someone calling for Mrs. Waterston and look around to see where Michael's mother was.

"Maybe we should go back to the bleachers and pretend to be just watching the practice," Evan said. "We don't want Biff to think we're plotting anything."

We all arranged ourselves in the bleachers again — though now, instead of the fathers sitting at the far left and me at the far right, we were all in a clump in the middle.

"I have to say," Luis said. "Even though we thought he must be one of Biff's cronies, we had come to appreciate Michael. At least he has some skill at the game."

"Yeah," said another — Vince Wong, if memory served. "I don't think poor Chuck's ever played an inning of baseball in his life."

17

"All of us volunteered to be coaches," Evan explained. "But all of us have been blackballed because of past clashes with Biff."

"When our older sons were playing," Luis added. "Are Josh and Jamie your oldest?"

"And only," I said.

"That explains it," Luis said. "You haven't had any prior experience with Biff."

"That's good," another father said. "If he doesn't hate her, or Michael or Chuck, he won't try to mess with the team as much."

"Mess with the team?" I echoed.

"You'll see," Vince said.

"If you've met him, you probably think we're crazy," Luis added. "He can be very friendly. Talks a good game."

"And it's all talk," Vince said.

"He promises improvements to the field, but every year there's less grass and the bumps and ruts get worse," Luis went on. "Eventually, he says, we will use the profits from food sales to build real bathrooms and a new Snack Shack with running water, and still all we have is that miserable porta-potty." He pointed to the object in question, painted in a color of brown that was unfortunately all too reminiscent of its intended purpose. "Apparently it takes all the profits the Snack Shack earns to keep

18

the field in its current miserable state."

"He must not be managing the money very well," I said. "Has anyone ever taken a look at the books?"

"No, and asking to is what got several of us blackballed," Vince said. "Don't even think of it."

"So Biff's teams will continue to win all the playoffs," Evan said. "And he'll coach the All-Star teams, which will always include his kids. And we'll all do our best to make sure that Biff's antics don't spoil our kids' enjoyment of the game."

"If I didn't love baseball so much, I'd try to steer Henry to soccer," Vince said. "Here we thought we'd gotten away from Biff."

"If anything bad ever happens to him, I hope we all have alibis," Luis said.

"We should be so lucky," Evan sighed. "No, I'm afraid we're all in for six more years of him."

"Only five," Luis said. "His youngest is eight. Almost nine."

"You never know," I said. "Maybe he'll move away. Get transferred or something."

"Unlikely," Luis said. "He's his own boss. Owns a local construction company."

"A local construction company?" I echoed. I had a bad feeling about this. "Wait a minute — Biff *Brown*? Does he own

19

Brown Construction Company?"

"That's him," Evan said.

I winced. Biff Brown might not hate me yet. But only because he didn't yet know who I was.

CHAPTER 2

Just then Michael and Chuck called for a water break, and the herd of small boys thundered toward us. Some of them went straight to the dugout where they had left their water bottles, and the rest swarmed off the field to collect water bottles from their fathers and beg for Gatorade and bubble gum.

I found myself looking at the porta-potty. I'd been here half a dozen times before for practices — how had I missed BROWN CONSTRUCTION COMPANY stenciled on its side? To say nothing of the much more visible graffiti advising us, in bright yellow paint, that *Brown stinks!* Of course, usually when I was at practice, I was trying to shove the annoyances of my day job out of mind so I could focus on Michael and the boys. Well, and the annoyances of my volunteer job as Team Mom. Still — was it a good thing or a bad thing that until now I'd missed Brown Construction's connection to baseball?

With the fathers' attention elsewhere, I walked a little away from the bleachers, pulled out my cell phone, and punched another of my speed-dial buttons.

"I'm working on it," Randall Shiffley said.

"Working on what?" Technically, ever since I'd accepted the position of executive assistant to the mayor, Randall had been my boss. But he often behaved as if I was the one giving orders. Perhaps I'd done a better job than I thought of learning Mother's people-management skills.

"Whatever you're calling about," he said. "Everything you've asked me to do is on my to-do list, and I'm motoring through it. Don't want anything to interfere with my enjoyment of Opening Day tomorrow."

"What I'm calling about isn't on your to-do list," I said.

"Not yet anyway."

"How did the county end up giving Brown Construction the contract to do the renovations to the town square?"

"Damn," Randall said. "Yeah, that would have been before your time. What's Brown done now?"

"Absolutely nothing as far as I can tell," I said. "I know we still have six weeks before the Memorial Day celebrations, but it doesn't look as if he's even started. And he's dodging my phone calls. I've left daily messages on his voice mail for the last several weeks. And followed them up with e-mails, which he's also ignored."

"Yeah, that's Biff all right."

"So, getting back to my original question — why is Brown doing the town square? Instead of, for example, your family's company, which usually comes in on time and under budget and never fails to return my calls."

"I appreciate the vote of confidence," he said. "Trouble is, we started to get complaints about nepotism. Mainly from other companies we beat in a fair competition for contracts, but still — it's a problem. That's why I put my cousin Cephus in charge of the construction company for the time being. And then I decided we need to spread the work around a little. Award a few contracts to other firms, even if they weren't necessarily the absolute lowest bidder, as long as they weren't too far off. And even if those of us in the trade don't consider them the most qualified."

"Oh, great," I said. "So now we're hiring overpriced, unqualified contractors just to keep them from suing us?"

"Less qualified," Randall said. "And not for anything mission-critical like the school roof. No way I'd let them get that. I figured the town square's pretty safe — mostly regrading, resodding, doing a little spruce-up on the bandstand. Only so badly they can screw that up."

"You sure about that? Because under the circumstances, I suspect Biff's company's the one maintaining the county ball fields, and they're not exactly in a condition that would inspire confidence in Brown Contracting's landscaping abilities." The rehydrated kids were back on the field where, as we'd been talking, I'd already seen two kids miss balls that had taken bad hops, thanks to the extraordinary number of bumps, dents, divots, hillocks, tussocks, molehills, and patches of tall dead weeds afflicting the field. And was it just the angle I was viewing it from, or was second base a good foot too far to the left?

"Good point," Randall said. "And yeah, Biff's in charge of maintaining the ball fields — that's part of our contract with the league. If I'd known Lem was going to get sick on us, I wouldn't have agreed to that. Maybe you can figure out a way to wrestle that back from him. And if he does a half-baked job of renovations on the town square, or doesn't get around to it by his deadline, which as I'm sure you have already noticed is the Monday before Memorial Day weekend, I can send in my guys to get the work done in time for the celebration, and then we'll have solid evidence to show why we're never giving them any more contracts."

"So I gather the optimal outcome is having them fail so we never have to use them again," I said. "Under the circumstances, would you like me to stop bugging Biff so much?"

"No, you keep on giving him the benefit of all the encouragement and reminders you'd give any other contractor. I have every confidence that Biff's capable of hanging himself in spite of all your efforts."

With that we signed off. I looked back into the outfield where Biff was still leaning over the fence.

Great. If I did my job for Caerphilly, I'd probably end up angering Biff and ending what had apparently been a rare stretch of relative peace for the Eagles. Maybe I could explain to Randall and get him to take over nagging Biff?

No. Hell, no. If Biff wanted work from Caerphilly, he'd have to fulfill the terms of his contract, and that didn't just mean putting in a lick and a promise on the town square, the way he'd done with the ball field. The town square had damn well better be in pristine condition, or I wasn't going to sign off on payment. For that matter, I was going to have the county attorney take a look at the contract between Caerphilly and Summerball, to see if we had any scope for forcing Biff to improve the field. And if Biff thought he could take out his resentment on my boys — or my husband . . .

I drew myself up to my full five feet ten and glared at Biff.

Obviously he couldn't really see me, but I was almost convinced he felt the heat of my stare. He glanced at his watch and then started walking along the fence on the first-base side of the field. I looked at my own watch. Only five minutes to six, when practice was over, and the Eagles would be expected to clear the field promptly to make way for the team that would be practicing from six to seven.

The Eagles were occupying the third-base dugout. Over in the first-base dugout, another dozen or so kids were unpacking their gear. It was only practice, so they weren't in uniform, but at least half of them wore brown t-shirts or hats with the word STOATS in bright gold letters.

I strolled back to the Eagles' side of the field where, in my absence, one of the fathers had fallen off the bleachers and banged his head. No, actually one of the bleacher seats had come off and dumped him unceremoniously on the ground.

"I'll be fine," he was saying to the two others who were helping him up and dusting him off.

"Let's put that seat back on," I said.

"No, let's leave it where it fell," the fallen father said. "Maybe it will inspire Biff to get the bleachers fixed."

"Fat chance," another said. "We should probably leave it down there so no one else comes to grief on it. If we just stick it back on the way it was, someone else could really hurt himself."

"I actually had in mind putting it back properly." I rummaged through my tote, pulled out a wrench, and then picked up the bolt I could see had fallen on the ground. "I noticed at our last practice that a lot of things out here were falling apart, so I brought some tools. If a couple of you will hold the seat in place, I can bolt it back together."

We managed to find all but two of the bolts that had fallen out, and luckily I also had a slotted screwdriver large enough to tighten the loose screws on the side supports.

"That should hold for now," I said. "And I'm sure I have bolts the right size in my workshop. I'll bring some tomorrow to finish this off properly."

"Wow," one of the men said. "I don't think I know many women who travel with a full tool kit in their purses."

"You probably don't know many women blacksmiths," I said. "Is that Biff's team over in the other dugout, getting ready to practice when we finish?"

"Yeah," one of the fathers said. "As usual, we get the five-to-six slot, the one that means a lot of us have to leave work early to get the kids here."

"And Biff's team gets the six-to-whenever slot," another added. "This time of year, they get at least an extra half hour of daylight, and if you think they're not using it, drop by here at seven thirty and you'll see them still hard at work."

"Probably not a good idea, dropping by to spy on him," another said. "That's how I got blackballed."

"I thought it was because you complained about prices in the Snack Shack."

"Could be," the first said. "It's not like he ever tells you why you're out. Suddenly your

28

e-mails don't get answered and you can volunteer to coach or serve on the board all you like, you'll never get picked."

Michael and Chuck, surrounded by their team, were strolling back toward us. I was struck by the contrast between the Eagles and the group now occupying the first-base dugout. The Eagles, resplendent in their black-and-red uniform t-shirts, were chatting with each other and with the coaches, skipping about, tossing balls back and forth, laughing — they were all smiling and happy. The kids in the dugout were scurrying and anxious, jumping when Biff or one of the other coaches barked an order. Not happy kids.

"You know, I have an idea," I said. "Michael and I live just a few miles down the road. Why don't you all bring the boys over to our house for a while?"

"Against the rules to have outside practices," one of the fathers said. They all looked anxious, and some of them glanced over their shoulders as if afraid Biff might have heard.

"No, no," I said. "We're not going to break the league rules. There will be no unauthorized practices." The anxious faces of the fathers relaxed a little. "But there's nothing wrong with trying to let the boys get to know each other and build up a little more team spirit, is there? Michael and I are having a picnic tonight at our house to welcome some visiting relatives. Why don't you all come? And bring your families?"

"I suppose that could be fun," one of them said, sounding rather puzzled.

"No actual harm in it," said another, as if trying to convince himself.

"I'd have to check with the wife," said a third.

"After all, we should do something to celebrate the start of the holiday," I said, in case any of them had forgotten that they had both Friday and Monday off due to Founder's Day Weekend, a town and county holiday. "And Michael has set up a pretty nice little baseball field in our backyard. Well, in my parents' cow pasture, which is right across the fence from our backyard. So if the boys brought their bats and gloves — I'm sure they're tired of practicing, but if they felt like having a little pickup game . . . ?"

Light dawned in the circle of faces.

"Awesome," one said. As if they'd rehearsed the maneuver, the tight-knit knot of fathers split apart as each one pulled out his cell phone, took a few steps away from the others, and began punching buttons.

"Honey," I heard one say, "do we have anything on tonight? . . . Well, can we skip it? We're invited to a baseball team picnic at the Waterstons. Yes, it's important."

As I strolled toward our car, passing other fathers on their cell phones, I caught scraps of other, similar conversations.

"Great idea," Michael said. "I might have suggested it myself, but I had no idea we were having a picnic tonight."

"Well, we are now." I had pulled out my own cell phone and was speed-dialing again. "Mother? Do you think you could organize a picnic at our house?"

"Of course, dear." She was almost purring at the idea. Next to decorating, entertaining was Mother's favorite pastime. "When, and for how many people?"

"In about an hour," I said. "For three or four dozen people on top of however many relatives have come to town for Opening Day. A lot of them kids — we're entertaining the boys' baseball team and their families."

"About a hundred, then," she said. "No problem. See you in an hour, dear."

I hung up to find Michael staring at me and grinning.

"I'm not sure which surprises me more," he said. "That you just ordered your mother

31

to organize a picnic for a hundred people on an hour's notice, or the fact that she agreed to do it so readily."

"I didn't order her," I said. "I asked her. She sounded delighted. But a hundred people — did she think I was lowballing the number of baseball guests, or do we really have forty or fifty relatives in town for Opening Day?"

"Could be," Michael said. "I'm delighted by how many diehard baseball fans there are in your family."

Yes, we had a lot of baseball fans, and also a lot of Josh and Jamie fans. And when my relatives added in the likelihood — which I'd just made a certainty — of having at least one grandiose family party during their stay . . .

"I hope a hundred isn't an underestimate," I said with a sigh. "And that not too many of them are planning to stay at our house."

"We'll manage," Michael said. "I'd better go round up our three."

"Three?" I echoed. "Oh, right — we're giving Adam Burke a ride. Shall I call his grandparents to ask if he can come to the picnic?"

"He was coming over after practice anyway for a playdate," Michael said. "Why don't you call and invite them to the picnic?

I'm sure Minerva and the chief would both enjoy it."

With that he strolled off toward the dugout.

I pulled out my cell phone and was about to call Minerva Burke, Adam's grandmother. But it was Thursday. And 6:00 P.M. Minerva was director of the New Life Baptist Church's justly famous gospel choir, and Thursday evenings from six to eight were one of their regular practice times. So instead I called Chief Burke.

"Hi, it's Meg," I said when he answered. "Nothing's wrong," I added, because I'd long ago figured out that the chief was a bit of a worrywart when it came to his grandkids. "Adam's playdate with Josh and Jamie is still on, but I wanted to tell you that we're having a big picnic for visiting relatives, and a lot of the kids on the team are coming with their families, and you and Minerva are more than welcome to join us when you're free."

"Thank you kindly," he said. "We wouldn't be able to get there until after choir practice, but if you think it will still be going on then, we'd be delighted to visit a while before we take Adam home."

"We'll see you sometime after eight, then," I said. "And Adam's brothers are welcome, too. The more the merrier." And then, since the chief seemed to be in a mellow mood, I decided to lead up to a question that had just occurred to me. "And since we've got a bunch of sports-crazy kids coming, all armed with the equipment they brought to practice, it's possible that baseball may occur. It'll be nice to have another witness that it's just a pickup game, in case Biff Brown accuses of us of having an illicit practice."

"I will be happy to defend the Eagles' honor should the occasion arise," he said. "I see you've made Mr. Brown's acquaintance."

"Not formally," I said. "But his reputation precedes him. Does Biff have anything to do with Adam getting traded onto the Eagles?"

"He has everything to do with it," the chief said. "The boy shows signs of being a handy little ball player —"

"I'd noticed," I put in.

"Thank you. And there was no way in Hades Minerva and I were going to let Biff anywhere near him. I had a word with Michael, just to say that I'd rather have Adam playing for him, with a couple of kids he knew well, and we cooked up the carpool scheme to justify it. But I didn't give Michael the whole story because — well, I hate to speak ill of someone, and I thought I'd give him — and you — the chance to form your own opinions of Mr. Brown."

"I'm afraid my opinion is already a negative one," I said. "And I've never even spoken to the man. Although I've been trying to, ever since Randall assigned me the job of making sure Brown Construction fulfilled the terms of its contract with the town of Caerphilly."

"Good luck with that," the chief said. "Because you're going to need it. See you this evening."

I hung up and was about to head back to the Twinmobile, as we called the van we'd acquired when the boys were born. But as I turned, I almost collided with a woman who had been hovering nearby.

"Sorry," I said. And then I frowned slightly, because it occurred to me to wonder what she was doing here. She wasn't an Eagle mother — I knew all of them. Which meant she had probably dropped off one of the Stoats.

So what was she doing sneaking up behind me and eavesdropping on my conversation with the chief? Probably planning to tattle on us to Biff, I realized, as she backed away from me slightly, in the direction of the

Stoats dugout.

She was short and slender, and looked to be about my age, although her hair was graying and she was huddled into a thick brown sweater jacket as if braced against extreme cold, even though it was a warm April day. Was she ill? Her face was unlined, but pale and drawn. She was wearing her right arm in a sling, and in its folds I could see that her fingers emerged from a white cast or possibly a very bulky bandage.

"Can I help you?" I asked.

She shook her head, then turned and fled back to the parking lot. I saw her get into a battered, far-from-new compact car. But she didn't drive away.

Was she waiting till I left to tell Biff about our picnic plans? Maybe I'd absorbed a little too much of the Eagle fathers' anxiety about Biff. She was probably just waiting out her kid's practice. The ball field was only a couple of miles from our house, but some-one who lived at the far side of the county might find it more convenient to stay.

Just then, Michael and the boys came back, and I was plunged into the noisy chaos of making sure all three small Eagles were properly belted in and that their baseball bags were in the back and appeared to contain all the hats, gloves, batting gloves,

36

balls, sunglasses, cleats, and other equipment they'd arrived with. Michael showed up with a small armload of similar items that had been left behind in our dugout.

"We should be able to get all this back to the owners at the picnic," he said.

I glanced back at the field. I didn't see the woman who'd been eavesdropping. Biff's players were lined up along the first baseline, and he was walking slowly along in front of them with his hands clasped behind his back and a scowl on his face.

Michael followed my line of sight.

"The general inspecting his troops," he said, sotto voce.

"More like the warden putting the fear of God into the new prisoners," I said. "Josh and Jamie are never playing on any team he coaches."

"Agreed," Michael said, as we climbed into the Twinmobile. "Party time, guys!"

The small Eagles cheered excitedly as we lurched out of the ramshackle parking lot and headed for home.

CHAPTER 3

I wouldn't have asked Mother to organize a party on such short notice if I hadn't been pretty certain she could do it. But when I arrived home and saw the scale of what she'd pulled together, I was impressed. And more than a little suspicious that she'd been planning all along to surprise us with a party.

Someone had strung up a large GO EAGLES! banner on the front porch, and an even larger EAGLES RULE! banner draped the side of the barn. Our entire herd of picnic tables had been deployed in the backyard and covered with plastic tablecloths in black and red — the Eagles' uniform colors. The tables were already half-covered with food, and people were still arriving bearing plates or bowls of food and cans or bottles of beverages. Someone was cooking barbecue somewhere — I couldn't see the grill, but the tangy smell of the sauce filled the yard. And everywhere cheerful people were introducing themselves, as Team Eagle met the family Hollingsworth.

I realized that since I was, at least technically, the hostess, I should probably pitch in to help with some of the preparations. And as Team Mom I should make an effort to get to know all of the family members. And this might be one of my best chances to gather more information on the looming menace of Biff — some of the families had older children who'd played local baseball, so they probably had stories and insights to share.

I could do all of that. But I couldn't do it all at once. And I wasn't going to do any of it at the moment. I was going to find a place where I could keep an eye on things while doing the yoga breathing exercises my cousin Rose Noire was always urging me to use when something stressed me. Just thinking about Biff stressed me. And in case the breathing wasn't enough, I snagged a glass of white wine from one of the picnic tables and my jaw dropped at the selection of food. Platters of cold cuts and cheeses, several different kinds of bread, freshly grilled hot dogs, hamburgers and brats, tossed salads, pasta salads, congealed salads, potato salad, cole slaw, crudités and dip,

chili, roasted ears of corn, green bean cas-
seroles, cakes, pies, cookies, bowls of fresh
cut fruit — where had all this food come
from in such a hurry?

More and more people poured into the
yard — how many relatives had Mother
invited? Because most of these had to be
relatives; there were only twelve kids on the
team.

Chill, I reminded myself. I perched on the
back steps, sipping and breathing.

"Mrs. Waterston? Mrs. Waterston?"

I tried to remember the name of the small,
blond, freckle-faced Eagle who was dancing
from foot to foot in front of me. Luckily I
already knew four of the herd — Adam
Burke, Mason, and my two. Also luckily,
our crew was fairly ethnically diverse — I
was pretty sure this kid wasn't a Wong, a
Takahashi, or a Patel. And he wasn't Ben,
the second black kid on the team, after
Adam. I'd already made a note to ask Ben's
parents how to pronounce Nzeogwu, so I
could prepare a cheat sheet for announcers
at the games. And I could recognize Chase
by the black eye he'd acquired during
practice. So by process of elimination, this
was either Zack Thornton, Manuel Espinoza, or Tommy Davis. He didn't resemble
Chuck Davis or Luis Espinoza —

"What do you need — Zack, right?" I asked aloud.

"Yes, ma'am," he said. "May I use your bathroom?"

"Of course," I said. "Whenever you need to. Go in the back door; it's the door on the right-hand wall."

I jerked my thumb over my shoulder at the back door and smiled with satisfaction as he scampered past me, and I could clearly see THORNTON emblazoned across his back. Odds were within a few weeks I'd know Zack's cute, pug-nosed face as well as any of the boys' friends. And I'd have strong opinions about whether he was a friend I wanted to encourage, and I'd probably know enough about his parents to either rejoice that I'd made new friends or hope we didn't run into each other after baseball season was over. But for now I focused on fixing his face in my mind. Zack.

"Meg!" Grandfather barked, startling me out of my reverie about the joys of the rest of the baseball season. "You need to do something."

"About what?" I asked.

"Your grandmother!"

"What's she doing?"

"Making a spectacle of herself!" He snorted as if in disgust and clomped off.

"What's the matter?" I asked. "Stealing the limelight from you?"

But he was already too far away to hear me — probably a good thing for continued family harmony. And it occurred to me that perhaps I should see what my grandmother Cordelia was up to. After all, this wasn't just any party — at least half the people here were relatives, many of them eccentric if not downright peculiar. If Cordelia was managing to distinguish herself in *this* company, maybe I should be worried. Or at least forewarned.

The party was in full swing. My brother, Rob, had hitched Groucho to the llama cart and was giving people rides around the llama pen. A croquet game was in progress in the backyard — presumably an Xtreme Croquet game, since the playing field was dotted with lawn chairs, picnic tables, and free-range Welsummer chickens, and the players were using some of my wrought-iron flamingo lawn ornaments instead of mallets. But most of the crowd was gathered along the fence that separated our yard from my parents' cow pasture, where Dad and Michael had set up the baseball diamond — rough, but serviceable, and absolutely accurate to the Summerball league standards. At least half of them were wearing either red-and-black Caerphilly Eagles t-shirts or regular clothing in the team colors.

I didn't see Cordelia in the sea of faces lined up along the fence. But I heard her voice.

"Okay, point to your target! Eagle arm! That's it!"

Cordelia, looking quite at home in her Eagles t-shirt, was standing in the pasture with four small Eagles lined up facing her. All four boys were pointing with their baseball-gloved left hands toward the side of the cowshed, where someone had affixed six or seven paper archery targets. The players had their right arms drawn back and crooked into a J-shape. Cordelia was walking down the line, inspecting their form, making small corrections, and then nodding approval.

"Now let's throw." She took a position beside the boys, and adopted the same pose. "Pick a target on the shed wall. Ready! Aim! Throw!"

Five baseballs took flight across the pasture toward the cowshed. Four of the balls fell short of the targets, but not by nearly as much as I'd have expected from seeing the same four boys throw at practice. And all four were on a straight line to the target.

Cordelia's ball hit the bull's-eye with a loud thud.

The dozen or so people lined up along the fence behind the throwers cheered and waved little black-and-red pennants. I wasn't sure if they were responding to the boys' throws or my grandmother's. Maybe both.

"How'd the boys' grandmother learn to play baseball so well?" one of the fathers asked me.

"Great-grandmother, actually," I said. "And I plan on asking her that myself after the picnic."

He laughed, obviously under the impression I was joking. I was serious — since we'd only found my long-lost grandmother a few years ago, I really didn't know how she had acquired her baseball skills. We were all still getting to know one another. I hadn't even figured out what to call her. Grandmother? Grandma? Granny? None of the usual names seemed to fit, so I thought of her as Cordelia and mostly didn't call her anything. Occasionally I referred to her aloud as Cordelia, and I had the sneaking suspicion she knew this and didn't really mind.

In another part of the pasture, several of the fathers were hitting fly balls to half a dozen energetic little Eagles, including Josh and Jamie. And at home plate, batting practice was in session. Michael was tossing the ball — it was one of his outstanding skills as a baseball coach, the ability to toss the ball with astonishing accuracy at just the right speed for relatively inexperienced hitters. Since we were currently playing at the "coach pitch" level, in which the batters faced not balls thrown by pitchers their own age but the familiar gentle tosses made by one of their coaches, Michael's skill augured well for the team's success. One of the fathers was behind the plate — possibly Vince Wong, although it was hard to tell since his face was hidden behind a catcher's mask. In between, Adam Burke was at the plate, and beside him a whippet-thin blond woman in khaki shorts and a Caerphilly College t-shirt was making corrections to his grip and his stance.

"Tory's amazing, isn't she?" I turned to see that Chuck Davis had come up to lean on the pasture fence beside me and was beaming at the batting practice with visible pride.

"Your wife?" I guessed.

He nodded.

"She seems to know a lot about baseball." Not that I was an expert myself — except maybe when it came to the rule books, thanks to all my recent insomnia. But I could see that Michael and the father in catcher's gear weren't objecting to what she was showing the kid — if anything, they were nodding in approval.

"Yeah, she's definitely where Tommy gets his athletic ability," Chuck said. "Me, I have two left feet and more than the usual number of thumbs, but Tory's a whiz at any sport she plays. Baseball's always been her favorite, though. I think if this country had a really competitive, organized professional women's baseball league, she'd have tried out in a heartbeat, and I bet she'd have made it."

"So she went into coaching instead?" I asked. The more I watched Tory work with Adam, the better his swing got — clearly she had a gift for teaching the sport.

"No, she went into nuclear physics instead," he said. "Got her doctorate from Cal Tech. She teaches at Caerphilly College now. We just moved to town in the fall, when she got the post. I can't tell you how excited she was to see Tommy starting to play ball."

"Feel free to tell me to mind my own business, but was there a reason she didn't volunteer to coach Summerball? Workload at the college, for example? I mean, you're doing a great job, but —"

"No, I'm doing a wretched job," Chuck said. "Anything the boys have learned at practice, it's mostly because of Michael, and maybe just a little because Tory teaches me all kinds of drills to pass on to the boys. And the drills help, too, as long as Michael's there to help me run them. It should have been Tory, but the guy who runs the league never even responded to her application. So when they sent out the second or third call for coaches, I applied, and got accepted within an hour. Kind of discouraging, really. And we figured, okay, I'd be the coach in name and she'd do the actual work, but we quickly figured out that was a no go. Not if we didn't want to get kicked out of the league. It's frustrating. I mean, coming from Northern California we knew there would be trade-offs, moving to a small southern town, although we were hoping that since it was a college town — not that Caerphilly isn't a lovely place —"

"And we're not all Neanderthals," I said. "Just a few of us — including, unfortunately, the jerk who's running the local Summer-ball league at the moment."

"At the moment?" Chuck echoed. "Does that mean there's some hope he won't be running it indefinitely?"

"I have no idea," I said. "I only figured out today what a menace Biff Brown is, so I haven't yet had a chance to figure out what we can do about him. But I'm putting it on my to-do list."

I pulled out my notebook, flipped it open to the proper section, and wrote "find way to deal with Biff Brown" as a new task. I frowned slightly, because it wasn't really a very satisfactory task.

"Is that the famous notebook-that-tells-you-when-to-breathe?" Chuck said. "I've heard about that from Michael. I feel better already, just knowing Biff's in your sights."

"Coach Chuck! Coach Chuck!" Two of the Eagles were running toward us. "It's a Biff alert!"

I glanced out at the field. Suddenly, instead of a glove and a baseball, Cordelia was holding a bow and arrow, and the four players were gathered around her observing a demonstration of how to nock the arrow into the bowstring. Someone had led Harpo, another of the llamas, out to home plate and Michael, Tory, Adam, and Vince were stowing the last of the baseball equipment into the two hampers slung across the llama's back. Instead of shagging fly balls, the fielders were running about the outfield playing a noisy game of tag, while the three fathers who'd been hitting the flies were standing together in a clump. From the way they were pointing one would assume they were holding an animated discussion about several of Dad's Dutch Belted cows, who were hanging their heads over the fence from the next pasture as if they enjoyed watching our human antics while chewing their cuds. If you looked closely, you could see the small heap of baseball gloves by the fathers' feet, but no doubt Harpo would be making a visit there in a minute.

"Good job, boys," Chuck said. "We shouldn't have to do this," he added, turning to me. "But until you succeed in ousting Biff, no sense giving him anything to use against us. We want to spend our time playing baseball, not fighting with the league."

Until I succeed in ousting Biff. No pressure. And how had "dealing with Biff" escalated into ousting him? Though it could come to that.

"Well, this could be useful," I said. "Biff stopping by, that is. As it happens, I've been trying to talk to him for a while."

"Talk to him about what?" Chuck suddenly looked very, very anxious. "You're not going to do anything rash, are you? I mean —"

49

"Nothing about baseball," I said. "Don't worry."

I headed back toward the house, scanning the crowd for Biff.

He wasn't among the group doing Tai Chi under my cousin Rose Noire's direction. He hadn't snatched a wrought-iron flamingo to join the croquet players. He wasn't in the crowd gathered around my grandfather, who was showing off a hawk from the raptor rehabilitation program at his zoo. Or maybe the hawk came from the Willner Wildife Refuge — Caroline Willner, owner of the refuge and Grandfather's frequent ally in animal welfare missions, was beaming proudly as people inspected the hawk, but since she was as short and round as Grandfather was tall and gangly, I hadn't initially spotted her. And it was an unusual-looking hawk — I was tempted to go over to take a closer look, but watching the hawk wasn't getting me any closer to locating Biff. Remembering his pudgy shape, I headed for the picnic tables.

Sure enough, there he was, eyeing the dessert table. But not eating. He appeared to be yelling at two ladies who were standing behind the table. One was my monumentally shy cousin Priscilla, and the other was an elderly Indian lady in a pink-and-purple sari. Priscilla looked ready to faint. From the expression on the Indian lady's face, I suspected that while she might or might not understand what Biff was saying, she definitely didn't like his tone.

I looked around to see if the nondescript woman I'd seen at the ball field was with him. She wasn't, but I'd be willing to bet anything she'd told him about our party.

I headed his way. Mother beat me to it.

"I beg your pardon," she was saying as I reached her side. "Please stop bellowing at my volunteer helpers. If you have some problem with the refreshments, please bring it to my attention."

"Where's the baseball?" Biff shouted. "I know you're doing it, so where the hell is it?"

"Language, please!" Mother snapped. "There are impressionable children around, to say nothing of adults who prefer not to hear such language." She turned to me. "Meg, dear, this . . . person seems to think you're playing baseball here. Can you enlighten him?"

"Sorry to disappoint you, Mr. Brown," I said. "As far as I know, no one's playing baseball at the moment." I was pretty sure this was the truth, thanks to the Biff alert. "There was some talk of having a pickup

51

game later," I went on. "But at this point I doubt if they'll get that organized before it's too dark to play. Why don't you let the ladies fix you a nice plate to take with you when you leave?"

"You can't fool me," Biff said. "Your team's having a practice. Against the rules."

"No, we're not having a practice," I said. "Although even if we were, what's your problem? We'd be improving the kids' baseball skills and promoting greater fitness, which last time I looked were among the Summerball organization's official goals for the league."

"You can't have a practice outside your official assigned practice times," Biff said.

"Show me the rule," I said. "It's not in the official Summerball rule book, and you know it. And you have no right to come barging in here, uninvited, and try to tell any of us what we can do on our own time and our own property."

"You're going to regret this," Biff said.

No, I thought, you're the one who's going to regret it. But before I could say anything, Mother spoke up.

"Meg, dear, if Mr. Brown wasn't invited, perhaps we should ask one of your cousins to help him find his way back to his car."

Ranged behind her were three exceedingly

large young male cousins with excited looks on their faces, as if eager to show off their prowess as bouncers in front of Mother and the assembled family. Biff had seemed untroubled by Mother's glare — more fool him — but now he looked a little uneasy.

"No, actually it would be helpful if he stayed for a little bit," I said. "I need to talk to him, and I've had no luck reaching him over the past few weeks."

"Trying to get in touch with me?" Biff looked as if he was bouncing back. In fact, he was starting to look smug. "Sorry, Mrs. Waterston, but I think you're mistaken."

"Professionally, I go by my maiden name," I said. "Meg Langslow. Executive assistant to Mayor Shiffley. Since you're here, let's talk about your progress on the town square renovation contract."

Biff's jaw dropped, and he took several steps back.

"I'm not in my office right now," he said. "So I can't possibly give you an update on any particular project — we have so many going on. Call my secretary on Monday."

"I did, this Monday," I said. "And last Monday, and the Monday before that. Also the last few Tuesdays, Wednesdays, Thursdays, and Fridays. You could probably paper a wall with all the While You Were Out slips your secretary has written for me. Assuming she's actually writing them. Either you have an incompetent secretary, or you need to stop dodging customers who want to talk to you."

"Can't talk now — I have to be somewhere else," Biff said. Anywhere else, his face said. "At the ball field. A lot to do to get it ready for Opening Day tomorrow."

"That's great," I said. "Because it needs a lot of work. What's happening with that kid from one of the other teams, the one who sprained his ankle tripping over that big rock in the outfield at practice last week — are his parents really planning to sue?"

Biff backpedaled some more.

Caroline Willner strode forward with a tall paper cup in her hands.

"Here; you could use some lemonade," she said. She shoved it forward with one hand while patting him on the shoulder with the other. I'd have been mildly annoyed with the interruption if Biff hadn't reacted to the lemonade as if she'd tried to hand him a cup of poison.

"No, no," he said. "Not necessary. I'm not staying."

"I put it in a paper cup so you could take it with you," she said. "It's warm for this time of year — you need to keep hydrated."

54

Biff reluctantly allowed her to shove the cup into his hands and flinched slightly as she patted him on the shoulder again.

"So how about if I drop by to see you?" I went on. "Say, Monday morning at ten."

"I'll get back to you on that," Biff said over his shoulder as he strode — almost sprinted — away from me.

"Let's make sure he actually leaves," Caroline said. She took my arm, and we began strolling in Biff's wake.

"I was about to pin him down to an appointment time, you know," I said.

"And if you had, do you really think he'd have been there when you showed up?" she said. "I figured getting rid of him as soon as possible was the best thing."

"He could always come back," I said. "Or sneak back."

"We'll have a warning if he does," she said. "I tagged him."

CHAPTER 4

"Tagged him? You mean Biff?" Surely I hadn't heard Caroline properly. "And tagged him with what?"

"Your grandfather and I are testing a bunch of new geolocator tags for birds and small mammals." She held up a little lumpy metal gadget about the size of a nickel. "Miniature GPS device. The weasels have been regularly escaping from their habitat. We've attached these to the little devils, so the next time they pull a Houdini, we can not only find them faster, we can also figure out where they're escaping from. Should work for human weasels, too, so I dropped one in the jerk's pocket."

"Like belling the cat," I said. "But how do we keep track of him?"

Caroline pulled out her cell phone and punched in some numbers.

"Willner here. Two new tracking devices activated." She rattled off two long strings of numbers and letters. "That's right. Special short-term instructions on these two. Can you read my present position? . . . Excellent! Right now those two new devices should be near my position but headed away. If either of them comes within, say, two miles of our position, send an alert to my number and the following number." She recited a familiar string of digits — my own cell phone number — before thanking whoever was on the other end and hanging up.

"They'll call or text you if Biff comes anywhere near your house," she said.

"Biff and who else?" I asked. "You said two new devices."

"Well, I wasn't sure I'd manage to slip one in his jacket," she said. "And I almost didn't — had to try a second time. And there's a good possibility he'll find it eventually and toss it away, because it just looks like a little bit of junk. So I had one of your cousins attach one to his car. That'll stay put for a while, and its battery should last a couple months. I suppose it was wasteful, putting the one in his jacket — it's not as if he looks like the kind of guy who'd park his car a few miles away and try to hike across a couple of miles of farmland to sneak up on us from behind, but you never know."

"Awesome," I said. "But isn't it illegal?"

"Probably," Caroline said. "I'm sure any data we got from the trackers wouldn't be admissible in court as evidence. But we're not trying to sue him — we just want a little early warning if he tries to barge in again. Brilliant if you ask me. Here — call this number any time you want an update on his whereabouts."

She held out her phone and waited while I entered the number into my contact list. Then she strolled off, still chuckling at her own cleverness.

I still wasn't sure it was a good idea. But it was too late to stop her, and I doubted there was any way we could retrieve the devices without Biff catching on to what she'd done.

And since it was still part of my job for Caerphilly to track him down and extract an update on the progress (or lack thereof) on the town square renovations . . .

I called the number Caroline had given me.

"Zoo Security," a cheerful female voice answered. "How can I help you?"

"This is Meg Langslow," I said. "Can you give me a current location on those last two tracking devices Caroline activated?"

"Absolutely! Just give me a moment . . .

58

both devices are in the same location. On our maps, it's something called Percy Pruitt Park."

I thanked her and hung up. Percy Pruitt Park was still the official name of what we locals usually called the county ball field. Nobody had fond memories of the Pruitts, who had arrived in Caerphilly just after the Civil War and pretty much run the town as their personal fiefdom until a few years ago, when we'd finally figured out how to get rid of them and elected Randall Shiffley as the new reform mayor. No one had complained when one of the Brown Construction trucks had knocked down the park's signpost some time ago. Maybe it was time to propose a name change.

I scribbled an item in my notebook to that effect and then returned to the party.

"Biff gone?" Michael asked.

"Unfortunately," I said. "Before I had the chance to bug him about the renovations to the town square."

"Well, maybe you can catch him tomorrow," Michael said. "At the game."

"Yes, he'll probably be there for the opening ceremonies," I said.

"And the whole game," Michael said. "We're playing his team, you know."

With that, he dashed back to where the

boys were resuming their practice.

"Great," I muttered. I didn't much like the notion of ruining my enjoyment of the boys' first game by trying to tackle Biff at the ballpark. But was he going to continue dodging me indefinitely?

An idea came to me. I strolled into the barn where it was a little quieter, sat on a hay bale, pulled out my cell phone, and called the town clerk's office. To my surprise, I got a live voice.

"Caerphilly Town Clerk's Office, Phineas T. Throckmorton speaking."

"Phinny, what are you doing there this late? What happened to that vow to start working sane hours?"

"Oh, don't worry," Phinny said. "Because I'm not working — I'm hosting a role-playing game. Call of Cthulhu — it's like Dungeons & Dragons, only based on H.P. Lovecraft."

"Yes, I know what it is," I said. "My brother's a game lord, remember?"

"Yes, we're hoping he can join us later tonight. I should get back to the game — was there a reason you called?"

"I was planning to leave you a voice mail asking you to do something for me when you're back at work next week," I said.

"Is it important? Urgent? I could do it now."

"Important, but not urgent." After all, I'd been trying to reach Biff for weeks now. A few more days wouldn't matter. "Any chance you could give me a list of recent construction permits issued to Brown Construction?"

"Those wretches who have yet to do a lick of work on the square? Absolutely! Will this help you get us out of the contract with them?"

"At the moment I just want to talk to other people who've used them," I said. "Maybe get some tips on the best way to work on them. And if it comes to getting out of the contract — well, the more information we have, the better." I was also thinking that if I knew what other jobs he had going, I could show up to badger him at his work sites, but I'd keep that idea to myself.

"Not a problem," Phinny said. "I probably won't have time to do it tonight — oh, splendid, the pizza just arrived — but I'll get it to you as soon as possible. I've got to go before Dr. Smoot collars all of the bacon and anchovy."

"Not on your own time," I said. "Next week will be soon enough." But he'd already hung up.

Pizza and role-playing games in the basement of the courthouse. It might sound tame to some, but for Phinny it represented a massive expansion of his social life. And the basement's ancient stone corridors probably made a pretty cool atmosphere for gaming.

I scribbled a reminder in my notebook to check with Phinny if I hadn't heard back from him in a few days. And then I closed my notebook, took a deep breath, and tried to banish Biff from my thoughts. I often teased my cousin Rose Noire that she'd never met a New Age concept she didn't like. Her latest one for dealing with stresses and worries was the mental eraser.

"Picture the source of your stress," she'd said. "Now pick up an imaginary eraser and rub whatever's stressing you out of the picture."

Of course, all the examples she used were inanimate objects, like bills and malfunctioning appliances. Was it quite ethical to imagine erasing a human being?

I tried it anyway. I pictured Biff, leaning on the outfield fence. Then I pulled out my mental eraser and gently but thoroughly removed him from the scene, leaving only the chain-link fence, the exuberant green of the woods behind it, and the Stars and Stripes rippling in the breeze against a perfect blue sky.

"I feel better already," I said.

I was searching for the best possible image of Biff in our backyard, to repeat the erasure exercise, when bright light suddenly spilled through the gap where I'd left the barn door open. Bright light accompanied by cheering outside.

"Have they set something on fire?" I muttered, as I hurried over to the barn door. Even for my family, cheering on a conflagration seemed a little strange, but you never knew.

I stepped outside to find Mother beaming with approval at the backyard, where a brilliant if slightly harsh light was illuminating the buffet table and the Xtreme Croquet game. I spotted a portable light tower, the sort construction companies used when they had to work into the night.

"Wasn't it nice of Randall to bring the lights over?" Mother said, as I stepped to her side.

"Very nice." I had to shade my eyes against the brightness. "Although we usually manage with a scattering of luminarias."

"But those wouldn't have done for the ball

field." Mother pointed beyond the yard, where our makeshift baseball diamond was illuminated by another three light towers.

"Oh, great," I said. "And if Biff comes back to spy on us again, we'll just hand him a pair of sunglasses and hope he doesn't notice."

"If he comes back, I'm sure you'll be able to chase him away again," Mother said. "And if he thinks he can bully the Eagles into not practicing when they want to — well! He'll learn. I've been talking to some of the other team families. Everyone knows he just makes up all those rules as he goes along. People are getting tired of it, and asking what can be done about it. You can put me down as another charter member of NAFOB."

"NAFOB?" Caerphilly was rife with acronymed action organizations, from SPOOR — Stop Poisoning Our Owls and Raptors — to CAP — Citizens Against Prohibition, which after achieving its original mission with the repeal of Prohibition in 1933 had reorganized itself into a rather dipsophilic social organization. NAFOB was a new one to me.

"Not a Friend of Biff," she said.

"Count me in on that one," I said.

But still, I pulled up my mental image of

the ball field and unerased Biff. Right now, I hoped he was there leaning on the outfield fence. Better yet, doing something over there that took a lot of concentration. We were only a couple of miles from the field — for all I knew the sudden glow in our backyard might be visible all the way there.

I walked over to the pasture, where it was now obvious from pretty far away that practice was taking place. Michael and Chuck were assisted by Tory, Cordelia, and at least half a dozen team fathers.

Josh came running over when he spotted me leaning against the fence.

"Mommy, look at the lights," he exclaimed. "Isn't it cool? Just like the big leagues!"

He went running back into the outfield.

"They haven't played under the lights at the ball field yet?" asked a cousin who was standing beside me, holding a glass of wine in her hand.

"We don't have lights at our field," I explained.

"And that's a pity, isn't it?" Randall Shiffley had come to lean against the fence on my other side. "Because I think the kids would enjoy a few night games, don't you?"

"You think you could see your way to

lending those light towers for the games?" I asked.

"I could," he said. "Of course, Biff hasn't scheduled any night games, but if the spring continues as rainy as it has been, we might need a few night slots to get in all the make up games."

"Night games are more fun sometimes," the cousin said.

"I agree," I said. "Although I suspect Biff won't, unless the suggestion comes from someone he gets along with."

"Which wouldn't be me," Randall said.

"Or me. I assume you'll be there to throw out the first ball tomorrow."

"No, apparently Biff has invited some bigwig from Summerball's national organization to do that." Randall's tone seemed light and neutral. Maybe a little too much so.

"Are you bummed about that?" I asked.

"I'm ticked off he didn't ask me first," Randall said. "Or even notify me. If he'd called me up and said he wanted to invite a bigwig from Summerball National, maybe thrown in a little flattery about how great it's going to be to show off our brand new league, I'd have said 'Great; look forward to meeting him.' But to tell me the day before Opening Day that he doesn't need me for the ceremonies . . . not cool."

"Disrespectful," the listening cousin put in.

I found myself wondering if Randall and Biff had had words. Oh, to be a fly on the wall.

"You know, it wouldn't be that hard to put up permanent lights at the field," Randall said. "Assuming the county can wrestle control over our own field back from Biff."

"I'll put that on my list," I said.

"And put it on your list to meet the Summerball National guy tomorrow," Randall said. "I don't know how Biff managed to snow the Summerball folks into letting him run the league, but I'm hoping they haven't really seen him in action. But they will tomorrow, and if Biff runs true to form and meanwhile you and I do our level best to charm the socks off the visitor . . . you never know."

"My money's on you," said the cousin. "But I'm confused about something — Meg, I thought you worked for the mayor."

"That's me, ma'am," Randall said, tipping an imaginary hat.

"And I thought the ball field was in the county, not the town."

"It is," I said. "But the town and county

are working together a lot more coopera-
tively these days. They used to have completely separate and often actively hostile
governments."

"The town was run by the Pruitts, a
bunch of greedy carpetbaggers, for over a
century," Randall said. "But people finally
got wise and voted them out."

"And with the Pruitts gone, we came up
with a proposal to join forces to save everybody time and money," I explained.

"Meg's doing, actually," Randall said.

"So Randall is mayor and also the county
executive," I said. "The town council is also
the county board. The chief of police is also
the deputy sheriff."

"The only people not completely happy
about the change were a few folks who were
on both payrolls," Randall said. "And we
gave them big raises to sweeten the pill."

"That's why we're having a four-day
holiday weekend instead of a three-day
one," I explained. "The county used to
celebrate Founder's Day on a Friday and
the town on a Monday. And neither would
budge. So now we celebrate both."

"So the town and the county are merged
now?" the cousin asked.

"For the time being, they're still separate
entities," I said. "And citizens of both have

the right to vote the plan out if they don't think it's working."

"Keeps us honest," Randall said. "But confusing to outsiders, since we locals have gotten pretty loosey-goosey about using town and county interchangeably when we talk about the government. But it works for us, and pretty well."

"Nice to know both town and county are in such capable hands!" The cousin lifted her wine glass as if to salute us.

"Looks as if you've got a vote of confidence from the Hollingsworth clan," I said.

"I think the hands she was talking about were yours," Randall said. The cousin giggled slightly. "But since I'm the one who was smart enough to hire you, I will bask in my share of the compliment. By the way, one of my cousins told me something that you might find interesting. Even useful."

Randall, like me, was blessed — or afflicted — with a remarkably large and close-knit extended family.

"Cousin Cephus has a kid on the Red Sox," Randall went on. "He was there picking his kid up when Biff's Yankees were starting their practice, and he overheard a regular knock-down drag-out between Biff and one of the Yankee parents. One of the Pruitts, as it happened."

"Did he hear what they were arguing about?" I asked.

"They shut up as soon as they realized he was nearby." Randall shook his head. "But it was a real doozy — they weren't just arguing; a couple of the other Yankee dads had to pull them apart. And Cephus was pretty surprised, because up to now, Biff and his team parents have been tight as ticks. Especially the Pruitts. If there's a crack happening . . . well, might be something that could be exploited to fix some of the problems we're having."

"In the league, or with Biff and the town square?" I asked.

"Either," Randall said. "Both."

"I'll keep it in mind," I said. "Of course, exploiting a possible rift between Biff and the Pruitts would be a lot easier for someone the Pruitts didn't already hate. Which wouldn't be me."

"Or me," Randall said. "Just keep it in mind."

I nodded.

Just then Cordelia strode over holding an empty plastic cup.

"Any chance of a refill on the lemonade?" she asked.

"I'll get it!" The cousin grabbed the glass and scampered off toward the picnic tables.

Cordelia leaned against the fence to survey the action on the field while she waited.

"So where did you learn to play baseball?" I asked.

"In Peoria," she said. "I was on the Redwings. In the All American Girls Professional Baseball League," she added, seeing my slightly puzzled frown. "Under my maiden name, since we weren't quite sure people back in Richmond would find it quite respectable."

"Meg, why didn't you ever tell me your grandmother had played women's professional baseball?" Randall asked.

"I didn't know she had," I said. "Why didn't you tell me?" I asked, turning to Cordelia. In the past year or so, I'd often tried to get Cordelia to sit down and talk about her life in the decades between her giving up Dad for adoption and our discovery of her, but every time I thought I'd mapped out her life she'd drop another biographical bombshell.

"Didn't know you'd find it all that interesting," she said. Just then the cousin returned with the refilled lemonade. "Let's talk about it later," Cordelia said. "We've got a lot of work to do with these kids."

"I'll hold you to that," I said as she strolled back onto the field.

The practice ended around eight o'clock. The zoo security desk called at eight thirty to tell me that the tracking devices were on the move. Even though practice was over, I was relieved to hear that Biff was headed away from us. Out of curiosity, I asked her to text me the location when he stopped moving. When she did, a little quick online research revealed that Biff had gone back to his construction company's offices. By that time all the baseball players had gone home or been sent to bed, and Michael was gently suggesting to the last few die-hard Xtreme Croquet players that everyone needed their rest to be up bright and early for tomorrow's game.

"No classes for four days," Michael exclaimed as we were settling down to sleep. "And the picnic was a great way to start off the holiday."

"I wish we'd done it weeks ago," I said. "All those parents I was complaining about as unfriendly and uncooperative and lazy — they're very nice people who were simply scared of having it backfire on their kids if they crossed Biff. Now that we know what the problem is, I'm sure we can figure out a way to deal with him."

"And if you need an alibi, just ask," Michael mumbled, already half asleep.

"That shouldn't be necessary," I said —
but softly enough that it wouldn't wake him
if he was already asleep. "I don't want
anything to happen to Biff. I just want him
to behave."

CHAPTER 5

Friday dawned bright and clear — and I was up to see it, unfortunately, since we had to be at the ball field by eight for the pregame practice. Getting both boys and Michael into their uniforms was astonishingly tiring and time-consuming. And then came loading the Twinmobile with all the gear and supplies we needed.

As Michael worked to fit everything into the back of the van, I flipped open my notebook and scanned my checklists. Waters. Juices. Snacks. Ice. First aid kit. Sunscreen. Insect repellent. Hand sanitizer. Even toilet paper, because Biff didn't seem to have assigned anyone to restock the porta-potty from week to week.

I suddenly had a dizzying premonition that this was the first of who knew how many early morning expeditions to the ball field. I could almost see the boys in their red-and-black shirts and white baseball pants getting taller and taller until they approached Michael's towering six-foot-four frame, and myself spending who knew how much time in the bleachers. It wasn't a bad prospect — I shared Michael's love of baseball, and never got tired of cheering the boys on no matter what they were doing. But it was a curiously daunting prospect. This was an occasion. A momentous occasion. The boys' first real baseball game. I felt we should mark it somehow. And —

"Meg? You ready? We don't want to be late."

I hopped into the van and gave up trying to mark the momentous occasion. As with so many other parenting milestones, I focused on making sure we all survived it. I turned on my phone and tried to find the e-mail from Mother in which she'd sent me a list of which cousins were working what shift in the Snack Shack.

At the ballpark, the bleachers on our side of the field — the third-base side — were already a sea of red and black, worn by a cheerful mix of Eagle families and my relatives. The overflow were settling into a sea of brightly colored folding camping chairs. My cousin Rose Noire and a sari-clad Indian woman that I now knew was Sami Patel's grandmother were staffing the Snack

Shack, and Osgood Shiffley, one of Randall's cousins, was warming up the grill. I could smell the charcoal already, and long before lunchtime the smell of the hot dogs and hamburgers would begin tempting people to have a second breakfast.

The crowd on the first-base side seemed a little more subdued. Most of the Stoats fans were also wearing their team colors, and the overall effect was drab and dispiriting. I could understand why Biff had chosen the color, but it really didn't make for a very decorative crowd.

I thought of going over and introducing myself to my counterpart on the Stoats. I spotted a woman holding a clipboard who seemed to be passing out something to people sitting on their bleachers — probably the Team Mom. But just as I was about to put a cheerful expression on my face and head over, she turned around, spotted me looking at her, and glared at me. Maybe I'd have gone over anyway and tried to establish friendly relations, but I recognized her: one of the Pruitts, the family who had run Caerphilly until a group of concerned citizens had helped organize the popular campaign that broke their stronghold on the town government and sent some of the worst Pruitt crooks to prison. From the look on her face, I suspected she recognized me as one of those concerned citizens.

Okay, maybe not so great an idea to wander over and try to strike up a casual conversation. Sooner or later I'd have some concrete reason to talk to her — coordinating Snack Shack schedules or something. In the meantime, I'd keep it civil. So I smiled back as if she'd blown kisses instead of glaring, and hurried back to my team's bleachers as if I had some task to do there.

"Where's Biff, anyway?" one of the parents on the bleachers asked.

"I hear he's wining and dining some bigwig from Summerball National," another said.

"No, that's the bigwig out there on the field with Randall," the first one said.

I strolled over to the chain-link fence that separated us from the field and looked around for Randall and the bigwig. They were standing on the pitcher's mound, gazing at the outfield, where the Stars and Stripes rippled gently against the cloudless blue sky. The breeze also rippled the colorful banners hung on the outfield fence, advertising a dozen or so local small businesses — I noticed that while Brown Construction had a banner, rival Shiffley Construction was absent. The loudspeaker system was blaring out a steady stream of music — already we'd heard "Centerfield," "The Boys of Summer," "Celebration," "We Will Rock You," and now "Start Me Up."

While tapping my feet to the Stones, I studied Randall and the bigwig. The bigwig was actually more than a head shorter than Randall, and his well-cut gray pinstripe suit couldn't conceal the fact that he was pretty scrawny and hollow-chested. Randall gestured at something to their left, and when the bigwig turned his head to look, I got a sideways view of the remarkably thick lenses in his wire-rimmed glasses.

If the bigwig's expression was anything to go by, Randall hadn't yet succeeded in charming him. Randall spotted me and nodded — no doubt suggesting that perhaps it was time I tried my hand with the bigwig. I sighed, and squared my shoulders. Damn Biff for inviting the bigwig, anyway. All I wanted to do was watch the game with my family and friends and —

"Mrs. Waterston?"

I turned around to see Mason, looking highly anxious.

"What's wrong?" I asked.

"I need the porta-potty," he said. "And someone's in it."

"I'm sure they'll be out soon," I said.

78

"It's been occupied all morning," he said. "And I finally went and stood outside the door and I knocked, and no one answered, and I really need it. The game starts in five minutes."

"If you really can't wait, you could go into the woods," I suggested.

"I can't," he said. "I . . . um . . . I don't just need to pee."

"Let me see what I can do."

I'd go see Randall and the bigwig when I'd taken care of Mason's problem. I strode toward where the porta-potty stood in its solitary splendor. Mason scurried along behind me, face contorted with discomfort that was probably approaching actual pain.

Damn Biff Brown anyway. Was he really so stupid that he thought one porta-potty enough for the number of spectators we expected today? As I hurried through the crowd I mentally called Biff several names I wouldn't have wanted to say aloud with Mason around. When I was finished helping Mason, maybe I'd tackle Biff on the question of more porta-potties. Or maybe I'd just call Randall and have him deliver some and charge them to the league. Get the health inspector, who happened to be one of Randall's cousins, to find some health or safety violation to justify it.

First things first. I arrived at the porta-potty and knocked briskly on the door.

"Is anyone in there?" I called. Stupid question, obviously, since the word OC-CUPIED appeared in the slot above the door handle, showing that the latch had been turned from the inside.

Or was it a stupid question? No one answered. And I heard no signs of stirring inside. I knocked again, even more loudly.

"If anyone's in there, speak up," I said. "Otherwise I'm going to pick the lock."

No answer. I unslung the tote that I'd been carrying over my shoulder and rum-maged through it. Yes, as I'd hoped, I still had the tools I'd been carrying yesterday, including the large-sized screwdrivers, both Phillips and slotted, plus a hammer and an assortment of screws, nails, and bolts. Everything I'd need to give the bleachers and the dugouts and anything else that looked rickety a once-over when I had a chance. The slotted screwdriver should be just the thing to tackle the porta-potty door.

I stuck the screwdriver blade into the crack of the door, just under the level of the OCCUPIED sign, and moved it up until it hit something. It took a couple of tries, and if my blacksmithing hadn't given me good hand and arm strength, I couldn't have managed, but eventually the latch gave way and I succeeded in flipping it up.

"Ready or not, here I come," I said to give anyone inside a last warning — though by this time I was pretty sure the porta-potty was empty. If there had been anyone inside, they'd definitely have spoken up since my efforts had not only made considerable noise but had also rocked the porta-potty. I fully expected to find that this was just someone's idea of a joke — figuring out how to flip the lock closed from outside, and then doing it on Opening Day. When I found the culprit, I was going to give him or her a piece of my mind — and I'd already thought of several likely suspects. In fact, one of them, my brother, Rob, was lurking nearby, no doubt pretending to be waiting his turn to use the porta-potty while in reality chuckling to himself.

But I was wrong. When I jerked the door open, I found someone slumped facedown on the floor in a crumpled heap. Male, pudgy, wearing khaki pants and a mud-colored Brown Construction t-shirt. A Yankees baseball hat had half fallen off his head.

"Biff," I muttered.

One arm had flopped down into the doorway when I opened it. I grabbed the wrist. No pulse, though I could tell the second I touched it that there wouldn't be. The skin was cold.

My first thought was that at least now there'd be no one to complain if I arranged for a whole flotilla of porta-potties. Not a very nice thought, but an honest one.

First things first. I stepped back, making sure to keep my body between Mason and the porta-potty door. I pulled out my phone, but before dialing 911, I shouted "Rob! Come here."

"What's wrong?" Rob asked as he strolled up.

"You know Mason," I said. "Take him somewhere and find him a real bathroom. Our house might be the closest place. The porta-potty's out of order."

"How can a porta-potty be — holy cow!" He had gotten close enough to see over my shoulder. "Okay. Can do. Come on, Mason."

"But the game's starting any minute," Mason protested.

"Not now it isn't," I said. "I'll explain later, but you'll be back in plenty of time for the game. Go. And Rob, on your way past the bleachers, send Dad over here."

Rob and Mason hurried off. I dialed 911 and prepared to tell Debbie Ann, the dispatcher, that there was a dead body at the ball field.

CHAPTER 6

"You found the body *where*?" Debbie Ann sounded incredulous. Or was it disgusted?

"In the porta-potty here at the youth baseball field," I said. "I think it's Biff Brown. I haven't looked at the face yet — I didn't want to disturb the body."

"Are you sure it is a body?" Debbie Ann asked. "Maybe I should send an ambulance, unless you're really sure he's dead?"

"Reasonably sure," I said. "His skin's cold, and I can't find a pulse. I'm trying to get Dad over here to make it official. Adam Burke's on the boys' team, so the chief should be somewhere here at the field. Could you —"

"Here I am." I looked up to see the chief standing at my elbow.

"Never mind," I told Debbie Ann. "He's here."

"Don't hang up," the chief said. He squatted just outside the doorway and checked

84

Biff's wrist. He looked surprised.

"He's cold," he said.

"Body temperature drops around a degree and a half per hour after death," I said. "Sorry; I know you know that better than I do. Force of habit. When I was a kid, Dad used to quiz us about stuff like that around the dinner table."

"Must have made for some interesting meals," the chief said. "It's just that I could have sworn I saw Biff an hour or so ago doing something in the outfield. He couldn't possibly have gotten that cold that quickly. I suppose I must have seen one of his workmen instead. Tell Debbie Ann we have a suspicious death. She knows the drill."

"I heard that," Debbie Ann said. "I'm on it."

As I was putting my phone back in my pocket, the first few bars of "Dixie" sounded out from somewhere in the porta-potty.

"Cell phone," the chief and I said in unison.

"It's in his back pants pocket," I added, pointing.

The cell phone trilled again. Wincing, the chief pulled out his handkerchief, reached over with it to tug the phone out of the corpse's pocket, and pressed a button to answer it.

"Shep!" snapped a voice on the phone. "Where the hell are you? The game was supposed to start five minutes ago, and you haven't even put on your uniform yet. I've got it in my car. Answer me, you son of a —"

"That sounds like Mr. Brown on the phone," the chief said to me, drowning out a torrent of words from Biff that was in serious violation of the posted field rules against using unseemly language in front of the kids.

"Then who's this?" I asked, pointing to the body.

"Is this Mr. Brown?" the chief said into the cell phone.

A few moments of silence on the other end.

"Yeah, this is Biff Brown," the voice on the cell phone said. "I was calling my brother Shep's phone. Who the hell is this? Let me talk to Shep, dammit."

"There's no call for strong language," the chief said. "This is Chief Burke. If this is your brother's phone, I'm afraid I may have some bad news. Could you meet me by the porta-potty?"

"You mean now?" Biff asked.

"Right now," the chief said. Then he cut the connection and wrapped the phone in his handkerchief before pulling out his own

86

phone and dialing a number.

"Horace? Are you here at the ball field
. . . ? Good. Bring your crime scene kit.
Meet me by the porta-potty. . . . Good question. Meg," he asked, looking up from his
phone. "Are there any other porta-potties
here at the field?"

"With Biff in charge?" I asked.

"No, there's only the one," he said into
the phone. "And if you see Dr. Langslow
—"

"I'm here."

The chief and I looked up to see that Dad
was right behind us.

"Never mind," the chief said to Horace.
"Just hurry."

The chief and I stepped aside to let Dad
see the body. Dad repeated the quick touch
to the wrist that both the chief and I had
already performed, although somehow it
seemed a lot more authoritative when he
did it. A faint frown creased his forehead,
followed by a look of concentration, and I
could almost trace his thinking. The sad-
ness of seeing a fellow human dead battled
the fascination of a puzzle, and then both
emotions gave way to a determination to
see that justice was done.

Or maybe I was tracing my own emotions.
Even if the dead person had been Biff —

"Gunshot wound," Dad said. He pointed toward the dead man's forehead. The chief leaned in to take a look and nodded. I couldn't see from where I stood and was happy to take their word for it.

Which probably meant it was murder.

I stepped back, pulled out my cell phone again, and hit another of my speed-dial numbers.

"Meg, what's up?" Randall Shiffley said when he answered. "Any idea why the game's not starting as scheduled?"

"We found a dead body in the porta-potty," I said. "Notice I said *the,* as in the only one out here. And it just became a crime scene, which means we have several hundred people out here drinking coffee and sodas and —"

"I'll have a couple brought over ASAP. Anything else I can do?"

"Maybe you could come over and check with the chief. I think we're going to have to postpone the first game, unless Horace decides that the crime scene is limited to the porta-potty, which seems unlikely, and —"

"Wait — crime scene? It's a murder?"

"Gunshot wound," I said. "So murder, suicide, or seriously weird accident."

"Who's the victim?"

"Probably Biff Brown's brother Shep," I said. "Biff's on his way to ID him."

"Well, that explains why the game hasn't started," Randall said.

"With Biff not there to coach his team."

"Well, that too, but Shep was scheduled to be the umpire."

"Wait — my sons' team was going to play Biff's team, and Biff's brother was going to be the umpire? Outrageous! In what universe is that fair?"

"Welcome to the Biff zone. And Shep's only his half brother, so it's only half outrageous. I'll go order the porta-potties and head right over."

I hung up, still fuming, and turned back to see what was going on around the porta-potty. Cousin Horace, Caerphilly's official crime scene technician, had arrived. He might not look very professional, wearing his Eagles t-shirt, Eagles hat, and faded blue jeans, but I could tell from the look in his eyes that he was one of the few people for whom today was going to turn out utterly satisfying. Not just baseball, but a crime scene followed — we hoped — by baseball! He and Dad were a matched set sometimes.

At the moment, Horace was standing in the doorway of the porta-potty, talking over his shoulder to the chief, who was making notes.

"What's going on here?"

Biff had arrived.

The chief turned around. I saw him start to hold out his hand to shake Biff's and then stifle the impulse.

"Mr. Brown?" he said. "I'm afraid I may have some bad news for you. It appears that your brother is dead."

"Heart attack, right?" Biff shook his head. "The doctor kept warning him those bacon cheeseburgers would get him in the end."

"I'm afraid it looks like homicide," the chief said.

"Homicide?" Biff's mouth fell open in astonishment. "Is this some kind of a joke?"

The chief gestured to the porta-potty. Horace stood aside, and to my relief both he and Dad had solemn, concerned looks on their faces. Biff stepped closer and peered in.

"That's him," he said. "Son of a . . . yeah, that's him. Shep Henson. My brother. Half brother, technically. Damn."

"When did you last see Mr. Henson?" The chief had flipped to a fresh page in his notebook and was scribbling.

"Yesterday afternoon, or maybe you'd call it early evening," Biff said. "He works for me at the construction company. I got there at about six thirty — no, make that closer to seven — and shortly after I arrived he told me he was taking off. I stayed on and worked for a couple of hours in my office, and then — well, I'm sure you heard about the break-in at my supply yard."

"I've read the reports from deputies Shiffley and Butler," the chief said. "I thought it was a false alarm."

"Depends on your definition of false alarm," Biff said. "There was definitely someone stumbling around out there. I heard them, and when I went to investigate, I found Shep had left the side gate unlocked. At least I assume it was Shep; locking up's his job most days. I didn't know if it was thieves or just kids playing a prank, so I called nine-one-one. Couple of your officers helped me check the whole supply yard. We didn't find anything missing, but it's a big yard, and there's a lot of random stuff out there. I called Shep a couple times to get him to come back and help out, but he never answered. You don't suppose he was already . . ."

Biff's voice trailed off, and he frowned down at his dead brother as if angry with him. But maybe he was just one of those men who hid real feeling under a pretense of irritation.

"Damn," he said. "He was supposed to umpire today. How am I supposed to find someone else on such short notice?"

The chief and I glanced at each other. His face seemed to show the same surprise I felt. Then, with a visible effort, he assumed his usual calm, professional expression.

"I'm sure there will be plenty of time to arrange something," he said. "Right now, this whole field could be the crime scene, and we may need to send all these people away for a few hours. We'll have to delay the first game — possibly cancel today's games, depending on how our investigation goes."

Biff looked up, frowning more deeply, as if about to protest. Then he seemed to deflate like a balloon.

"All right," he said.

"If you don't mind, let's go over there where we can have some privacy." The chief was pointing at the stretch of empty field between the porta-potty and the woods. "I'd like to get some more information about your brother."

"You want to know who his enemies are," Biff said. "Look around you! All those entitled parents, demanding luxury accommodations and preferential treatment for their miserable untalented kids."

92

To me that sounded more like a list of Biff's enemies. Apparently Biff realized this.

"Every call he made, someone would argue with," he added. "It could get pretty vicious."

"I'd be happy to hear your thoughts on anyone who might have had a grudge against Mr. Henson," the chief said. From the look on his face, I could tell he planned to take Biff's thoughts with more than a few grains of salt. I noticed Randall Shiffley had arrived, and was observing Biff with the expression of deadpan impartiality he normally wore when trying not to laugh at unusually outrageous citizen complaints. "This way."

"But I have a league to run," Biff protested.

"Perhaps I could be of assistance." It was the bigwig. I hadn't spotted him standing there beside Randall. Up close he looked even scrawnier, and his eyes behind the thick lenses were squinting against the sun and watering. "James Witherington. I'm a vice president with Summerball National. It's part of my job to troubleshoot problems for our local affiliates. I'm sure assisting Mr. Brown in his time of sorrow comes under my job description. You go on and help the local authorities with their investigation," he said, turning to Biff. "I'll make sure everything's done strictly according to Summerball policy."

"I'm not sure I'm allowed to offload my Opening Day responsibilities to anyone else," Biff said.

"Of course you can," Mr. Witherington said.

"Rule 13.4.1," I said, perhaps a little more loudly than I had intended. Given all the hours I'd spent fighting insomnia with the Summerball rule book, bits had begun to stick in my mind, and the rule in question struck me as something that might prove useful to know. Mr. Witherington turned his head and studied me for a few moments with a gaze of mingled surprise and approval.

"Precisely," Mr. Witherington said. He turned back to Biff and the chief. "Essentially, an official of the national league can fill in temporarily if a local official is incapacitated for any reason. I think bereavement is an appropriate reason for incapacitation. Mr. Brown, allow me to extend official condolences from Summerball National, along with our assurance that we will do everything we can to keep things running smoothly."

Mr. Witherington extended his hand

toward Biff, who appeared not to see it. He was staring at the porta-potty.

"And all of us appreciate your thoughtfulness at this difficult time," Randall said. "May I introduce my executive assistant, Meg Langslow?"

"Pleased to meet you," I said as I shook the hand Biff was ignoring. Witherington's handshake was firmer than I'd have expected.

Randall introduced the chief and Horace. Biff, meanwhile, had recovered himself enough that he was glaring with visible annoyance at all this polite handshaking.

"Why don't the two of us go and make the announcement together?" Randall said to Mr. Witherington. "Show the people that the town and the league are cooperating harmoniously on this. And we can relocate our opening ceremonies to the town square. Get the crowd out of the way of the investigation."

"Good thinking," Mr. Witherington said. "I don't suppose there's another ball field to which we can relocate today's games?"

"Well," Randall began, and looked to me for help.

"There's the elementary school field," Biff said.

"But it's in pretty bad condition," I said.

"Worse than here," I added, seeing Mr. Witherington glance back at the field behind us with a small but definite frown. Biff glowered at my statement, but I ignored him. "And besides, it's nowhere near the Summerball regulation size even for the youngest kids — the base paths are only forty-five feet, the distance to the outfield fence is only about a hundred and eighty feet, and there's no pitcher's mound to speak of."

"Not suitable, then," Mr. Witherington said. "Well, let's hope your local law enforcement will be able to let us have the field back in time to get in this weekend's games. I wish you success in your sad endeavors, Chief Burke. We will do our part by clearing the field for you."

He and Randall strode off. At least Mr. Witherington was striding — Randall didn't have to work too hard to keep up with him. Though it did look as if Randall was making a little more progress at charming the Summerball rep. Not surprising; when he set his mind to it, Randall could be quite the charmer. I saw Biff watching their departure with much less satisfaction than I felt.

"Mr. Brown? If you please?"

Biff followed the chief into the open field

beyond the porta-potty.

I glanced over at the bleachers. Should I go and fill in Michael and Chuck?

Aida Butler, one of my good friends, and also one of the chief's deputies, strode up.

"Taking charge of the crime scene?" I asked.

"Yup," she said. "Randall and that mousy little guy from the league are about to address the crowd. Not sure what they're going to say."

"That we've had a murder, and we're relocating the Opening Day ceremony to the town square," I said.

"Good idea," Aida said. "But of course we both know as soon as they announce that, at least half a dozen people will wander over here to rubberneck."

"Or to use the porta-potty before they go." I pulled out my phone. "Let me just text Randall to remind him to announce that it's out of order."

"So how bad is this one, anyway?" Aida asked, when my thumbs had finished tapping out the message to Randall.

"A lot worse than it needs to be," I said.

"Come again?"

"A porta-potty's never going to be anything but a porta-potty," I said. "But at least if you clean them regularly and use enough disinfectant, they're merely sort of yucky rather than downright gross. But evidently Biff doesn't share that philosophy."

"Um . . . yeah." Aida looked as if she was smothering a giggle. "Actually, since a couple of my nephews have played on this field, I know how bad the porta-potty is. I meant how bad was the crime scene — since I know you've seen a few in your time."

"Sorry," I said. "Except for the location, not too bad. Then again, if there was badness, I may not have seen it. Dad said it was a gunshot wound and pointed to the guy's forehead, but he was facedown when I found him, so I didn't see anything."

"That's odd," she said. "Not a lot of blood?"

I thought about it for a few moments.

"I don't remember seeing any blood at all," I said finally.

"Even odder." She glanced over at the porta-potty, where both Horace and Dad were crouched in the doorway, discussing something in an undertone. For some reason, the sight of them squatting there in front of the porta-potty with such serious looks on their faces struck me as . . . well, not quite funny so much as utterly in character. I held up my phone and snapped a couple of shots of them. Mother would probably balk at having a picture with a porta-potty in the family album, but Dad would love a picture of him and Horace on a case.

"Hey, Horace," Aida called out. "Was he actually killed in that thing?"

"No," Dad said.

"Unlikely," Horace said, almost at the same time.

Aida nodded as if she'd expected as much.

"Not good," she said, turning back to me. "That could mean this is the crime scene." She spread her arms wide and looked around at the busy ball field.

So much for my hopes of a crime scene followed by baseball. If the field was the crime scene, we'd be lucky to get it back before the weekend was over.

Randall and Mr. Witherington made their announcement that the opening ceremonies would be held in the town square at noon, and the great exodus began. The river of black-and-red–clad spectators from the Eagles' bleachers surged toward the parking lot, where it mingled with the smaller stream of brown-clad Stoats fans. I made sure the boys had all their gear, helped Michael and Chuck gather all the team equipment, and saw them all loaded into the

Twinmobile.

"I'm going to stay here a little longer," I said. "I'm sure I can catch a ride back to town."

"Or just call and we'll come back out to pick you up," Michael said, giving me a quick kiss on the cheek. "As long as you're staying, could you give the dugout one last check for stray items?"

After waving good-bye to them, I hiked back to the dugout, where a quick search produced an insulated bottle, half a pack of gum, and a single batting glove. I stowed it all in my tote and turned to see the chief standing by home plate, staring out at the field. I leaned against the fence that separated the dugout from the field, wrapped my fingers through the chain link, and watched for a few minutes. The chief pulled out a pair of binoculars and trained them on the outfield, where Horace and Sammy Wendell, another deputy, appeared to be inspecting the ground inch by inch. As we watched, Sammy picked something up and held it up to show Horace. I couldn't hear what they said to each other, but Sammy pulled a brown paper evidence bag out of his pocket and stowed the item, whatever it was.

"A vital clue?" I said.

"Probably another Gatorade bottle cap," the chief said, lowering the binoculars. "I hate crime scenes like this, where several hundred people were tramping around for several hours before we even knew it was a crime scene. Odds are we won't find anything relevant, but we have to try."

"Since Randall's Pied-Pipering the baseball crowd over to the town square, I thought I'd stick around a bit," I said. "See if there's anything useful I can do for you wearing my executive assistant hat."

"Is the parking lot mostly empty?" he asked.

"Do you want it to be?" I asked. "I can go tell anyone who's still hanging around to clear out."

"Not just yet," the chief said with a smile. "We're trying to figure out how Mr. Henson got here. He lives over in Clay County. According to Sheriff Whicker, his truck's not in his driveway, but it's not here, either. Could be he drove some other vehicle, but I figured there was no use checking till everyone was over at the town square."

He headed for the dugout, putting his binoculars in their leather case as he walked. I joined him when he left the field and we headed for the parking lot. Only eight vehicles were parked there, and four of them were police cruisers.

"My car, your dad's car, Vern's truck, and Biff's truck," he said, pointing to the four civilian vehicles as he named them.

"Biff's still here?" I said.

"Apparently." He didn't look thrilled at the notion. He strode off. I was about to follow, when I was distracted by a shout from somewhere near the first-base dugout.

"What the hell are those doing here?"

CHAPTER 7

I turned to see who was bellowing. Biff, of course — and he was pointing at something behind me. I turned to look.

"Porta-potties!" I exclaimed. "Sweet!"

A truck had arrived bearing not one but three porta-potties. And they were the extra-large-sized ones, which meant not only were they handicapped-accessible, they were also a lot less unpleasant to use for women, who more than men tended to be weighed down with purses, totes, diaper bags, and other baggage that made negotiating a coffin-sized standard porta-potty challenging. Best of all, instead of muddy brown they were painted bright blue with a Shiffley Construction Company logo on them. In a decade of attending outdoor events in Caerphilly, I'd come to appreciate the superior maintenance that Randall's company gave to their porta-potties. Biff's porta-potties started out nastier than Randall's porta-potties ever got.

"I thought you'd be pleased," Randall said, jumping down from the cab of the truck. "Now let's find the chief and ask him —"

"I've got the contract to supply porta-potties to the ball field," Biff said. "What kind of a scam is this, Shiffley?"

"Scam!" Randall exclaimed. Normally he was pretty easygoing, but apparently Biff knew how to push his buttons. "Scam! If you think you —"

"Of course we know that you have the contract," I said to Biff in my most soothing tones, before Randall could say something that would be satisfyingly insulting but probably unproductive. "But Randall didn't think it was right to bother you in your time of sorrow just to take care of a problem with porta-potties."

"That's right." Randall appeared to have recovered his temper thanks to my interruption. "You need to be spending this time with your family. And let us take care of this. After all, it's not your fault the police have to rope off your porta-potty as a crime scene, and you shouldn't have to suffer for it. So I arranged temporary replacements at the town's expense."

104

Not so temporary if I had anything to do with it.

"We only need one," Biff said. "League can't afford to pay for three. Especially not three of those luxury numbers. This is a ball field, not the Taj Mahal."

I was opening my mouth to give Biff a piece of my mind on the subject of porta-potties but this time Randall saved me from being undiplomatic.

"I know you only had the one," Randall said. "But as long as my truck was making the trip, I thought I'd try a little experiment. We get a lot of complaints about the ball field porta-potties down at the Town Hall."

"Some people —" Biff began.

"Are just not satisfied unless you give them a marble bathroom with rose-scented toilet paper," Randall said. "We both know that. Some of the citizens are always going to complain as long as there's porta-potties. But I bet if we give them the fancy kind, and more than one of them so there won't ever be much of a line, we can keep the complaining down to a minimum. And when you consider the amount of time my staff spends listening to people complain, it might be a savings in the long run. So let's keep the three porta-potties for now, at no cost to the league, and see how it goes. If it

105

works out, when we renegotiate the contract between the town and the league, maybe the town can foot the bill for two or three of your deluxe models."

"Well . . . we'll see how it goes," Biff said.

He strode off, still grumbling, but in a pro forma kind of way. I suspected he was already calculating the profits to be made from renting three high-end porta-potties to the town.

"I'd rather have one of your standard porta-potties than three of his so-called deluxe models," I told Randall when I was sure Biff was out of earshot. "Assuming he even has any deluxe models, which I seriously doubt. And I bet those three of yours would cost the league less than he's charging for that one nasty standard one."

"You did hear me say 'maybe,' right?" Randall shook his head as if Biff still amazed him. "When we negotiated terms for the ball field, my uncle Lem was still in charge of the league. We thought we were dealing with a sane individual, and we didn't do nearly as good a job on the contract as we should have. I'm going to contact the county attorney and have her start working on something a lot more useful for next year."

"Does that mean you're not expecting your uncle Lem to recover?" I asked. Quite apart from being one of my friend Randall's favorite uncles and reputedly a pretty competent league head, Lem had always impressed me as a very kind and thoughtful man, and I wished him well on all accounts.

"No, he's doing great and looking forward to getting back," Randall said. "Though probably not till the fall season. But he could completely recover from cancer and be hit by a bus next week, and then we'd be in the same boat, so let's draw up a contract so solid that we'd be in good shape even if Attila the Hun showed up and kicked out Biff and Lem both. A contract that gives the town, not the league, control of the facilities. Would I be correct in assuming you and the rest of the team parents might have a few ideas about how that contract should read?"

"Tell the county attorney I'll be in touch," I said.

"Will do." Randall was studying his deluxe, handicapped-accessible porta-potties with much the same look of disgust and annoyance I usually bestowed on the Brown johns. "And will someone tell me why in tarnation we're still using porta-potties out here? Water and sewer lines came by this way twenty years ago. We could just as easily have flush toilets."

"I gather there's an arrangement between the league and the town that once the league raises the money to pay for them, the town will arrange to have them built."

"Yeah, and it seems pretty strange that neither the Little League nor the Summerball League under Biff can save enough profit from the Snack Shack after all these years. Lem and I were talking about tossing that agreement aside and just having the town build them — our park after all — but Biff has been resisting that idea."

"Maybe it's a matter of pride to him to raise the money instead of asking for a government handout," I said.

"Then why not let us build them and pay us back gradually?" Randall said. "You get some real flush toilets in here and business at the Snack Shack will boom. Right now, half the people who come to a game sit nursing a small water for two hours cause they'd rather faint from dehydration than use the porta-john. Not to mention the people who drive back to town for a bathroom and buy their snacks there while they're at it."

"You're preaching to the choir," I said. "Why don't we get these unloaded before Biff thinks of some other reason to turn them away."

"Let's talk to the chief," he said. "We can't put them over by the old one. Let's see how much distance he wants between them and his murder site."

"Body dump site, actually," I said. "But yeah."

After consultation with the chief, we arranged to put the porta-potties all the way at the other side of the field from where the old porta-potty was, and the truck lumbered off to the far end of the parking lot.

Randall had brought three of his workmen to help unload the porta-potties. He and one of the men climbed up on the truck and shoved a porta-potty onto a little elevator platform at the back of the truck bed. Then the driver lowered the platform until it was at ground level, where the other two men could shove the porta-potty off the platform and wrestle it into place. If I'd been doing it, I'd have tried to back the truck as close to the desired spot as possible, to avoid quite so much manual labor, but I didn't want to suggest it, lest the volunteers take that as an insult to their physical prowess. So I merely watched and praised their efforts when all three new porta-potties were neatly lined up and ready for customers.

Just then another truck lumbered down

the road, towing a bright blue object that I recognized as one of Randall's job site trailers.

"I thought the chief could use it as a mobile investigation headquarters for however long he has to spend out here," Randall said, when he saw my puzzled stare. "Let's go surprise him with it."

The chief seemed charmed by the loan of the trailer, and supervised unloading it at the far end of the parking lot, near the new porta-potties.

"That was very thoughtful, Randall," he said. "I'm much obliged to you."

"Let me show you around," Randall said, leading the way into the trailer.

Inside, to the right of the door, a built-in U-shaped banquette provided seating around a table at one end, while a desk and chair stood on the left side. I took a seat around the table and watched as Randall gave the chief a tour. A brief tour, since the trailer was only about eight feet wide and twenty long, meaning someone sitting behind the desk wouldn't have to raise his voice much to be heard by anyone on the banquette.

"And you can lock up when you leave," Randall said, handing the chief a key ring. "And —"

"Chief?"

We looked up to see Horace and Dad peering in the door of the trailer.

"Come in," the chief said. "Do you have some information for me? Time of death, for example?"

"From my initial examination, between ten p.m. and two a.m.," Dad said, as he seated himself at the table and I scooted along to the center of the U-shaped seat to make room for Horace. "That's based mainly on body temperature and lividity. I may be able to refine that further when I get him on the autopsy table."

Dad sounded almost cheerful at the thought of doing the autopsy. Luckily, everyone now in the trailer completely understood that his enthusiasm arose from his passionate desire to solve Shep's murder, and that he'd have been infinitely happier if it were a case of performing hours of heroic life-saving measures on a wounded victim. Still, even Dad seemed to realize his tone might upset the uninitiated.

"Chief, you'll notify Mr. Brown that we're doing the autopsy, right?" Dad added. "People seem to take that so much better coming from you."

"Of course." The chief nodded, scribbled something in his notebook and turned his gaze to Horace — who, from his expression, had something to report.

"He definitely wasn't killed in the porta-potty," Horace said. Not a surprise to me, since I'd already heard what Horace and Dad had told Aida. And from the chief's expression, not a surprise to him.

"Not enough blood spatter?" the chief asked.

"No blood spatter at all, technically," Horace said. "Blood drops on the floor and a little smearing on the walls, all consistent with his being killed somewhere nearby and stuffed almost immediately into the porta-potty."

"Why nearby?" the chief said. "Couldn't the killer, for example, have killed him somewhere else — just about anywhere else — and driven the body over here to use the porta-potty as a body dump?"

Both Dad and Horace were already shaking their heads.

"Livor mortis," Dad said. "That's the way the blood settles in a body after death," he added, presumably for Randall's benefit, since the chief and Horace were familiar with the term from their jobs, and I'd grown up listening to Dad's peculiar ideas of proper dinner table conversation. "The livor mortis is entirely consistent with the position in which Meg found him, which means he either was killed in the porta-potty —"

"Which is not possible," Horace interrupted.

"— or he was put into the porta-potty very soon after death," Dad went on. "Livor mortis can start to show between twenty minutes and two or three hours after death."

"More important, the body's not going to be dripping blood for more than a few minutes," Horace said. "He was killed somewhere around here, and then hidden in the porta-potty while he was still bleeding."

"So we need to search the area to find the actual murder location," the chief said. "Which means we need to keep everyone away for a while."

"Mr. Witherington — you met him, right?" Randall said. "The man from the Summerball national office?"

The chief nodded.

"We've been strategizing on how to re-arrange the schedule." Strategizing in the absence of Biff, apparently. "Be nice if we could announce the new plan at the end of the opening ceremony."

"Which starts at noon," the chief said.

"But we don't have to announce the schedule first thing," Randall said. "We can keep people busy for a while with the speechifying."

"How much time will you need?" the chief asked, looking at Horace.

"At least a few hours," Horace said. "If you think you can get people to sit still for a couple of hours of speeches . . . well, count me as glad I'll be busy out here."

"Read out the names of all the kids," I suggested. "And have them come up on stage to shake Mr. Witherington's hand and pose on stage with him for group pictures. That will eat up some time, and all the families will stay."

"And maybe Minerva could round up some of the choir members and give them a few songs," the chief said. "Though 'Take Me Out to the Ball Game,' might be the extent of their baseball repertoire."

"They could do a few patriotic songs," Randall said. " 'God Bless America' and such. Good ideas, all. Be nice if we could get in at least one game today, though, even if we have to bring in the lights to do it."

"Why don't we tentatively plan to release the field at six," the chief said. "And if it looks as if we won't be ready by then, we'll let you know."

"Thanks," Randall said.

"And before you leave," the chief went on,

"can you arrange to leave that truck here, or maybe send it back later? The one you used to haul the new porta-potties here. We need to take the old one away."

"Back to Biff's?" Randall asked, sounding puzzled.

"No, it's still potential evidence," the chief said. "We'd like you to haul it down to the station and put it in the vehicle impound lot. We can lock it up there in case we need to do any more tests on it."

"The far end of the impound lot," Horace added, grimacing as if he wasn't looking forward to the possibility of going near the porta-potty for those additional tests.

"Can do," Randall said. "I'll tell my driver to stand by till you're ready."

He nodded in farewell and left the trailer.

"And I should leave you three to your police work," I said to Dad, Horace, and the chief. "I can get a ride back to town with Randall." I picked up my tote and started to slide toward Horace's end of the seat, and he hopped up to let me out. But before I could get up, the chief spoke up.

"Just one more thing." He looked down at his notebook and frowned.

I sat down on the banquette again.

CHAPTER 8

"Just to clear something up," the chief said. "Mr. Brown claims he's been receiving threatening phone calls from someone. A woman."

"I bet he means me." Just like Biff to try causing me trouble. I took a deep breath before going on. "I've been calling him for weeks — at least once a day for the past few weeks. His company is supposed to be renovating the town square, and so far I haven't seen a single workman on site. But I'm not sure it counts as threatening phone calls since I've never gotten past his secretary."

"You never used . . . intemperate language?" the chief asked.

"Of course she didn't," Dad chimed in.

"I might have to him if I'd ever reached him," I said. "But not to his secretary. I always tried to be polite to her. Not her fault he's dodging me. Couple of times I told her to tell him it was no use sending any more invoices because we weren't paying a red cent until we saw some progress on the town square. Made her write it down. I suppose that might have sounded like a threat to him. But I never said that to him — never got a chance to. Is there such a thing as threatening While You Were Out notes?"

"I rather doubt it." The chief was fighting a smile. "You never called his cell phone?"

"I don't think I have his cell phone number." I pulled out mine, looked at the contact list, and shook my head. "No. Hard as he was to reach, if I'd had a cell phone number I'd have used it, but I don't. I only have what I believe is his office number."

I repeated the number. The chief scribbled it down, then flipped to another page and nodded.

"Yes, that's his office number," he said.

"If making one or two calls a day to his office in a vain attempt to find out if he's ever going to do a lick of work on the town square is harassment, then guilty as charged," I said. "I've also sent him a couple of e-mails a week, and the occasional snail mail. But that's all I've done, and I'd be happy to share my phone and e-mail records if you want them. I have no idea how one goes about doing that, but I'm sure you can tell me."

"No need," the chief said. "Since Mr. Brown raised the issue of threatening phone calls, we should have no difficulty getting a warrant to examine all his phone records." He sounded rather pleased at the prospect — almost smug. I wondered if Biff realized how useful his complaint about harassment might be to the chief — or how inconvenient for himself, if he had anything to hide. "Given the business relationship between your employer and Brown Construction," the chief went on, "I would be surprised not to see your number there."

"You'll see my office number as well as my cell," I said. "I don't recall ever trying to reach him from our home phone, but I can't swear I never did. So does this mean you're operating on the theory that Biff, rather than his brother, was the intended victim?" None of my civilian business, technically, but since the chief seemed to be in a mellow mood, I risked asking.

"I'm not operating on any theory yet," the chief said. "What was it Sherlock Holmes said about theories?"

" 'It is a capital mistake to theorize before one has data,' " I rattled off. And as I continued, Dad chimed in so we were reciting in unison. " 'Insensibly one begins to

118

twist facts to suit theories, instead of theories to suit facts.' "

Sherlockian trivia had been as much a part of my childhood dinner table conversations as fascinating medical facts.

"Precisely." The chief looked only mildly startled by our Holmesian duet. "It's much too early to speculate on whether Mr. Henson was himself the target or whether he was merely the victim of an unfortunate physical resemblance to the killer's real target."

"Did Randall mention that one of his cousins saw Biff having a fight with one of the Pruitts?" I asked. "And he didn't mean just an argument; they had to be pulled apart. I only got it third hand, but it stuck in my mind."

"I'll look into it." The chief made a few more notes. "Did Randall happen to say which cousin? Or which Pruitt?"

"His cousin Cephus, and I don't know which Pruitt, but probably one whose kid is on the Yankees."

The chief nodded and scribbled.

"My money's on Biff as the target," Dad said. "After all, people don't very often yell 'Kill the umpire' in real life."

"And when they do, they're usually just venting," Horace added. "Has anyone ever really killed an umpire?"

"Not since 1927, to the best of my knowledge." Yes, the chief would know something like that. "And baseball was a much rowdier game in the late eighteen-hundreds and early nineteen-hundreds. I doubt if this murder has much to do with baseball — historically, most of the violence against umpires, or for that matter players and coaches, has been committed in the heat of the moment — during the game or shortly thereafter."

"Yeah," Horace said. "And there's not much baseball going on around here between ten p.m. and two a.m., so heat of the moment won't fly as a mitigating circumstance."

"And remember," the chief added, "Lem Shiffley didn't use Mr. Henson as an umpire in the fall season, so to my knowledge, Mr. Henson hasn't officiated at a game since the end of last year's spring Little League season, a good nine months ago. I'm sure a few parents are still complaining about some of his more egregiously bad calls in the playoffs, but I have a hard time believing that any of them would still be in the throes of homicidal rage. I'm not discounting Shep's — or Biff's — involvement in baseball as a possible motive, but I suspect we'll need to look off the diamond for the killer's motive."

And I suspected he'd be relieved to find the motive outside baseball. After all, the chief was such a passionate Baltimore Orioles fan that he'd named his sons after his favorite ballplayers. And at least one of his sons had followed suit — the one whose untimely death, with his wife, in a car crash had made Henry and Minerva the custodial grandparents of Frank Robinson Burke, Jr., Calvin Ripken Burke, and Adam Jones Burke.

"Well, idle speculation won't solve this," the chief said. "Horace, if you're finished here for the time being, why don't you head over to Mr. Henson's place to search there?"

"You've made arrangements with Sheriff Whicker, then?" Horace slid out of the banquette and picked up his forensic kit.

"No," the chief said. "If at all possible, I'd like for you to see it exactly the way he left it, not the way it will look after some nosy Clay County deputy finishes contaminating anything that might have evidentiary value."

"Yeah," Horace said. "They're not so good on subtleties like chain of custody."

"So I'll make my call once you're parked in front of the house," the chief said. "And you can be there waiting to keep an eye on them."

"Might help if you could send Vern along, too," Horace said. "He's better at handling those Clay County deputies." Probably because, in spite of the longstanding tension between inhabitants of the two counties, Vern, like his counterparts in our neighboring jurisdiction, was a good old boy who'd grown up hunting the local woods while Horace, like me, was not originally from around here.

"Good idea," the chief said.

Horace waited while the chief called Vern to issue his instructions, then nodded to us and left the trailer.

"I should go, too," Dad said. "I'm going to see how soon I can arrange the autopsy."

He slid out of his end of the banquette, nodded farewell to us, and dashed out of the trailer with a look of happy concentration on his face.

"You know one thing I like about your dad as a medical examiner?" the chief said. "He's stopped asking me if I want to watch the autopsy. He'd love it if I did, and he's quick to call me in if there's something I really need to see, but he doesn't badger me about watching. Unlike his predecessor, who seemed to think I was falling down on the job if I wasn't right there looking over his shoulder every second. Definitely an improvement."

He didn't have to mention the fact that, unlike Dr. Smoot, his predecessor, Dad was not obsessed with vampires and didn't show up at crime scenes wearing a black velvet cape with a red satin lining and sporting fake fangs. But I knew that was another big factor in his approval of Dad.

"He hasn't stopped asking me to the autopsies," I said. "But that's because he still hasn't entirely given up hope that I'll suddenly change my mind and apply to med school so I can follow in his footsteps."

The chief chuckled at that.

"And speaking of following in his footsteps, I'm going to see if he can give me a ride." I slid out of the banquette, stood up, slung my tote over my shoulder, and turned for the door. "If he's going to the hospital he'll have to pass by the town square. The still completely unrenovated town square."

"I can arrange a ride if your father leaves you behind." The chief closed his notebook and folded his hands on top of it. "Just one more thing — are you at all exaggerating your difficulties in contacting Mr. Brown?"

"No," I said. "Randall put me in charge of managing the contract with him about six weeks ago, and last night, when he crashed our party, was the first time I ever saw him or spoke to him."

"A pity," the chief said.

"Yeah, I'm starting to get a little anxious about whether the town square is going to be usable for the Memorial Day festivities," I said.

"Actually, I meant a pity because I would have liked to have heard your opinions on Mr. Brown and his business practices. In fact, I still would, if you manage to see enough of him to form opinions."

"What exactly do you suspect him of?" I asked.

The chief pursed his lips and frowned slightly. I could see he was torn. On the one hand, I was a civilian, and he strongly disapproved of amateur interference in his police work. On the other hand, as a member of the town and county government, I wasn't just any civilian, and I hoped he knew from past experience that I wasn't like those annoying amateur detectives in the mystery books Dad was so fond of reading. If I found evidence I'd bring it to him, not hide it and try to conduct my own investigation.

"We've received complaints about him," the chief said finally. "Anonymous complaints, which makes it blasted difficult to know whether to pay any attention to them or not."

"What were the complaints about?" I asked.

"At first, that Brown was cheating people," the chief said. "The letters told us to look at his company's books and see how badly he was cheating people."

"And was he?"

"Blessed if I know," the chief said. "Since a few anonymous hate mails didn't exactly give me cause to demand to see Mr. Brown's financial records. I talked to a few people who'd hired his company to do projects. None of them were falling over themselves to recommend him, but no one had any specific complaints. A little grumbling about how long everything took and how expensive it all was, but you get that with almost any contractor. Not much more I can do without him finding out I'm investigating him and complaining of harassment."

"The letters don't give any clues?" I asked.

"Apart from the fact that they were all mailed either here or in Clay County, no."

"What about people who work for Biff?" I asked. "Or even better, used to work for him?"

"So far everyone I've found still works for

him, and is from Clay County to boot —
which gives them two reasons not to talk to
me, even if I wanted to tip my hand. And
something like half of them seem to be
related to him, which makes three reasons.
Apparently he uses a lot of transient labor
— immigrants, many of them; legal as far as
I can tell, but even if I could track them
down, they might not feel inclined to speak
to law enforcement, so I didn't try too hard.
I'd done what I could and found nothing,
so I put it aside."

"In that part of your brain where you keep
stuff that bothers you because right now
you can't do anything about it," I suggested.
"But there's always hope for the future?"

"Yes," the chief said, with a slight smile.
"Nothing I can do without evidence, but I
was definitely going to keep my eye on him.
And I filled in Randall when all this first
happened, about six or seven weeks ago,
which might mean he took the accusations
of cheating seriously enough to want your
eagle eye on Mr. Brown."

"Could be," I said. "Especially since if
Randall accused him of cheating, Biff could
try to pretend he was doing it to discredit a
rival."

"Whereas you would be perceived as a
more impartial witness."

"Impartial." I shook my head at that. "I'm Randall's friend and Randall's employee, and last night I made it pretty clear how I feel about Biff's management of the Summerball League. Not sure anyone will buy that I'm impartial."

"You'd be surprised," the chief said. "At any rate, after a few weeks our anonymous complainant switched tunes and began accusing Mr. Brown of using his business as a cover for running a drug trafficking enterprise."

"I'm not sure I see how a construction business makes a good cover for selling drugs," I said.

"He also runs a scrap metal and used equipment parts business," the chief said. "A glorified junkyard, really. And no more thriving than his construction business."

"But I bet it's mostly a cash business."

"And one that gives people a reason to go out to his premises," the chief said.

"Still," I mused. "Does it really sound all that plausible, or does it just sound as if the anonymous letter writer is saying anything he can think of to cause problems for Biff?"

"Most likely the latter," the chief said. "And I think if Mr. Brown really were running a drug business here in Caerphilly, I'd have noticed by now. But at least this accusation was both more concrete and more capable of being proven — or disproven. So I have had my officers keeping a close eye on Mr. Brown's establishment for the last several weeks."

"I'm dying to ask what they've learned," I said. "But I know better than to ask nosy questions about police business. Although if you're about to arrest the head of the boys' baseball league as a drug kingpin, it might be nice to give the parents a heads-up so we can figure out how to explain it all to the kids."

"And make plans for the celebration, no doubt," the chief said, with a chuckle. "No, either Mr. Brown is considerably more clever than I give him credit —"

"Fat chance," I muttered.

"— or he's not Caerphilly's leading drug lord, and our anonymous informer was either misinformed or, more likely, just trying to cause trouble for Mr. Brown. And ironically ended up doing him a favor."

"By giving him an alibi for the murder?"

"Exactly." The chief took his glasses off, leaned back in his chair, and rubbed his nose thoughtfully. "Not that he would have been our only suspect, or even our primary one — Mr. Henson had a complicated domestic situation and a volatile personality

— but we'd have looked closely at Biff in any case."

"I expect you still will," I said.

The chief cocked his head slightly and raised one eyebrow.

"Doesn't he look to you like the kind of guy who'd hire someone to do his dirty work?" I said. "He does to me."

"I've always found contract killing a particularly troubling crime," the chief said. "There are few things as evil as callously killing another human being for profit."

"Or hiring someone to do so," I said.

"Agreed," the chief said, nodding. "Just as evil, and also remarkably stupid. People who are willing to commit cold-blooded murder rarely have qualms about turning their hand to blackmail. Yes, we will definitely be considering whether Mr. Brown might have reason to want his brother dead."

"Isn't hired killing a hard crime to solve?" I asked.

"Only in the movies," the chief said. "And maybe in the kind of lofty socioeconomic circles where rich people hire contract killers for fees larger than most third world countries' gross national product and transfer the funds via bank accounts in the Caymans. I doubt if Mr. Brown would have any idea how to find such a killer, even if he could afford to hire him. No, if Mr. Brown hired the killer, someone will have seen him handing some shifty character a thick wad of money. Or some good old boy will turn up with a huge, brand-new truck when everybody knows he's got no money and even less credit. Or someone will get drunk down at the Clay Pigeon and brag about doing it."

"The Clay Pigeon?"

"That's the latest incarnation of that unsavory drinking establishment next door to the Clayville Rifle Range," the chief said. "They still haven't figured out that no matter how often they change the name, the state and federal authorities will still find them."

"I don't get over to Clay County much," I said. "And I can't say I've ever been to a bar there."

"I strongly recommend that you remain unacquainted with its loathsome premises." He shuddered slightly. "No, if Mr. Brown hired someone to kill his brother, we'll find him out sooner or later. Look, I realize that in the course of your work with the boys' team and for Randall you're probably going to encounter Mr. Brown. I'd appreciate any information you happen to run across, but be circumspect. He may not have committed the murder himself, but there's still a very real possibility that Mr. Brown engineered it and, if that's so, he will tend to be very intolerant of people asking questions about his affairs."

"Understood." I stood up and shouldered my tote again. Then a thought hit me. "So, you were able to get a list of his customers."

"Only in Caerphilly County," the chief said. "Building permits are a matter of public record, so Mr. Throckmorton in the town clerk's office was easily able to supply me with a list of those issued to Brown Construction."

"I asked him for the same list last night," I said. "I was planning to talk to some of Biff's clients, to see if I could get any tips on how to work with him. I assume getting a similar list of his building projects in Clay County would have been almost as easy."

"But considerably less discreet," the chief said. "For all I know, Mr. Brown could have friends or even family in the Clay County clerk's office. I wouldn't risk it."

Was he warning me off, or just explaining why he wasn't asking for such a list?

"When I get my version of the list, I'll probably still contact a few people on it," I said. "Purely for the purpose of seeing if any of them have a magic formula for mak-

ing Brown Construction do its blasted job."
Unless he wanted to warn me off. The possibility seemed to hang in the air between
us for a few moments.

"Good luck," was all he said.

I nodded, and left the trailer.

CHAPTER 9

When I stepped outside I looked around to see what was happening. The chief's deputies were still combing the baseball field and the parking lot. I had the feeling the department was going to go way over its budget for brown paper evidence bags this month. Nearby, Dad and Aida were still conferring about something.

"Definitely a lot of blood," Dad was saying. "And of course, since he was shot in the head —"

I decided this was not a conversation I needed to overhear. I tuned them out, pulled out my cell phone, and called Michael.

"Coach Waterston of the fabulous Caerphilly Eagles!" he answered. I could hear juvenile cheering and giggling in the background.

"The boys handling this okay?" I asked.

"Fine," he said. "Let me take a few steps

to get away from the small pitchers with big ears. Okay. I think they're doing fine, mainly because most of the adults around them are taking this whole thing pretty much in their stride. No idea how Biff's teams are taking it — we're making sure we keep our distance just in case. I mean, for all I know, Shep could have had a kid on one of those teams. If he has kids — does he?"

"I have no idea," I said. "If he did, I assume they'd be playing in Clay County. Apparently he lived there. So what's the plan?"

"Everyone was planning to spend all day at the ball park," he said. "And we have no idea whether baseball is canceled for the whole day or not. So I invited the team to hang out at our place. Your mother's organizing the food — we've got tons of leftovers anyway. The kids can practice a little, and swim in the pool, and go for rides in the llama cart, and they'll all be together, bonding as a team."

"And if you get a call that the team has to be at the field in ten minutes or forfeit the game, you'll be ready," I said. "Because I bet that would be Biff's style of doing things."

"Bingo," he said.

"I'm catching a ride in with Dad and will join you for the ceremony. Got to run!"

Actually, the reason I was in such a hurry to hang up was not that Dad was leaving — he and Aida were still talking animatedly about something — probably something gory. As I watched, Dad pointed to a spot right between his eyes, and then to a spot on the back of his head. Yes, they were discussing bullet trajectory. More conversation I didn't want to overhear.

But the conversation Biff was having — *that* I wouldn't mind overhearing. He was standing toe to toe with a tall, skeletally thin man with gray hair and a gray Amish–style beard, full all around the face but with the upper lip and chin shaved bare. Though I doubted if the man was Amish — he was dressed in faded jeans, a green John Deere t-shirt, and a bright red baseball cap.

And they were clearly not having a friendly discussion. Biff was shaking his fist, and I could see spittle flying from his mouth and landing on the man's shirt. The taller man's hands were by his side but his fists were clenched, and if I were Biff I'd have taken a step or two backward before those fists came into play.

Not for the first time, I wished I could read lips. But since I couldn't, I decided to move a little closer. I set off toward Dad's car in a diagonal that would take me closer to the two of them, but so gradually that I hoped they wouldn't notice.

It worked at first. I began picking up the odd phrase.

"— wouldn't put it past you," Biff sneered.

"You'd better watch what you're saying," the tall man said.

"Or I'm next — is that what you're saying?"

Just then they both appeared to notice me, broke off their conversation, and headed in different directions. Biff stormed over toward his car, which was in the far end of the parking lot. The tall man hopped into a battered truck that stood near the entrance to the parking lot — a truck that hadn't been there when the chief and I had surveyed vehicles a little while ago.

The tall man drove off. I went and leaned against Dad's car. After about ten minutes, Biff left.

About that time, to my relief, Dad came trotting over. We hopped in his car, and I deliberately started a conversation about baseball's designated hitter rule, a subject on which I knew Dad had firm opinions. I did not, but by playing devil's advocate, I succeeded in distracting him so that he wouldn't tell me any of the gorier details of his preliminary medical examination.

As we were reaching the outskirts of town, and Dad was waxing eloquent on the batting skills of a retired Major League pitcher named Carlos Zambrano, my cell phone rang. Randall.

"I should take this," I said.

"Hey, Meg," Randall said. "How much longer are you going to be out at the ball field?"

"I'm already on my way into town," I said.

"Great! Mr. Witherington and I are making some plans for how to get this weekend's games back on track. We could use your help. Can you meet us on the steps of the town hall?"

"Can do," I said.

"Oh, good," Dad said as I was putting my phone away. "Because I'm sure poor Shep wouldn't want his death to interfere with the game."

"You knew him, then?" Sometimes it surprised even me how much Dad got around.

"Well, no," Dad said. "I've seen him officiate at a few games, though."

"Was he a good umpire?"

"I think it takes a special kind of person to be an umpire," Dad said. "Someone who has both a passionate love of the game and a willingness to do a difficult and unpopular job."

Evidently Dad wasn't going to give me an honest verdict on Biff's umpiring skills.

"I think that's one of the most important things we can teach the kids," Dad went on. "That it's important to respect the ump's position, even when we don't agree with his decision."

Then again, maybe Dad had just made his verdict pretty clear.

We pulled up in front of the town hall. I hopped out and waved as Dad drove off toward Caerphilly Hospital. In the town square, the crowds were already assembling on the benches that formed a half circle at the foot of the bandstand, though some people were still coming and going from the various shops and restaurants that surrounded the square on three sides. And a few people had discovered that the white marble town hall steps provided a good vantage point. Randall and Mr. Witherington were seated near the top.

I stopped halfway up to scan the town square, and felt my frustration rising. The bandstand, draped in red, white, and blue bunting in honor of the Founder's Day Weekend, looked festive from a distance, but if you looked close you could see all the peeling paint and broken bits of woodwork. And what should have been a lush, green lawn, broken only by the neatly raked paths, was a piebald muddle of green, brown, and red clay. Biff Brown ought to have been ashamed of himself for not having made at least some progress in the renovations. But I suspected he didn't even care.

I took a few of Rose Noire's calming breaths and continued my climb, nodding greetings to friends, relatives, and neighbors along the way.

"We're in a pickle," Randall said, as I reached the top step. "If you count all the levels, from t-ball through intermediate, we had sixteen games scheduled, four a day from this morning until Monday afternoon, and we're not going to have nearly enough daylight to get it all in."

He showed me the schedule, which had games posted for nine, eleven thirty, two, and four thirty on each of the four days of Founder's Day Weekend.

"And that's assuming we don't have any rain delays," Mr. Witherington said. "Unfortunately we're under a threat of scattered thunderstorms from tomorrow on."

"There's a whole bunch of daylight you're not using," I said. "The early kind. Start the games at eight instead of nine. And if you

139

have Randall bring a whole bunch of his portable construction lights to the field, you can keep the games going till eight or nine at night."

On one margin of the schedule I scribbled a possible alternation, with games starting at eight, ten thirty, one, three thirty, and six. Randall and Mr. Witherington studied it briefly and then they both nodded.

"We might even be able to get in a sixth game, at eight thirty," Randall said. "If it's one of the majors teams — those games tend to move faster anyway, and the parents won't be quite as vexed if the kids are up late, especially on a holiday weekend."

"That seems sensible to me," Mr. Witherington said. "Though I would like to discuss the issue with Mr. Brown. He seemed averse to the thought of an early start when I suggested it — I gather he didn't think the local folk would like it."

"I think under the circumstances people would understand," I said.

"Mr. Brown may not be as knowledgeable about how the locals feel as he thinks he is," Randall said.

"Yes." Mr. Witherington's tone had grown just a shade less warm. "I gather there has been a certain amount of . . . tension in the league. I do hope I can help resolve that —

140

but first we need to get these games back on track — preferably with Mr. Brown's co-operation, or at least consent. And if we can ever manage to reach him, I would also like to discuss with him the possibility of doing just a little bit of maintenance at the field before the first game. I realize that he inherited a field that had been left in fairly poor condition thanks to years of neglect by the local management of another youth baseball organization, and that he has had to spend a great deal of time and money getting it into the shape it is now but — I beg your pardon? Have I said something amusing?"

Both Randall and I had burst into laughter. In fact, Randall was leaning back on the steps, clutching his stomach as he uttered howls of laughter. I recovered first, perhaps because I could see the look on Mr. Wither-ington's face.

"I'm so sorry," I said. "This weekend is already going very far from the way you wanted it to, isn't it? You arrive expecting a quiet weekend of baseball, and instead you find yourself out in the boonies watching something that looks like the Hatfields and the McCoys going at it, complete with a genuine murder, and you're probably look-ing around, wondering which of these lunatics can be trusted, or maybe whether any of them can."

"Well, I wouldn't go quite that far," Mr. Witherington said, a tremulous smile returning to his face. "But yes, the weekend has not gone as expected."

"Sorry," Randall said. "We weren't laughing at you. It's just that — well, Biff's right that the newly organized Summerball League inherited the field in pretty poor condition, thanks to neglect by the previous management."

"Yes," Mr. Witherington said. "That's easy to see."

"What he doesn't mention is that he was the previous management," I said.

"I beg your pardon?" Mr Witherington looked puzzled.

"Biff used to hold the same position with the previous league that he does in our Summerball League," Randall said. "For about six or seven years. So I give you the pretty poor shape thanks to neglect, but if he tried to suggest that it was someone else's fault, then shame on him."

"The reason we're with Summerball is that everyone dropped out of the other league to get away from Biff," I said.

"Then how did he get elected head of our league?" Mr. Witherington demanded.

"He never did," Randall said. "Not in any meeting or election I ever heard about. My uncle Lemuel Shiffley was elected president, and people were pretty happy with how he ran things for last year's fall season, but during the winter break he took sick and had to cut down on things."

"And suddenly we got an e-mail saying that Biff was head of the league," I said.

"There should have been a meeting of the league," Mr. Witherington said.

"Neither my husband nor I heard about a meeting," I said.

"I hear rumors that there might have been a meeting," Randall said. "But apparently, through some oversight, only a small portion of the league parents heard about it in time to attend."

"Or heard about it at all," I said.

"We were told there was a meeting," Mr. Witherington said. "And we received half a dozen glowing letters of recommendation for Mr. Brown."

"Match the names on those letters against the names of the parents on the two teams he's coaching," I said. "The Yankees in the majors and the Stoats in coach-pitch."

"He's not without friends," Randall said. "He takes care of his friends, and his friends take care of him."

"These are very disturbing allegations," Mr. Witherington said.

"Don't take our word for them, then," I said. "Take your time. Do your research. Talk to as many parents as you like — though you might want to keep in mind that a lot of people are afraid to speak up for fear of hurting their kids' prospects in the league. I'll try to spread the word that it's okay to talk to you, but some people will still be wary."

Mr. Witherington nodded, but I could see he was still a little uneasy.

"In the meantime," Randall said, "I'm going to get some lights ready to bring over to the field tomorrow, and I'm going to have a crew on standby who can sweep in and fix things up a bit as soon as the chief releases the field. If you talk to Biff and the two of you decide you don't want any of that, just tell me and we'll stand down."

Mr. Witherington studied us for what seemed like a couple of years. He definitely had a good face for a corporate guy — the thick lenses made it hard to read his eyes, and the rest of his features didn't give away a thing. I wouldn't have wanted to play poker against him.

"Thank you," he said. "I appreciate the offer, and I'll let you know my decision very shortly." He turned to go, then looked back. "And thank you for your candor."

He picked a cautious path down the steps, carefully looked both ways at the street, and made his way toward the bandstand.

"Did we come on too strong?" Randall asked.

"Time will tell," I said.

"I'm an impatient cuss," he said, with a laugh. "You know that. What's your best guess?"

"We haven't convinced him," I said. "But we've planted a seed. We need to give it space to grow."

"Just space? No encouragement?"

"Time and space," I said. "I think if we give it those, Biff will do the encouraging we need, all by himself. Let him make our case for us. By the way — on another subject, though not really unrelated, I gather Biff and Shep are both originally from Clay County?"

"And Shep still lives there," Randall said. "Lived, that is. Biff bought a house over here for his family about ten, twelve years ago."

"And he moved his business at the same time?"

"He never moved his business," Randall said. "Just his driveway." He laughed at the

145

puzzled look on my face and continued. "His office and scrapyard have always been right along the Caerphilly/Clay County line. Eventually he came up with the notion that he'd have better odds of getting business over here if he had a Caerphilly address, so he bought ten acres of useless swampland off my cousin Porterfield — land that just happened to be right next to his, but on this side of the border. And he made himself a brand new driveway that came out to the same road, but on the Caerphilly side of the line."

"And contracts poured in from grateful Caerphilly residents?"

"Not so's you'd notice." Randall shook his head and grimaced slightly. "He's real good at schmoozing when he's trying to get a job. Hasn't figured out that it also matters how you treat folks during the job, not to mention at the grocery store and the town square."

"And at the ball field," I added.

"Precisely," he said. "Want to bet he tries to use Shep's death as an excuse not to meet his deadline?"

With that he shook his head and headed down the steps toward the bandstand.

"Not on my watch," I muttered.

I headed down the steps myself, more

slowly, scanning the crowd as I went; looking for Biff. I realized I needed to talk to him today. Ask him if the loss of a key employee — and a family member at that — was going to interfere with his completion of the contract. If he said yes, I could offer to let him out of it, suggest we'd keep him in mind for the next available bit of town or county work. If he said no —

"What in the world is your fool grandfather up to?"

CHAPTER 10

I looked up to see Cordelia standing at the foot of the courthouse steps, with her hands on her hips, frowning at something over in the town square. I followed her gaze and saw that Grandfather had arranged to have his portable booth set up — the one he used during Caerphilly's various festivals to support his efforts to raise public consciousness of environmental or animal welfare issues. Today, the banner over the booth read THE EAGLE HAS LANDED!

"Oh, that's right," I said. "He mentioned that he was going to bring a bald eagle to exhibit. In honor of the boys' team, and to help raise awareness of the environmental issues threatening the species. And before you ask, it's not a wild eagle — he's bringing one from the zoo's raptor rehabilitation unit that's too badly injured to be safely returned to the wild."

"Bald eagle, eh?" Cordelia uttered a sound

that might have been either a snort or a sharp chuckle. "You might want to tell the old reprobate to get his eyesight checked."

With that she strode off. I sighed, closed my eyes, and took a few of those deep, calming breaths Rose Noire was always recommending I take when dealing with our family. It didn't seem to help much. Of course, maybe it would have helped more if thinking of Rose Noire didn't remind me of how she was such a consummate romantic and believed Cordelia and Grandfather, having been reunited, were eventually going to become a couple again, in spite of having gotten along perfectly fine without each other for well over half a century. I'd be satisfied if they just started speaking to each other again, instead of sniping at each other from a distance, using me as an intermediary.

I strolled over to see what Grandfather was doing that had so provoked Cordelia's scorn.

I found him glaring at two uniformed zookeepers, one tall and blond, the other short and very tanned. From the anxious looks on their faces, I suspected he'd been doing more than glaring.

"What's up?" I asked.

"I'm planning some remedial training for

Axel and Manoj," Grandfather said.

"We know what an eagle looks like," said the short, dark zookeeper. His faint Indian accent suggested that he was probably Manoj. The tall blond, provisionally identified as Axel, just rolled his eyes.

"Oh, really?" Grandfather said. "Meg, what do you think of the fine eagle they brought me?"

He strode over to a tarp-shrouded object to the left of the booth and whisked off its covering, revealing a large bird hunched on a perch in the center. It was almost three feet tall with dark feathers and the unmistakably naked red head of a —

"Turkey vulture, right?" I said. "Not an eagle, of course, but a very fine specimen of his species. Unusually large, isn't he?"

"Yes, a very fine specimen." Grandfather seemed pleased by my praise. "He had an unfortunate experience with a barbed wire fence — damaged his left wing so badly that he's unable to fly. But otherwise a very healthy specimen." His face grew thunderous again. "Of *Cathartes aura.* Not *Haliaeetus leucocephalus,* which is what Axel and Manoj were instructed to bring."

"Nobody instructed me about anything except to bring the truck around to the aviary," Axel said.

150

"The message I was given didn't say to bring an eagle," Manoj said. "It specifically said to bring Alexander Hamilton."

"Alexander Hamilton?" I echoed.

"We name the eagles after famous patriots," Manoj said.

"Then why didn't you bring him?" Grandfather demanded.

"Alexander Hamilton is molting, and also off his feed," Manoj explained.

"Perhaps he's sulking about the plans to kick him off the ten-dollar bill," I suggested.

"Did you call Dr. Rutledge?" Grandfather's face changed from anger to concern.

"I did," Manoj said. "And he said Alexander Hamilton will be fine, but he also said to leave him at the zoo to rest, and take another bird instead. And as you have said yourself, even when they are in good health, the bald eagles are timid with crowds and easily stressed. So since I did not know there was a particular reason for bringing an eagle, I considered all the birds in the raptor refuge and asked myself which would put on the best show and actually enjoy being admired by the public. And the answer, of course?" He flung out his arm toward the vulture. "Escoffier!"

"Gesundheit," Axel muttered.

"We name the vultures and buzzards after

151

famous chefs," Grandfather said.

Escoffier appeared to recognize his name. He shifted slightly, and then hunched his neck lower, uttered a low hissing sound, and spread out his wings in a gesture eerily reminiscent of a B-movie vampire preparing to pounce on his cowering human prey.

"A real crowd-pleaser, I can tell," I said. "So what's the problem?"

"My great-grandsons play for the Caerphilly Eagles!" Grandfather exclaimed. "Not the Caerphilly Vultures!"

"So call the zoo and organize another eagle," I said. "And in the meantime, cover up the eagle sign and let people enjoy the vulture. Unless for some reason you're just in the mood for yelling at people about every little mistake," I added, frowning at Grandfather.

"Or explaining another dozen times why the mistake wasn't your fault," Axel put in, although it was unclear from the direction in which he was looking whether he was aiming this barb at Grandfather or Manoj. "You mind helping with this?" he asked me, holding out one end of an oversized sheet of paper. "You're tall enough. Of course, so's your grandfather, but I guess he's too important to hang up signs."

Grandfather harrumphed. Which, in his

present mood, was actually a pretty positive sign. Maybe he was starting to like this Axel kid. I knew I was.

Grandfather and Manoj watched as Axel and I spread out the paper and taped it along the top of the booth.

"Vulture Culture," Grandfather read. His voice sounded faintly disapproving.

"You do remember that I asked if you had a better suggestion, right?" Axel said. "Manoj, how about if you stay here and explain the vulture to people. I'll go back and see if I can liberate an eagle."

Without waiting for an answer, Axel strode off.

"Escoffier and I will endeavor to be a credit to the zoo until his replacement arrives," Manoj said. I could tell that he was trying to stand up straight and proud — all the zoo personnel knew that Grandfather approved of people who stood up for themselves when he challenged them. But his shoulders were hunched so tensely that his posture bore an unfortunate resemblance to Escoffier's.

"Sounds excellent," I said. "Grandfather, let's go watch the ceremony." I took Grandfather's arm and steered him toward the bandstand, partly to get him out of Manoj's hair, and also in the hope that if I had him

153

in tow some kindly soul would offer us some of the limited available seats. Though I'd settle for getting him one.

"I suppose you think I was too hard on them," Grandfather said. "Well . . . I will go back later and praise Manoj's work with Escoffier. He's a good lad. A little more seasoning and he'll make a fine head keeper for the aviary."

"And Axel shows management potential if you ask me," I said. "Good problem-solving skills."

"He's not a zoology student," Grandfather said. "He's only working at the zoo part time. I think he's studying *business.*" From his tone, you'd think Axel was pursuing the academic study of cannibalism, necrophilia, or identity theft.

"Even better," I said. "Who do you want running the practical side of things? Someone who knows the proper diet to feed the naked mole rats or someone who knows how to manage your finances so you don't bounce the check that pays for your Purina Naked Mole Rat Chow."

"We don't feed them commercial food," Grandfather said. "They eat tubers and roots. And —"

"Kidding," I said.

"Point taken."

We found some family members near the front who had saved us seats. Randall, Mr. Witherington, Biff, and a couple of other local dignitaries were seated in folding chairs at the right side of the bandstand, and Fred Singer, the owner, editor, and pretty much entire staff of the *Caerphilly Clarion,* had set up a big photo backdrop on the left and was occupying himself during the wait by taking crowd shots. The red, white, and blue FOUNDER'S DAY banner still hung over the stage, and someone had added a SUMMERBALL! banner beneath it. A contingent of New Life Baptist Choir members in their maroon satin robes were hovering near the left side of the stage. In various parts of the crowd you could see small patches of color where some of the teams were sitting — the red and blue of the Red Sox, the black and gold of the Pirates, Wombats in blue and gray, Sandgnats in green and white, Grasshoppers in orange and green. I took out my phone and snapped a few shots of the multicolored sea of people.

"Oh, great," someone murmured behind me. I recognized one of the Eagle parents. "Brace yourself for an hour of hot air when *he* gets started."

I assumed he meant Biff, since Mr. Witherington was an unknown quantity and Randall had earned a reputation for making speeches that were entertaining, pithy, and above all short.

But when it came time for the ceremony to start, Mr. Witherington stepped forward to the microphone. He thanked the community for joining the Summerball family, offered a few platitudes on sportsmanship, and ventured a rather dry joke at which we all laughed with enthusiasm once we realized it was supposed to be funny.

"At this time I'd like to bring up someone who needs no introduction to those of you who live here," Mr. Witherington said.

Biff bounded out of his seat and over to the microphone.

"Mr. Biff Brown." In a surprisingly deft maneuver, Mr. Witherington managed to place himself between Biff and the microphone, while appearing to be merely placing a consoling arm around Biff's shoulder. "I'm sure all our thoughts are with Mr. Brown in his time of sorrow," he went on. "And I know better than to tax him further at such a stressful time. Ladies and gentlemen, may we have a moment of silence for the late Mr. Shep Henson, who served his community so well as an official in our national pastime."

He bowed his head, so of course Biff had to follow suit. Some of us in the audience did, but I think most were sneakily watching to see what happened when the moment of silence was over.

Biff moved slightly, as if about to make a break for the microphone, but before he could do so, Mr. Witherington abuptly grabbed both of Biff's hands with his and shook the resulting ball of hands up and down a few times before throwing his arm around Biff's shoulders again and steering him gently but firmly back to his seat. While that was going on, Randall stepped up to the microphone.

"All you ballplayers get ready," Randall said. "When Mr. Witherington calls your names, I want you to file up onto the stage here, and then you'll all stay here while Fred from the *Clarion* takes your pictures for the paper. Let's start with the t-ball players. Oh, and for those of you who might be tempted to sneak out after your team comes up on stage, keep in mind that a contingent from the New Life Baptist Choir will be singing a melody of patriotic songs at the conclusion of the ceremony, and with any luck by the time they're finished we'll have a revised weekend baseball schedule for you."

It did take a while for all the teams to

traipse across the stage and have their pictures taken — especially since Randall allowed time for all the parents and grandparents to take plenty of photos of their ballplayers. But even without the promise of the concert, I think our innate small town sense of fair play would have kept most people in their seats.

That and the chance to gawk at someone who might be either Shep's murderer or the murderer's intended victim.

We all behaved ourselves and stayed quiet while the names were called, but during the photo sessions a pleasant hum of conversations arose as the Caerphillians exchanged theories.

Biff had killed Shep because Shep was having an affair with Biff's wife.

Shep had tried to kill Biff because Biff was having an affair with Shep's wife, and Biff had killed Shep in self-defense.

Some other enraged cuckolded husband had killed Shep, with or without mistaking him for Biff.

Shep's enraged ex-wife had killed him in a drunken rage.

An enraged ex-customer had killed Shep, either mistaking him for Biff or for his own sake.

Or an enraged ex- or current employee.

An enraged unpaid vendor.

An enraged baseball parent.

There was even a theory that Shep had been killed in retaliation for Brown Construction's many and varied outrages against the environment. False claims to be using green building materials. Dumping waste materials in local woods and streams. Cutting down a tree in which a pair of eagles had built a nest.

When the last set of rumors crept down our row, I stole a glance at Grandfather. If anyone in Caerphilly was apt to take offense at Brown Construction's environmental sins it was Grandfather. In fact, I could see him frown and I knew he was taking note. Odds were he'd investigate the rumors, and if he judged them to be true, he'd take action. Organize a protest rally, or a boycott of Brown Construction. Denounce them in the local paper. Even march up to Biff with a camera crew and provoke a confrontation he could use on *Crimes Against Nature,* his ongoing series of documentaries exposing people who willfully caused damage to the environment. He hadn't done one on the construction industry yet. Maybe he was thinking it was time. And he could easily have mistaken Biff for Shep — I'd done it, and my eyesight was a lot better than his.

But shoot someone in the head, stuff him in a porta-potty, and then slink off? Not Grandfather's style. And while he was in good shape for a man in his nineties, I wasn't sure he was capable of lifting Shep and stuffing him into the porta-potty. And he certainly wouldn't have been down at the ball field doing so between 10:00 P.M. and 2:00 A.M., when Dad estimated the murder had taken place. He'd have been fast asleep in one of our guest rooms, snoring loud enough to be heard down in the kitchen. I was pretty sure I recalled hearing him.

The one interesting thing about all these rumors was that with the exception of the few about possible jealous husbands and ex-wives, all of them seemed to find Biff a much more likely target for murder than his half brother. I studied Biff as he sat, squirming impatiently while Mr. Witherington read out the names of the players with Randall prompting in an undertone before anything hard to pronounce. Biff didn't look very happy. Of course, he rarely did. But still. Was his the face of a man grieving the loss of a brother? Or merely one annoyed at having to give up the spotlight? The face of a man worried that he was the real target of a killer? Or the killer himself?

He didn't look worried. Maybe a little grumpy. And someone should explain to him that when you're sitting on a stage in front of several hundred people, it's downright rude to keep checking your cell phone every five minutes.

I'd been going back and forth on whether to tackle him after the ceremony. Open up a discussion on the town square contract, and maybe on the ball field maintenance contract. I'd been leaning toward giving him a pass until tomorrow or even until the four-day weekend was over. But after watching him in action, I decided he wasn't that grief-stricken. I'd tackle him.

I glanced around to see how other people were reacting and spotted someone.

The woman who'd almost certainly told Biff about the Eagles' so-called unauthorized practice. Ms. Nondescript, as I'd begun to think of her.

Chapter 11

I studied Ms. Nondescript as discreetly as I could. She was talking with someone — another woman who seemed to be paying more attention to the stage than their conversation. The final team was lining up for its photo op — the Yankees, including Biff as head coach, and a stocky, smaller version of Biff scowling from his place on one end of the back row of kids. The second woman was probably a Yankee mother. Yes, once the team was in place, she pulled out her phone and began taking photos. Ms. Nondescript appeared to be waiting to resume the conversation. But when the picture taking was over, the Yankee mom smiled, patted Ms. Nondescript on the arm, and hurried toward the steps leading to the stage.

I'd been studying the Yankee parents myself, trying to pick out the one who'd had the fight with Biff. Pruitts were easy to identify, since like the Shiffleys they nearly all shared a strong family resemblance. But while the Shiffleys tended to be tall, lanky, and lantern-jawed, Pruitts were almost always short, stout, and possessed of necks so short that their heads appeared attached directly to their bodies. By my count there were at least three Pruitt fathers snapping photos at the foot of the stage.

Ah, well. No doubt Cephus could finger the guilty one for the chief. And if he should happen to be guilty of more than just picking a fight with Biff . . .

While the Yankees were shuffling offstage, Randall grabbed the microphone.

"Ladies and gentlemen," he said. "Chief Burke tells us that his officers are still working over at the ball field, and some forensic technicians from the State Bureau of Investigation are coming up this afternoon to help out. So our tournament will recommence at eight a.m. tomorrow morning. Wish I had better news, but I hope you'll all enjoy this fine performance by the New Life Baptist Choir."

The stage filled with maroon as Minerva Burke and some of her choir began taking their places for the concert. Much as I would have liked to stay and listen, I realized I'd feel antsy if I didn't get a few

163

things done.

"See you back at the ranch," I whispered to Grandfather.

My original plan was to collar Biff before he left the bandstand. But by the time I pushed my way through the crowd, I caught a glimpse of him disappearing in the direction of the nearest parking lot, dragging the junior version of himself behind him.

I pulled out my cell phone and called him. Got his voice mail, of course.

"Hi," I said. "It's Meg Langslow. I just thought as long as there's no baseball this afternoon, maybe this would be a good time to talk briefly about the town square renovation contract."

I wouldn't hold my breath waiting for him to answer. Never mind. I'd catch up with him sooner or later.

I glanced around and saw Ms. Nondescript pushing her way through the crowd. I trailed along behind her. I was sure Biff was planning to take advantage of the postponement to get in some more practices with his two teams. If, as I suspected, she had a kid on one of those teams, she might lead me to him.

Although when we hit the sidewalk along the north side of the town square, it occurred to me that she might be heading for the parking lot behind the courthouse. And if she got into her car and drove to this theoretical practice, I'd have no way of following her, since my car was back at home and Michael and the boys were out in the Twinmobile.

But she didn't turn into the parking lot. She kept walking north, with a brisk, determined air, although her legs were so much shorter than mine that I had no difficulty keeping her in sight without appearing to be in a hurry.

And I cheered silently when she turned into the walkway of Ideen Shiffley's bed and breakfast. Definitely a lucky break.

"Ideen takes such an *interest* in her guests," Mother was fond of saying. Which was a polite way of saying that Ideen was nosy to a point that seemed excessive even to Mother, with her keen appreciation of the advantages of a small town's grapevine. And Ideen's bed and breakfast rarely got much repeat business, in spite of Caerphilly's legendary shortage of hotel rooms, because she tended to suspect most of her guests of being potential ax murderers or terrorists and kept them under close and completely unsubtle surveillance.

If Ms. Nondescript was from out of town, I was probably wrong in my assumption that she was the mother of a kid on one of Biff's teams. Of course, that raised the question of why she'd been at the field and the town square — but with any luck, Ideen would know.

Luck was definitely on my side today. Ideen was out in her front yard, weeding.

"Morning," I said. "Your flower beds look lovely."

They really did — her azaleas were blooming, and she had beds of daffodils, tulips, and a host of other flowers whose names I didn't remember, though you wouldn't catch me admitting it to Mother. Of course, Ideen's flower beds always looked lovely, mainly because weeding them gave her a perfect excuse for keeping an eye on everything that happened on her block.

"Yes," she said, with a complacent smile. "They are starting to shape up, if I say so myself. Big doings at the town square."

"Yes." I definitely didn't want to get trapped into giving her a recap of the whole ceremony. "I expect your guest's told you all about it."

"Not a whole lot." Ideen shook her head. "I'm sure she will when she feels up to it. Migraine. I'm a martyr to them myself, so I know better than to badger her at a time like this."

166

"Oh, dear," I said, trying to include Ideen as well as Ms. Nondescript in my sympathetic look. "And so terrible to have one when she's traveling — because no matter how comfortable your surroundings, it's always better to be home when you feel unwell."

Actually, I couldn't imagine a more uncomfortable place to be unwell in than Ideen's bed and breakfast. It was a vintage bungalow from the 1920s, complete with striped awnings over all the windows and painted aluminum furniture on the porch. It still looked much as it had when Ideen's grandmother had turned it into a tourist home during the Depression; I suspected the mattresses and plumbing hadn't been updated since. But Ideen preened at the implied compliment.

"Does she need any medical help?" I went on. "Because I could talk Dad into stopping by if she does."

"Thank you," Ideen said. "I'll suggest it. Because if you ask me, Edna — that's her name, Mrs. Edna Johnson — doesn't know much about taking care of herself. Didn't bring any medicine — I don't go across town without my headache pills, and here she came all the way up from Richmond and left them behind. And I'd have offered her mine, but — well, I know better than to tell a doctor's daughter about the dangers of taking someone else's prescription medicine."

"Richmond?" I echoed. "That's only what — an hour and a half away. Odd that she'd be staying overnight so close to home."

"She's job-hunting," Ideen said. "Had an interview yesterday afternoon at the college, and driving in traffic sets off her head, so she decided to stay here for a few days and see if she could arrange a few more interviews. Apparently she forgot about so many places being closed for Founder's Day Weekend."

"Not something you'd expect a Richmonder to know," I pointed out.

"Yes, but she used to live here," Ideen said. "She worked for the Pruitt's bank up until they fired her a couple of years ago, and she couldn't find any work closer than Richmond. But she loved it here and is hoping to move back." She glanced over her shoulder as if to make sure her guest hadn't crept up to eavesdrop on us. "I don't think that first interview went well. She took to her bed when she got home yesterday afternoon at five or six — didn't even want a bowl of soup or a cup of tea — and suffered for hours. I checked on her a couple times an hour, and it was nearly two a.m. before she finally said that yes, she was starting to feel better, and thought a cup of weak herbal tea might help her fall off to sleep."

"Poor thing," I said, trying to imagine enduring both a bad headache and Ideen's well-meant but intrusive sympathy for eight or nine hours.

"And this morning didn't help — finding out that an old friend had been murdered."

"Shep Henson was a friend of hers?"

"No, Biff Brown," Ideen said. "But we first heard it was Biff, and she was that upset — her son was on one of his teams. Not that it was much of a relief when she heard it was Shep instead of Biff. She knew him, too. She wanted to go down to the town square — she seems to have thought it was more of a memorial to Shep."

"There was a moment of silence," I said.

"Set her head off again, going down there," Ideen said. "When's the funeral happening?" Ideen never missed a funeral.

"No idea," I said. "I don't think they can schedule it until they find out when Dad's releasing the body. But I'll give you a call if I hear."

"I'd appreciate it." Of course, the odds were she'd hear before I did, but my offer seemed to please her. "If they're having it soon, Edna might just stay over, but if they put it off till after the holiday, she'll probably just go home as soon as she feels well enough to drive." She glanced over her shoulder again. "Frankly, I suspect she wants to ask Biff for a job, or at least a reference, and she can't very well bother him about that at a time like this, now can she?"

"Of course not," I said.

I noticed that Ideen seemed to be distracted by something down the street. I glanced that way and saw a stout lady I recognized as one of Mother's garden club cronies trotting briskly down the street and waving to Ideen — and giving me a chance to escape.

"Well, I'll leave you to your weeding," I said.

"Thanks," Ideen said. "And I'll try to talk Edna into seeing your dad."

I continued down the street in the direction I'd been traveling — no sense letting Ideen suspect that I'd been shadowing her guest. I was just turning the corner when I heard the garden club lady's voice. "Ideen, you should have been there for the ceremony!"

I rounded the corner and set out in the direction of the town square.

I made my way back to the town hall, went inside, and took the elevator up to the third floor, where I had a small office not too far from Randall's.

"Wasn't expecting to see you quite this soon," I said to my desk. It declined to reply, so I had no idea whether it resented the interruption to its peaceful four-day weekend or welcomed the company on a day when the town hall was so quiet that dropping a pencil seemed to echo all up and down the corridors.

Though not quiet for long. Outside, in the square, the choir struck up "Take Me Out to the Ball Game." My window looked down over the square so I cracked it open a bit, the better to hear the singing, then went back to my desk and turned on my computer.

While it started up, I noted in the appropriate page in my notebook the date and time of my latest attempt to reach Biff. I had a whole page dedicated to documenting my attempts to reach Biff. Was it insensitive to call about business on a day when he might be busy making funeral arrangements for his brother? Well, if it was inconvenient, he could always ignore it, the way he'd ignored my previous fifty-seven calls.

I noticed something new in my in-basket

and found, to my delight, that Phinny had dropped off the information I'd asked for about Biff's clients. Perhaps I should have chided him for falling back into his workaholic ways, but then again, maybe he'd disobeyed my instructions not to bother until next week because he thought this could be related to the murder. And for that matter, it could well be that he already had most of the information from fulfilling the chief's earlier request.

I glanced down the report, which showed all the construction permits Brown Construction had filed in Caerphilly County in the last seven years. I made a note to ask Phinny, just out of curiosity, if he'd only gone back seven years for any particular reason. My organized side would have gone for either five or ten. Maybe he felt seven was lucky. Or, more likely, Biff had only been doing business in Caerphilly for seven years.

And it wasn't a very fat report, actually. Either Brown Construction was a pretty small-time operation or he was doing most of his business someplace else. Clay County, for example — which would make sense, since he was originally from there.

I poked around in the various official databases until I came up with Biff's home address and jotted it in my notebook. Then I grabbed my file on the town square renovation project. I made sure it contained a copy of the contract and that the contract included the business address of Brown Construction. A quick call to the number Caroline had given me showed that both of the tracking devices she'd planted on Biff were now out at that address. Which didn't guarantee that Biff was there — he could have other jackets and other vehicles — but I figured the odds were good.

Of course, now I had to find transportation — my car was at home, and Michael was probably on his way there with the Twinmobile.

I pulled out my phone and texted Randall.

"Taking the Behemoth if that's okay," I said. "Official business." The Behemoth was an old but serviceable pickup that Randall kept in the courthouse parking lot for times when he got tired of driving the sedate and respectable sedan he'd adopted as his official mayoral vehicle.

"Keys on the hook," he texted back.

I entered Biff's office address into my phone's GPS program, tucked the file into my tote, and after tidying my desk again — because I suspected it enjoyed being tidy — I picked up the keys from their hook on the wall of Randall's office and set out.

Of course, Biff's place of business was about as far from the center of town as it could be and still be in Caerphilly County. Although from what Randall said, most of it wasn't technically in Caerphilly County at all. When I turned off the Clay Swamp Road onto the driveway beside the Brown Construction Company sign I was only a mile or so from the Clay County line. I was already tired of driving the Behemoth by that time, but the road was in such horrible repair that I was glad not to be risking my own axles. The Behemoth seemed to relish the rough ride. Clearly Biff didn't want to make it easy for clients to visit his place of business. The road's mud and grass surface had plainly been slashed out of the swamp not too long ago, and the trees along either side, choked with Virginia creeper and poison ivy, looked as if they were plotting to take it back any time now.

I finally emerged from the woods into a cleared area bisected by a tall chain-link fence topped with razor wire. The placement of the fence seemed somewhat arbitrary, since almost as many ramshackle vehicles and rusty bits of unidentifiable equipment and debris lay outside the fence as inside. The gate was closed with a chain and padlock. There wasn't anything like a sign to tell you this was Brown Construction, but enough of the equipment had been painted the same color as Biff's porta-potty, with the word BROWN stenciled on in flaking white paint, that I figured I was at my destination.

I pulled the Behemoth up close to the gate and looked around for something resembling a doorbell or an intercom. I felt curiously reluctant to get out of the truck. I honked the horn and then flinched at the sound and scanned the clearing around me and the edge of the woods, more than half-afraid . . . of what? Not the distant barking that informed me Biff kept one or more dogs on his property. After life with Spike, our eight-and-a-half-pound furball, the canine world held few terrors for me. In fact, although by the sound of his bark this beast was probably considerably larger than the Small Evil One, the familiar sound of a dog snarling himself into a frenzy added a curiously homey touch to the otherwise forbidding landscape.

"This whole place is as creepy as its owner," I said aloud. Saying it made me feel slightly better. But it also made my reluctance to leave the safety of the Behemoth seem more reasonable. Biff struck me as the sort of paranoid person who wouldn't trust dogs alone to protect his domain. There could be well-camouflaged booby traps. Or, more sensibly, security cameras that would reveal my presence.

And if they did, so what? I was here on legitimate business.

I spotted what looked like a buzzer of sorts — at least it was a button with a hand-lettered sign saying WAIT HERE FOR ENTRY over it. I pulled the truck closer to it, got out, and pressed the button. A loud buzzing sounded somewhere back in the complex, and the dog's snarling reached new crescendos of fury. Apart from that, no response. After several minutes, I pressed the button again and held it down longer. Still no response, except from the dog, and a sort of thudding noise that suggested perhaps he was hurling himself against something. Just in case it was something in bad repair that stood between him and freedom, I got back into the truck.

I studied my surroundings through the windshield. I even pulled out my phone and took a few random pictures. If I'd been admitted past the padlocked gate, I'd have crossed half an acre of vehicle- and equipment-littered gravel parking lot to arrive at one of the ugliest and most dilapidated buildings imaginable. It was a huge hulk made of sheet metal, cinder block, and faded wood, and looked as if it had been built hastily and out of spite, and then abandoned to fall apart in well-deserved solitude.

Not exactly a good advertisement for Brown Construction's building and maintenance skills. Or maybe too accurate an advertisement. Would it hurt to tidy up a bit? Maybe plant a few daffodils to soften the edges?

The chain-link fence disappeared into the woods in either direction, and as far as I could see, on either side of the huge building and behind it, the fenced-in area was filled with untidy piles of building materials, rusted hulks that might be either outdated equipment or scrap metal, abandoned-looking vehicles, and unidentifiable detritus. Well, Randall did say Biff was running a scrapyard along with his construction business. Though it looked more like a graveyard for unwanted machinery and lumber. I spotted a couple of porta-potties in even worse condition than the one he'd brought to the ball field, which I wouldn't have imagined possible. And a few of the cars or trucks, inside or outside the fence, looked as if they might be capable of running if someone did a little repair work on them instead of leaving them to rust with their older siblings.

At least now I understood how Aida and Vern could have spent several hours searching the premises for Biff's intruder. They could easily have spent several days.

I pulled out my phone and checked my mail and messages — not that I was expecting anything urgent, but I was stalling my departure. There was always the chance that Biff would return. Or that I'd get up my nerve to stroll along the perimeter and spy on the inside of the junkyard.

Not that I could think of any good reason why peering into the junkyard would be useful. I already knew more than I wanted to about Biff's business. I'd be spying out of sheer, useless nosiness. That, more than the continued barking of the dog — or dogs, perhaps? — was what kept me inside the Behemoth. As long as the dogs were inside the fence, they couldn't hurt me, no matter how hard they barked, but in case Biff's fences were in the same dismal state of disrepair as the rest of his domain, I decided caution was wiser.

I was just about to start the engine and depart when I heard another vehicle. My spirits rose — maybe this trip hadn't been useless after all. And then a sudden thought struck me — had it been really wise, coming out here into Biff's territory. Yes, it was broad daylight, but that didn't mean much out here in the vine-infested woods. I quickly fired off a text to Michael, telling him where I was. And then one to Randall, in case Michael was too busy with the Eagles.

A Caerphilly County police cruiser crept into the clearing. I didn't know whether to be relieved or annoyed. I recognized Aida Butler at the wheel. She pulled the cruiser to a halt near the gate. I got out of the Behemoth and went to meet her and she rolled down her window.

"What are you doing here?" she said.

"Hoping to catch Biff in," I said. "Not that I'm ever sorry to see you, but I got all excited, hearing a car coming down the lane. Thought it might be him."

"Fat chance," she said. "Have you tried the ball field?"

"Wouldn't they chase him away if he showed up there?" I asked.

"True," she said. "But if you're looking for him . . ." She pressed a button or two on her radio. "Sammy? Is Brown there at the field?"

"Haven't seen him since he left for the

ceremony," the radio crackled back.

"He's probably figured out I'm looking for him," I said, "and is avoiding all his usual haunts so I can't catch him."

"Heaven only knows where he's got to, then," she said. "Maybe over in Clayville seeing to the funeral."

"Definitely in Clayville?" I asked. "The funeral, I mean."

"Well, Shep lived in Clayville," Aida said. "And all their people are there. You'd think the Clay County people would take it hard, him changing his address to a Caerphilly County one, but no one seemed to care. Maybe they thought it was a good joke, him pulling the wool over all us Caerphillians. Not that he ever did that much. Everybody already had his number."

"Not that I'm snooping or anything," I said. "But what are you doing out here? Anything I should worry about?"

"Just checking on things." She was getting out of her car. "Apparently after the Opening Day ceremonies Biff got the wind up and made a big fuss. Complained that the chief wasn't taking last night's burglary seriously enough. So I get to come out here every few hours and make sure everything's secure. Not that anyone but him could tell if anything was stolen, and for heaven's sakes, who'd want any of it?"

"He can't come check himself?" I fell into step beside her as she approached the gate.

"Scared to, I guess." She rattled the padlock to make sure it was still secure, causing the distant dog to bark all the more furiously. "He's panicking. Convinced that whoever killed Shep was actually gunning for him."

"Not unreasonable," I said. "From what I've heard talking to my fellow baseball parents, Shep wasn't really liked, on account of his biased umpiring, but everyone knew he was only doing it because he didn't dare cross Biff."

"Exactly," Aida said. "Killing Shep won't do anyone any good, because Biff will just find another stooge to ump for him. But killing Biff — a lot of people might consider that a good deed for the community. Me included — I have nephews who played in Little League under him. You know they'll have to learn hard lessons, playing sports, like sometimes even their best efforts won't be enough to win. What you don't expect to have them learning is that the fat cats who run the world can do what they like and there's nothing they or anyone else can do about it. I'd just as soon they didn't have to learn that lesson quite so young."

"Maybe this time will be different," I said. "Because a lot of us are determined not to let things go on like this."

"Good luck to you," she said. "Lord, I wish that miserable mutt would stop barking! I know he won't though. Three and a half hours we were out here the other night, and I don't think the blasted cur shut up for more than five minutes at a stretch. If I were a better person, I'd walk all the way round the junkyard, but I don't see any signs of anything amiss. You see anything hinky when you got here?"

I shook my head.

"I'm going to pass on the long walk in the woods." Although she had returned to her cruiser, she was spraying herself from head to foot with Rose Noire's all-natural essential-oil mosquito repellent, which actually worked a lot better than most noxious chemical products as long as you remembered that it had a really short half life and you'd pretty much need to respray yourself every hour.

"If you're not circumnavigating Brown Construction, what's with the bug repellent?" I asked.

"If there was some way to breed ticks and mosquitoes for profit, Biff would have that market cornered," she said. "And I figure I should at least walk the fence as far as the back gate and make sure that's secure. Then I'll do something actually useful, like check for tire tracks in all the places people might have hidden their cars if they decided to sneak in the back way last night."

"What does he need a back gate for?" I asked, looking at the dense woods surrounding the yard. "Does he have much call to dump bodies out there in the swamp?"

"Used to be the front gate," she said. "He's still got something that loosely resembles a road back there. Leads straight to Clayville. Nearly all of his employees live over there, and I expect they use the back way to get here. Long as you've got four-wheel drive and don't worry too much about your axles and your shock absorbers, it's doable."

"Let me have some of that stuff." I held out my hand for the bug spray. "And I'll keep you company."

I'd be the first to admit that it was sheer curiosity that made me stay — curiosity about Biff's lair, and also about any other tidbits Aida might drop about the investigation. But the perimeter hike wasn't conducive to casual conversation. Between climbing over fallen tree trunks and hacking through bushes, avoiding the swampy bits, and warning each other about snakes, we didn't have time or wind for much else.

"Here we are," Aida finally said as we stepped out into another clearing. "The original grand entrance to the thriving commercial enterprise that is Brown Construction."

It looked a lot like the current front entrance, except that a couple of centuries ago someone had painted a word in foot-high brown letters along the rusty corrugated metal side of the building. Enough paint had flaked off that if I hadn't known Biff's name I could never have guessed that the letters spelled out "Brown." The clearing was littered with rusting cars and trucks. The area inside the fence had the same air of neglect and dilapidation I'd already seen, and was filled with the same apparently random piles or clusters of items. A mountain of old car batteries. A front-end loader that appeared to have had a collision with something even larger. Another gaggle of repulsively dilapidated porta-potties.

"Seeing all these luxury vehicles reminds me — have they figured out how Shep got to the field?" I asked. "He didn't have a vehicle in the parking lot at the ball field."

"His truck's here," Aida said. "That one," she added, looking up from her phone and pointing to a battered Ford pickup, distinguishable from the rest of the hulks mainly by the fact that it still rested on tires rather than blocks. "Apparently he got to the ball field on his Harley. They found it abandoned in the woods not far from the field."

"Dumped by the killer?"

"Most likely."

Aida rattled the gate, sending the distant dog into frenzies again, and then without a word we turned to go back to the new front gate.

"Hope you weren't expecting anything exciting out here," Aida said when we got back to our vehicles and were cleaning the burrs and bits of stickweed off our pants legs.

"Just studying up on how to tackle Biff," I said. "Wish I had some idea where he's gone."

"Lying low somewhere, I expect. Hoping we catch the killer before the killer finds him."

"Unless he is the killer," I suggested.

"Yeah, he could just be pretending to be terrified so we don't suspect him. If you really want to talk to him, I'd go see if he's home."

"That will be my next stop," I said. "Even

if he doesn't know anything, maybe his wife will."

"Good luck."

Aida got back in her car and appeared to be filling out some kind of paperwork. Or maybe she was waiting to make sure I left. She wouldn't have to wait long.

Although before climbing back into the Behemoth, I used the camera on my phone to take a few more pictures of my surroundings. I wasn't quite sure why — maybe if Brown ever tried to sue Caerphilly for not giving him more work, we could show the photos and make it obvious to any sane judge or jury on the planet why we weren't falling all over ourselves to hire him.

Something struck me.

"I think one of the trucks is gone." I pointed to an area where a series of abandoned pickups lined the side of the road, ranging from one only eight or ten years old to one that looked as if it could have been used for the movie version of *The Grapes of Wrath.*

"One of those trucks?" Aida sounded dubious. I could see her point.

"I could have sworn that when I first got here there was another one beside this one," I said, pointing to the newest of the hulks. "That one's completely off the road, and I remember having to kind of swerve around the last truck in line when I drove in."

"Whole place is like an obstacle course," she said.

I flipped back through the photos on my phone, but I'd been focusing on taking shots of the gate and the building, not the junk jungle around it.

"I'm probably imagining it," I said with a shrug.

"I'll keep my eyes open," Aida said. "If I see any zombie trucks that look as if they could have escaped from back here, I'll pull them over and check their registration."

I nodded. Then I programmed my GPS with Biff's home address — near the center of town, thank goodness! — and set out, waving at Aida as I went.

CHAPTER 12

Biff's house, like his business, definitely illustrated the old saying about the shoemaker's children having no shoes. Maybe he thought it didn't matter how his business looked. And maybe he was right — a construction company went to its customers, not the other way around, and his ramshackle office building was so far out in the boonies that no one would ever just happen to pass by. But his house was right in the middle of the town of Caerphilly. Not in a snooty upscale neighborhood like Westlake, where people would wonder how much of their construction costs went for supplies and salaries and how much for the owner's exorbitant lifestyle. No, if I'd been a small business owner, I might very well have chosen a modest but comfortable frame house like his, on a similarly solid but unpretentious street.

But then I'd have made at least a half-hearted effort to keep it up.

Biff's house was surrounded with a white picket fence that, when new, could have starred in one of those homey paintings of wholesome small town American life. Unfortunately, it was badly in need of a coat of paint, and at least a dozen pickets were broken or missing entirely. Tree roots had buckled the flagstone front walk, making it more of an obstacle course than a path. The grass was in need of cutting, though calling it grass was an insult to respectable fescue and zoysia. The white frame house could also use paint if not new siding. A basketball backboard with no net on its hoop leaned drunkenly to one side beside an asphalt driveway so cracked and pitted that it was obvious no one had dribbled there in years.

I picked my way over the helter-skelter flagstones, held carefully onto the railing while climbing the ramshackle front steps, and rang the doorbell. I didn't hear any ringing inside, but then one doesn't always. After a minute or so I rang again. Then I gave up on the bell and knocked firmly.

After another minute or so, during which I tried to look nonchalant in spite of the uneasy feeling that someone inside was scrutinizing me at length through the door's peephole, the door opened perhaps a foot.

"Yes?" A small, slender woman peered out. She had graying blond hair pulled back into a pony tail and large eyes that would have been pretty if they hadn't held such an anxious expression. I couldn't easily tell her age — she could have been anywhere from thirty to fifty.

"Mrs. Brown?" I tried to make sure my face was calm and businesslike; friendly, but not overly so.

"Yes," she said. "May I help you?"

"I'm Meg Langslow, special assistant to the mayor," I said. "I was actually trying to find your husband."

"He's not here," she said. And then her face turned into a frightening scowl. "As you horrible people already know. He's not here! He hasn't been here for the past month, not since I kicked the sorry bastard out! I stopped caring where he was the day I filed for divorce, and I'm not calling off the divorce, no matter how many of his friends he sends out to harass me! If you think —"

"Mrs. Brown!" I said, when she had to take a breath and I could get a word in edgewise. "I'm not one of your husband's friends, and I'm not here to harass you."

She frowned, suspicion replacing fury in her expression.

"In fact, I was actually dropping by in the hope that I could harass him," I said. "So since he's not here and not likely to be, allow me to compliment you on making such a positive change in your life, and remind you that if you ever need it, the Caerphilly Women's Shelter is available. Just call Reverend Robyn any time, day or night. And unless you have any idea where I could find Biff so I can make his life a little more miserable, I'll be on my way."

She just looked at me for a few seconds. Then her suspicious look gave way to a tremulous smile.

"You must be the witch from the county he's been complaining about," she said. "The one who's actually trying to make him live up to the terms of that contract for the town square."

"I bet he didn't say witch," I said, with a chuckle.

"No, but I don't stoop to his level." She held the door wider. "Come in for a minute. I can give you a few places to check if you really want to find him."

"Thank you, Mrs. —" I began.

"Gina," she said. "Just Gina. Or Ms. Crocker if you want to be formal. I'll be legally getting rid of the Brown part as soon as I can, and I'd rather not hear it in the meantime."

Inside, everything was shabby, with more than a few things in need of repair or replacement, but neat and clean — remarkably so for a house with kids. Try as I might to keep things tidy, the boys' toys and sports equipment and clothes tended to end up in the living room, dining room, and kitchen. And yet the Browns had kids — four of them, to judge by the multiple pictures on the walls and the mantel.

Multiple pictures of the kids, but hardly any with Gina, and Biff was conspicuous by his absence — though a few unfaded spots on the light blue walls suggested that parts of the photo gallery had been removed. And there were other absences in the room. A small old-fashioned tube TV stood on a stand clearly designed to support one of its big, modern, flat-screen cousins, and nearby, in the corner that offered the best view of the tiny television, a worn-looking side chair occupied a space that could easily hold a huge armchair or recliner. I suspected a few of Biff's favorite toys had gone with him.

"Have a seat." She gestured to the sofa. I sat, and had to smile when I saw that a glass bowl on the coffee table held not only pens and pencils but also a scattering of Legos.

"He might be over at his brother's place." Gina had picked up a small address book covered in floral fabric and was leafing through it. "I'll write down the address. He's been staying in the caretaker's room out at his construction company, but now that poor Shep's out of the way he'll probably just move on into his house."

Out of the way? Was she suggesting Biff had knocked Shep off for his house? Her head was bent over the notepad on which she was writing, so she didn't see my look of surprise, but maybe she realized how it sounded.

"It was actually their mother's old house," she went on. "Shep moved in when she died, which seemed pretty fair to me, since he was the only one of them who actually lifted a finger to help her the last few years of her life when she was so sick. And it's a tiny little one-bedroom bungalow on the outskirts of Clayville, so it's not as if they could easily share. When I filed for divorce and kicked him out, Biff had trouble finding a place to live — you know how scarce housing has always been in Caerphilly, and these days Clayville's just as bad. Biff tried to convince Shep to move into the caretaker's room so he could have the house — can you imagine? For once Shep stood up for himself. And now Biff gets it after all."

For a few moments, I found myself remembering the days when Michael and I had been househunting in Caerphilly — particularly the day when we found out that one of his colleagues had snatched a promising house out from under our noses by offering a price significantly more than the house was worth — or than we could afford. I'd experienced a few minutes of white-hot anger at the colleague, and I might have even exclaimed "I could kill him!" But actually murdering someone for a house?

Stranger things had happened.

"He has two cousins over in Clay County," she was saying. "He might be speaking to one or the other of them at the moment. One's a minister, so I guess Biff will probably ask him to do the funeral."

"Which church?" I asked. Thanks to helping out at various interfaith volunteer service projects, I knew a lot of the local clergy from Caerphilly and adjacent counties.

"Not sure what they're calling themselves these days," she said. "Holy Vessels of Clay, or something like that. It's that group who decided all of the local Baptist churches were too liberal and permissive and went off on their own."

"It's not that church that does the snake handling at their services, is it?" I asked. Dad had recently developed an alarming fascination with the subject. Only from a medical point of view, but I took a dim view of any fascination that brought him into close contact with rattlesnakes.

"Not that I've heard of," she said. "But they're Biff's cousins, so who knows?"

If Biff was hoping for a reconciliation, he was doomed to disappointment. She had paused, hands still holding the pencil and the address book, eyes staring into space.

"Do you know if they're going to arrest him?" she blurted out. "For the murder, I mean."

"Biff?" I asked.

"If it was just me and him, I wouldn't care," she said. "In fact, the way I feel about him right now, I might even gloat if he got arrested. But there's the kids to think about. He's a rotten father, but he is their father. How am I supposed to break the news to them if their father is arrested? For murder? Of their uncle Shep?"

She looked so distraught that I wanted to reassure her. But what if the chief hadn't interviewed her yet?

"I don't know anything definite," I finally

said. "But I did hear a rumor that he has an alibi."

"That's good." She let out a heavy sigh. Was that relief or disappointment on her face. Probably a mixture of both. "Good for my kids, anyway. But if Biff didn't do it, who in the world did?"

"The rumor mill seems to think there's a good possibility someone mistook Shep for Biff in the dark," I said. "And if that's so, then the police will be a lot less interested in Shep's enemies than Biff's."

Her face puckered briefly in a slight, puzzled frown, then smoothed into an expression of startled, anxious comprehension.

"Yes," she said, nodding slightly. "I never thought of that but — yes, of course. The notion of someone killing Shep just didn't make sense — I mean, who kills someone just because they're clumsy and annoying? But Biff? Lord. The chief's going to have his hands full, chasing down all the people who had it in for him. Starting with me, of course. Guess I better get my alibi in order."

She grimaced. And then her face fell.

"What if whoever did it tries again?" she asked. "Are my kids in danger?"

"I don't know," I said. "Talk to the chief. And tell him everything you know. The sooner he figures out who killed Shep and why, the sooner we can all feel safe."

"Yes." She was doing the mile-long stare again. Then she snapped out of it. "Thank you," she said. "You've been helpful. I wish I could do the same for you."

"If you have any helpful hints on how to get him to do the work we've hired him to do down at the town square, that would be nice," I said.

She chuckled mirthlessly and shook her head.

"If you'd asked me that yesterday, I'd have said 'Put a gun to his head.' Probably not something I should say today." She studied my face for a few moments, than appeared to make a decision. "He's probably having cash flow problems. He never did tell me much about his business, but I overheard things. I'm pretty sure he's got a client who's taking his own sweet time paying for a big job. Not sure who. But I know he's worried about whether he's ever going to get paid. So it's possible he hasn't started the town square job because he doesn't have the cash to buy the materials. No way he'd want to admit that. He's probably ransacking his supply yard, trying to see if he can come up anything he can use to get the job done with."

"Good grief," I exclaimed. "We certainly don't want that."

"Oh, so you've seen his supply yard?"

"Only from the outside," I said. "That was enough. So what if we happened to find all the materials he needed in one of the county supply warehouses?" I reached into my tote and pulled out my copy of the contract. "And asked if he'd renegotiate the contract into one where the county supplies the materials and he provides the labor? Of course, that's assuming he can get the labor. If he's that broke —"

"The labor wouldn't be a problem," Gina said. "All his usual workers know he's good for it eventually. At least they'd assume that because he always has been up till now. But a lumberyard wants cash on delivery — especially from someone who's bounced a few checks lately."

"This doesn't have a materials list." I indicated the contract I'd been flipping through. "But I'm sure Randall Shiffley could figure out what supplies are needed."

"And get them at a better discount than Biff can," Gina said. "Just don't let on to Biff that a Shiffley had anything to do with it. He'd pitch a fit."

"Duly noted," I said. "And it is one of my main missions in life to avoid provoking people into fits."

"He has such a temper." Was it just by chance that she was rubbing her jaw as she said that, or was she recalling some bit of damage Biff's temper had inflicted? "He's going to have a hard time getting along without Shep. He always says — said — Shep was the carrot and he was the stick. If he needed to sweet talk anyone into something — lending him something, hurrying up a supply delivery, paying an overdue bill — he'd send Shep. And people would usually do what Shep asked them to do, partly because he was pretty likable most of the time, and partly because they knew if they didn't, they'd have to deal with Biff."

I mulled that over for a few moments while she did the long blank stare again. Probably something I should just tell the chief about. But since I was here . . .

"What if Biff sent Shep out to talk to someone who was really mad at Biff?" I asked.

"It happened," she said. "More than once. You think maybe this time someone shot the messenger?"

I shrugged. She shook her head slightly, but it didn't look as if she was saying no to the idea. More like thinking it was all too sad and plausible.

"How did he get along with the parents of the kids on his teams?" I asked.

"Just fine," she said. "That's why I thought at first you must be one of the mothers. The harpies keep badgering me to take him back. No, he gets along fine with the team families. Well, except for some of the Pruitts."

Aha!

"Nobody much gets along with the Pruitts," I said aloud.

"Biff used to," she said. "Things got a little strained about the time the Pruitt's bank went under. Some of the Pruitts seemed to think the loans they'd made to Biff had helped bring it down, and to hear Biff talk, they went out of business just to spite him. But I think they'd mostly made peace with each other."

"I heard he had quite an argument with one of the Pruitts at a practice," I said.

"That would be Adolph Pruitt," she said. "He was one of the ones who ended up doing time for something or other he did while the Pruitts still had the bank. He seems to think Biff was the one who turned him in to the FBI."

"And he wasn't?"

"I doubt it." She shook her head firmly. "If Biff had something on Adolph, he wouldn't have taken it to the Feds. He'd have tried to use it himself."

"You mean he'd have blackmailed Adolph?"

She thought about that for a few moments.

"Maybe," she said finally. "But more likely he'd have just held it over Adolph's head. Expect a lot of favors in return."

And that didn't count as blackmail?

"But Adolph ended up in prison anyway," I said aloud. "I guess he's not in a position to do his buddies any favors now."

"He's a Pruitt." She shrugged. "They usually land on their feet."

I couldn't argue with that.

We sat there for a few moments, each lost in her thoughts. I wasn't sure what Gina was thinking, but I was contemplating the news that Biff was at odds with someone who'd spent time in prison. Someone who might not share Gina's belief that Biff wouldn't talk to the FBI.

"They'll probably have an open casket," she said suddenly. "And if they do, I'm not taking the kids. They'd freak, not just because he's their uncle, but he's going to look so much like their father."

"The resemblance is that strong?" I asked.

Gina got up, walked over to the coat

closet, and pulled something down from the shelf over the coat rod. A couple of framed pictures. She walked back to the sofa and handed them to me.

"You wouldn't think they were only half brothers, would you?" she said.

No, I wouldn't. Biff was maybe an inch taller, Shep maybe a few pounds lighter, but the resemblance was uncanny.

"I don't feel so stupid now about mistaking Shep for Biff," I said, handing the pictures back.

Gina nodded. She looked at the pictures. Her jaw tensed and her hand tightened on the frames as if she was fighting an urge to destroy them. Then she took a deliberate breath and walked back to the closet to put the pictures away again and her face returned to its former melancholy, almost vacant, expression. I decided it was time to hit the road.

"I should be going," I said as I stood up. She followed me to the doorway, and I had the slightly disconcerting impression that if I'd begun dancing the Charleston or hopping down the hallway like a rabbit, she'd probably have absent-mindedly done the same thing.

"Don't forget about Robyn," I said, as I opened the front door. "Even if you don't need the shelter, she's a good listener about stuff like this."

"I'll keep it in mind." She smiled, but I noticed that she'd picked up a dust rag and was already eyeing the hall table for specks. I deduced that she probably shared my tendency to clean when stressed.

When I got back to the Behemoth, I was undecided whether to call the chief first or Randall. Then I realized that making any calls while sitting in front of Gina's house would probably feed her anxiety. So I drove several blocks before parking and calling. Neither Randall nor the chief was in and I wasn't in the mood to boil down my conversation with Gina to a message, so I just left each a request to call me.

And when the chief called back, was there any subtle way to ask if Gina had an alibi? I hoped for her sake that she did. She definitely had a motive to kill Biff. The resemblance between him and Shep was uncanny in the daylight, and it had been full dark. What if she'd shot Shep before realizing he wasn't Biff? Or what if she'd pulled a gun on what she thought was her husband, realized her mistake, and shot Shep anyway, to keep him from revealing her attempted murder to the police — or to Biff?

The chief was no dummy. He'd have

thought of all this.

But it would be nice to know sooner, rather than later, if Gina was a victim or a killer.

I'd see what I could find out when the chief called. And mention to him that Biff might be on the outs with a vengeful Pruitt with a prison record. Meanwhile, since there was still plenty of time before dinner, I decided to make one more visit. This time to one of Biff's clients. I scanned the list Phinny had given me for someone I knew well enough to approach. I didn't recognize half of the names. A fair number of his projects had been for Pruitts, especially in the years before the rest of the town had risen up and kicked them out of the Caerphilly town government. I skipped over those names. Even if the Pruitts were willing to talk to me — which was unlikely, since they were well aware that I'd played a significant part in their downfall — I wouldn't trust a word they said.

Most of my friends and neighbors seemed to have avoided dealing with Biff. Probably because they were also friends and neighbors of the Shiffleys. I kept scanning the list for anyone I felt I could approach.

Aha. Willard Entwhistle. The last name sounded familiar. I pulled up the Summerball roster I kept on my phone. Yes, there was a Kermit Entwhistle on the Flatworms, another coach-pitch team. And I couldn't remember running into any other Entwhistles before, so odds were Willard was Kermit's father. Or grandfather. Either way, I might be able to play the Summerball family solidarity card.

And according to the building permit records, Brown Construction had built a pig shed and pasture fence for Mr. Entwhistle a year and a half ago.

I programmed Mr. Entwhistle's address into my GPS and set out.

CHAPTER 13

Mr. Entwhistle's farm was in the far south end of the county, where asphalt pavement gave way to gravel roads, making me glad once more that I was in the indestructible Behemoth rather than my own car. My GPS lost signal several times, and I was about to go back to the list to find a more accessible Brown Construction client, when I spotted a small, neatly painted sign that said: ENTWHISTLE ORGANIC PIG FARM. TAMWORTH AND GLOUCESTERSHIRE OLD SPOT.

"Cool!" I murmured. Not just a pig farmer, but an organic one — and raising what I recognized as rare heritage-breed pigs to boot. Not surprising, actually, in Caerphilly. A few years ago we'd begun hosting the Un-Fair, a regional agricultural festival showcasing heritage breeds and heirloom crops, and many local farmers and farm hobbyists had started raising heritage animals of all sorts — including Dad, with his Dutch Belted cows and Black Welsh Mountain sheep. This promised to be interesting.

I turned into Mr. Entwhistle's lane, and after a short stretch of woods I emerged into the open again with rolling green pastures on either side of me. The field on the left was dotted with tall, lean pigs with sleek ginger-red coats. No spots on the coats, so I deduced that these were the Tamworths. To my right, then, must be the Gloucestershire Old Spots, their white coats decorated with random splotches of black. The pastures positively swarmed with activity — pigs were trotting about, rooting in the ground, drinking from the stream that bisected both fields, and wallowing with abandon in the mud on the banks of the stream. Clearly Mr. Entwhistle's pigs were not only organic but free range. If I didn't know about the existence of such things as free-range bacon and organic pork chops, I could easily have envied these pigs their healthy and carefree life.

I pulled into the farmyard, parked the Behemoth in a spot where it didn't look as if it would be in the way, and stepped out. In town, I'd have marched up to knock on the front door of the house. But only a lazy farmer would be inside the house on a beautiful spring day like this, and from the look of things, Mr. Entwhistle was anything but lazy. Everything was neat, clean, and in good repair. It even smelled fresh, which must have been hard to manage with pigs. I turned around slowly, scanning the house . . . the barn . . . the Tamworth pig shed . . . the pastures . . . the Gloucestershire Old Spot pig shed. . . .

"Can I help you?"

I turned to see a sandy-haired man in jeans and a plaid shirt, standing beside the Tamworth shed. He didn't look unfriendly — just guarded, as if he and the pigs weren't quite used to seeing a lot of visitors.

"I hope so," I said. "You must be Mr. Entwhistle." He didn't deny it. "I'm Meg Langslow. I work for the county. And I think our kids all play baseball together. Your boy's on the Flatworms, right?"

He nodded. He was frowning. Maybe I shouldn't have mentioned the county. He might be one of those rural folks who distrusted the government on general principles. I should definitely push the baseball connection. But carefully. Even though his son wasn't on Biff's team, they could still be cronies.

"I was looking for someone to help me with something," I said. "And I figured, since you were a fellow baseball parent —"

"Why can't you people just leave me alone?" He didn't raise his voice, but there was a world of venom in his tone. "I paid my sponsorship money. What more do you want?"

"I beg your pardon?"

"Just go back to Biff and tell him to — tell him to leave me alone." I had the feeling he'd been on the verge of using saltier language and stopped himself at the last minute. "If he keeps harassing me I'll pull Fletcher and Kermit out of baseball entirely. Hell, I might anyway."

"Can we start over?" At least now I knew how to play it. "Because I didn't come from Biff, and I have nothing to do with Biff — well, as little as possible. Unfortunately, my job for the county includes managing the contract with Brown Construction to renovate the town square — a contract I frankly would never have signed. So far Biff hasn't done a lick of work — doesn't even return my phone calls. I looked in the town records to see what else he'd built, and saw the permits for your pig shed and fence, and I came out to see if you had any helpful hints on how to get the jerk to do his job, because obviously I don't have the touch."

He studied me for a few moments.

"So you're not a friend of Biff's," he said.

Hadn't I just made that abundantly clear?

"Not in the least," I said. "I am merely one of the many people who suspect the murderer got the wrong brother."

"Ha!" Not a very cheerful laugh, but it was progress. "Sorry I snapped at you. I jumped to the conclusion that you were the new collector for his extortion racket, but I guess Evie Pruitt's still doing that."

"Extortion racket?" My eyes must have been bugging.

"That's what some of us call the sponsorship ads we all end up having to buy in the opening day program," Entwhistle said. "I could advertise in the *Clarion* for six months for what Brown charges, and since I don't do retail sales, it's not as if I get much bang out of it. But I want to support the league my sons play in, so I ante up every year. And these days I do it by check, so there's no way he can pretend to have lost my contribution. Evie drops by to say I still owe for the ad, I can show the canceled check. Since you've never heard about this, I gather you don't own a small business."

"My husband teaches at the college," I said. "Technically, I do run a small business — I'm a blacksmith — but that's taken a backseat since the boys were born, so Biff probably only knows me as that annoying woman who keeps asking when he's starting work on the town square. I don't suppose you can share any tips on how to manage him as a contractor?"

"Wish I could help you, but I'm afraid Biff's never done any work for me."

"But according to the building permit file —"

"Oh, he pulled a permit all right," Mr. Entwhistle said. "And took a hefty deposit. And then did absolutely nothing for three months."

"This is starting to sound all too familiar," I said.

"And it gets worse," he said. "I needed the new pen because I was adding the Tamworths."

"Beautiful animals," I said, and he beamed.

"They're new since last summer," he said. "I've had the Gloucestershires for four years now. Guy I knew had been breeding Tamworths for years, but he had to sell because he's going into assisted living, and I bought his herd. Got a good price on them because he knew I was keen on keeping the breed going. But I couldn't just turn them in with the Old Spots."

"Or you'd have nothing but Gloucesterworth Tamspots, and there go two breeds," I said.

"Well, I'm not the only breeder of either," he said, with a chuckle. "But I want to do my part to keep the breeds alive, and my friend was getting close to the sale date on his farm, so I really needed the new pasture and shed. I kept bugging Brown, and he finally showed up to do the work, and then my problems really began. He dumped a couple of truckloads of *treated* lumber on my farm."

He said the word "treated" with the same mixture of outrage and disgust that Mother would use in uttering "manure" or "polyester." I was puzzled for a moment, and then I remembered.

"Oh, that's right," I said. "Treated wood's against the rules for an organic farm."

"And first he tried to claim using naturally seasoned wood wasn't in the contract," Entwhistle said. "Which was nonsense, because it was right there in black and white. And then he tried to claim it was a mistake, and I said, fine, just get it off my property before it contaminates my soil. And then he tried to claim he couldn't get any of the right kind of wood in time to meet my deadline, so how about if he just used the wood he had and gave me a certificate stating it was naturally seasoned wood to show the inspectors. That's when I fired him."

"Good for you," I said.

"And it's not just because he could have cost me my organic certification," he said. "Although that would have been a real danger if I'd let him get away with it — did he really think the inspectors wouldn't recognize treated wood? No, I just figured that a guy who would lie to the USDA's organic inspectors probably wouldn't be any more honest with me. I don't want to do business with someone like that."

"Wish the county didn't have to," I said.

"So that's my advice if you really want to get your project done," Entwhistle said, shaking his head. "Try to get him to live up to his schedule, and he's like the Invisible Man, but fire the sorry son of a gun and you'll never get him out from underfoot. Had to chase away his workers five or six times when they showed up and tried to start the project using that damned poisoned wood. Took a couple of weeks to get the lumber off my land, and then I only managed it by hiring the Shiffleys to build my shed and pasture and making it a condition of the job that they take the nasty stuff back and dump it in Brown's lumberyard. Should have hired them in the first place —

they came in ahead of time and under budget. I should never have listened to Brown when he said he could beat their price."

"But at least you're rid of him now," I said.

"I wish," Entwhistle said. "I'm suing him to get back my deposit, and he's suing me for not paying for the work he never even started, and you can definitely count me in as another one of the people who think the killer got the wrong brother. Probably lucky for me they didn't kill Biff or the chief would likely have me high on his suspect list."

"He might anyway," I said. "There's been a lot of speculation that whoever did this mistook Shep for Biff. It did happen in the middle of the night down at the ball field. And for that matter, since I'd never met Shep, I mistook him for Biff when I found the body in the morning."

"Pity," he said. "Shep never did anyone any harm that I know of, or if he did, you can bet Biff was really the one behind it. Shep had the good grace to look embarrassed the couple of times he showed up leading a team of workmen and tried to start building with that nasty treated lumber. So when do you think I can expect my visit from the chief?"

"No idea," I said. "Not necessarily all that soon. The more I learn about Biff, the more I realize what a long list of possible suspects the chief is dealing with."

"Safety in numbers, then," Mr. Entwhistle said. "And let's hope there's a few more farmers on the list so I'm not the only one with no alibi for the middle of the night."

"Yeah, I guess you have to get up pretty early to take care of them," I said, nodding at the pigs.

"Between them and my kids, I'm in bed by nine most nights," he said. "My wild nights are over."

He was gazing with fond pride at the Gloucestershire Old Spots as he said it. I had the feeling he didn't much resent either the pigs or the kids for getting him up early.

"They're a lot of fun to watch," I said. "Just tell me to mind my own business if you like, but does it bother you to eat your own pigs?"

"It would if I did but I don't," he said.

"Don't tell me you're a vegetarian?"

"Shoot, no," he said. "I'm a meat-and-potatoes guy, no question. But when you raise them free range — they seem so happy, and you get to know their personalities. Not something any self-respecting pig farmer ought to admit, but yeah, it would bother me to eat them."

"So you don't eat pork?" I guessed.

"I eat other people's pork," he said, with a laugh. "And I'm a picky son of a gun, too, because I know how nasty a badly run pig farm can get. But there's half a dozen free-range organic farms whose meat I'll buy."

"Which ones?" I asked, pulling out my notebook. He rattled off the names, and I recognized a couple whose products appeared in the local section of the Caerphilly Market. Any pig farm that passed Mr. Entwhistle's inspection would be high on my list. His pig shed was neat, tidy, and cleaner than some parts of my house — the parts frequented by Rob and the boys. For that matter, I put Mr. Entwhistle's farm at the top of my list.

"Thanks for being up front with me about Biff," I said. "And I'll see you at the next Flatworms/Eagles game. I think there's one coming up shortly."

"With only four teams at our level in the league, there's pretty nearly always one coming up shortly," he said. "I look forward to it. What I don't look forward to is cheering 'Go, Flatworms!' Can't someone convince Biff to come up with more normal names for the teams?"

"I guess I should feel lucky we've got the

Eagles," I said.

"I heard a rumor that it was originally supposed to be the Earwigs, only someone at the uniform company thought it must be a typo and changed it to Eagles."

"Yeah, Earwigs sounds a lot more like Biff's style," I said.

We shook hands, and I turned to go back to the truck. Then a thought struck me.

"By the way, could you do me a favor? If you happen to get talking to someone at the game who seems really interested in heritage animals, could you try to make pig husbandry sound as difficult as possible?"

"Well, it's a lot harder than people think," he said. "It's not as if you just turn them out in the field and nap. You worried that someone you know will get bit with the heritage pig bug?"

"My dad. He's got heritage-breed cows and sheep already, and I'm very much afraid he's getting ready to commit more animal buying."

"He shown any interest in pigs?"

"Lately he's been studying poultry," I said. "I was hoping he could be satisfied with a few rare geese or ducks. We've some experience with poultry, but none with pigs. I think he should work his way up to pigs."

"Good point," Mr. Entwhistle said. "If

anyone shows undue interest in my pigs, I'll talk up the hardships."

"Thanks," I said. "It was nice meeting you, Mr. Entwhistle."

"Just Will," he said. "See you at the game."

I got back into the Behemoth and drove slowly out, admiring the pigs on either side as I went. When I reached the road, I stopped and pulled out my list of Brown Construction customers. Were there any more here in the south end of the county? Yes, five years ago Brown Construction had gotten a permit to build a barn for a Mr. Samuel Yoder. When I programmed the address into my GPS, it seemed to think the Yoder farm was only ten minutes away.

I headed out. After a good twenty minutes of sporadic signal and missed turns, I arrived in front of the Yoder farm. Or at least what used to be the Yoder farm. Lush, rolling pastures empty of any livestock. No vehicles or equipment visible anywhere. A big farmhouse that looked a little unkempt, and to its left, a huge, half-finished barn. The ground floor of the barn was covered with tattered Tyvek construction wrap, with some loosened strips flapping in the faint breeze. The upper story and the soaring roof were nothing but naked frame.

Maybe I was jumping to conclusions, but

what if that sad, unfinished barn had driven Mr. Yoder into bankruptcy? If he was less wary than Will Entwhistle, less successful in getting satisfaction from Brown Construction, maybe a little less financially sound to begin with . . . ?

The Entwhistle farm was nearby — probably a good deal nearer than my roundabout route would indicate. Odds were Will knew what had happened to his neighbor, and if Biff had had anything to do with the Yoder's unfinished barn and abandoned farm, Will would probably enjoy telling me. I made an entry in my notebook to remind me to ask him.

And then a thought hit me. I pulled out my phone and called Mother.

"Where are you, dear?" she asked. "Some of the cousins were asking."

"Long story," I said. "I'll fill you in when I get back this evening. Speaking of cousins, is Festus still gung ho about buying a farm here in Caerphilly to serve as a weekend getaway?"

"Yes, if he can ever find a suitable place. Not that he isn't perfectly welcome to stay with us any time, and I'm sure you feel the same, but there is something about having your own place."

"Tell him to check out this place." I gave

her Samuel Yoder's name and the address of his farm. "I don't see any 'for sale' signs, but it doesn't look as if anyone's actively farming, and — long story, but I have reason to suspect the owner may be experiencing financial difficulties."

"I will, dear. Is it a nice place?"

I glanced back up at the huge old farmhouse, shaded by enormous oaks, and sitting on a hill with a sweeping view of the rolling pastures that surrounded it.

"With a little work it could be an enviably nice place." And given Festus Hollingsworth's thriving law practice, he could afford the work more than most. "I'll send you some pictures."

"I'm sure Festus will be very grateful, dear."

"That's good," I said. "Because it would be really nice if he could express his gratitude by telling me anything he can find out about Mr. Yoder and what happened to him and his farm."

"Ooh, a mystery." Mother pretended to make fun of Dad's obsession with mysteries, but she had her own sense of curiosity and was expert at teasing hard information out of the rumors that made the rounds of the local grapevine. "I'll call him right away."

I hung up, feeling pretty confident that if there was a story behind the vacant Yoder farm, between Mother and Festus they'd find it. I shot a couple of pictures with my phone, showing the house, the barn, and then a long shot of the gentle, rolling pastures. Then I e-mailed them to Mother.

Of course, it would take Mother and Festus time to report back. I pondered for a few moments, then pulled up the Summerball roster and dialed a phone number on it.

"Entwhistle," said a now-familiar voice.

"Will, this is Meg Langslow again," I said. "I had one more question, about your neighbor, Samuel Yoder."

"Another Biff casualty," Will said. "I don't know all the details, but I'm sure he'd be happy to fill you in."

"He's not here," I said.

"If you're over at his farm, yeah, he's not there. Bank's in the process of taking his farm. He moved in with his married daughter."

"Do you know where she lives?" I asked.

"No — somewhere in town, but I don't know the address, and since her married name is Jones, good luck finding her. But why don't you talk to him at tomorrow's games? His grandson's on the Wombats, and

221

he never misses a game. He's about six three, thin as a rail, with a bushy gray beard. Or if you have any trouble finding him, I'm sure one of the other Wombat parents can point him out."

A thought hit me.

"Mr. Yoder's beard," I said. "Is it one of those Amish-style beards, with the bare chin?"

"Yes — he's not Amish, but I think he's got some ancestors who were. You've met him, then."

"Seen him." Probably not a good idea to mention that I'd seen him having a bitter argument with Biff. "I think I'll recognize him again."

"Good. See you at the games."

With that he hung up.

Yes, I'd recognize Samuel Yoder. If I ran into him at the game, should I ask him why he'd been quarreling with Biff at the ball field? Probably a better idea to leave it to the chief.

I was about to dial the chief again, then I hesitated. Definitely a good idea to let him know that I'd probably found two more people with good reason to dislike Biff and that one of them had had words with him at the scene of the crime.

But I didn't want to tick him off by appearing to be snooping in his case. Probably a good idea to make my report in person, so I could gauge his reactions.

I programmed my GPS for the center of town and set off, hoping the machine was better at finding its way out of than into the trackless wilds of the southern end of the county.

After only a few wrong turns, I made my way back to town and parked the Behemoth in the nearly deserted lot at the police station. In fact, the chief's blue sedan was the only vehicle in sight.

I walked through the door of the police station to find the entrance room empty. No officers visible, no citizens waiting in front of the reception desk or in the battered orange or purple plastic chairs around the walls, and most important, no one behind the desk.

Why was the police station deserted in the middle of the day?

CHAPTER 14

"Hello?" I called, scanning the empty reception room.

A head popped up from beneath the desk, startling me so that I jumped slightly. Then I recognized the elaborate braids and round caramel-colored face. Kayla Butler, Aida's daughter. She looked nearly as startled as I did. And why had she been hiding behind the desk?

"I didn't know you were working at the police station," I said, while glancing around to see if there was anything visible to account for the hiding. All seemed clear, but then I began to worry for another reason — the last I'd heard Kayla had been completely immersed in the joys and sorrows of her senior year at Caerphilly High School. I hoped this was only a part-time job and not a sudden derailment of her planned career in music and drama.

"I work here part time when they're short

staffed," Kayla said. "We need every penny for the college fund."

I was relieved to hear that.

"But I don't usually work the front desk," she said, frowning slightly. "I wouldn't be out here at all except that some fool tourists ran into Merle Shiffley's pig truck just now, and they were already short staffed with the murder and they had to send Mom and Sammy to the accident scene."

"Oh, no," I said. "Was anyone hurt?"

"Merle is fine, and so are the pigs as far as we know, but Mom and Sammy are still helping round them up so it could be a while. Vern took the tourists to the hospital with cuts and bruises, but they'll live. And I spilled my slushie." She gestured toward her feet. "That's why I was under the desk. I need to mop it all up before the chief sees it. He's the only one here, so if you need to see him, you're fine, but if you want anyone else, they're all out somewhere." She waved her hand vaguely as if to suggest that the whereabouts of the rest of the force remained a profound mystery.

"I did want to see the chief," I said.

"Go on back, then," she said, disappearing under the desk again.

I thought of suggesting that Frankie, who usually manned the desk during the day shift, would have called the chief on the intercom to ask if it was okay to send me back. I decided my conscience would be served if I told her on the way out. I strolled down the hall and knocked on the chief's closed door.

"Come in, Kayla," he called out.

I opened the door.

"Although I thought I told you that you can use the intercom and not leave the front desk unattended," the chief went on as I stepped in. He didn't look up from the stack of papers in front of him, and I recognized a faint note of irritation in his voice.

"Shall I remind her of that on my way out?" I asked.

He raised his head and looked briefly startled before breaking into a smile.

"Come in." He sat up and pushed the papers away from him as if grateful for an interruption. "Not sure the reminder will do any good," he added as I shut the door and took a seat in front of his desk. "But she's a good kid, even though she can talk the hind leg off a donkey, and I appreciate her giving up part of her weekend on such short notice to help out here. What can I do for you?"

"Since there's to be no baseball today," I said, "I decided to console myself with work. I tried to find Biff, but no luck. He wasn't at his business, and apparently the soon-to-be ex-Mrs. Brown kicked him out a month ago."

"Yes," the chief said. "Vern reported that he appears to be living in bachelor squalor in one of the back rooms of the main building at his scrapyard. I know the housing market is tight here in Caerphilly, but you'd think he could find something over in Clay County."

"Evidently the housing market is tight there, too," I said. "Especially for someone who may be experiencing serious cash flow problems. Gina — the estranged wife, who seems already to have shed her married name — suggested that might be why he's procrastinating on starting the town square work — can't afford to buy the materials."

"Interesting," the chief said. "I do need to talk to her at greater length."

"I hope she has an alibi," I said. "Because she sure has motive."

The chief frowned slightly, and pursed his lips. I dropped the subject.

"So after not finding Biff in either place, I began to suspect that fate was trying to tell me something," I went on, "and decided to stop trying to badger Mr. Brown in his time of sorrow."

"Thoughtful of you," he said. "Although from what I've seen, Mr. Brown seems to be coping with his bereavement fairly well."

"Suspiciously well? Not that it's any of my business," I added hastily. "Anyway, I decided to talk to some other people who have worked with Brown Construction in the past. I wanted to find out if anyone else had had the same problems with him, or if anyone had any good advice for working successfully with him. Because I'm not having much luck getting him off the mark."

"Sensible," the chief said. "Am I correct in assuming that your presence here means you found some information you think I might find useful for my investigation?"

"You are." I described my visits to the Entwhistle Farm and the deserted Yoder Farm and the quarrel I'd seen between Mr. Yoder and Biff. I even mentioned that I was siccing Festus on the Yoder Farm. The chief listened without any visible signs of impatience, and took down the names and addresses.

"Interesting," he said when I'd finished. "I was aware that the Yoder Farm was vacant but hadn't heard why. I would be interested to hear anything else you and Festus learn. I'll have a talk with Mr. Brown and Mr. Yoder about the reason for their —

would you call it a quarrel?"

"Heated discussion, at the very least. Though in Mr. Yoder's defense, that seems to be Biff's normal form of interaction with the rest of humanity."

"Hmmm." He scribbled in his notebook. "I gather from your tone that you don't consider Mr. Entwhistle a prime suspect."

"He's a fellow baseball parent, a heritage animal fancier, and keeps his pig farm cleaner than most people's kitchens," I said. "So maybe I'm predisposed to like him. No idea if he's a suspect or not. But he's a nice guy."

"So are most of Mr. Brown's enemies," the chief said, with a sigh. "Which is more than one can say for him. I do beg your pardon," he added. "That was a very uncharitable thing to say. But this has been a trying day, and Mr. Brown has been a major factor in making it so."

"I understand," I said. "I was just going to ask —"

Just then both of us turned our heads toward the door. No doubt the chief was hearing the same thing I was — shouting, coming from the front desk.

"I should check on Kayla," the chief said. As he stood up, he opened a desk drawer and pulled out his gun, still in its holster.

He deftly attached the holster to his belt before heading for the door.

"I'm not getting in your way, but I'm coming, too," I said.

"Chief?" It was Kayla's voice on the intercom. "Chief?"

But just as he was about to reach for the knob, the door slammed open.

"Where'sa chief?" A remarkably tall red-headed woman — easily as tall as Michael's six foot four — was standing in the doorway. Make that slumping against one side of the doorway. The chief took a step or two back before answering.

"Chief Burke at your service, Ms. . . . ?"

It took the woman a few seconds to focus on him — time enough for me to realize that she wasn't quite as huge as she first seemed. At least four inches of her apparent height was due to her enormous hair, which was teased and upswept into a tousled mess that would have made Medusa look subdued. Another six inches came from the spike heels of her zebra-print sandals. Barefoot and with a normal hairdo, she'd probably be a couple of inches shorter than my five foot ten. And she was probably about my weight, too — a little heavier than optimal, but not fat. Someone should tell her that wearing skin-tight lime-green Lycra capris was not a good look for women with our shape. And either she'd forgotten to put on her blouse or fluorescent pink bras had somehow become outerwear.

"Callie Peebles," she said. "Please'ta meet-cha."

She stumbled across the office toward the guest chair I'd just vacated. As she passed me I could smell way too much musk, with an undertone of rum. That explained the slumping, and also her slurred speech. She settled herself in the chair, hoisted her suitcase-sized leopard-print purse into her lap, and looked up at the chief expectantly. As if suddenly remembering something, she smiled and batted her eyes at him. I was suddenly struck by how enormous her lips were. Next to hers, Mick Jagger's mouth would look understated. And I found myself fascinated by her hair, which had to be the brightest red I'd ever seen not gracing the body of a fire engine. Mother would probably have described it as "exuberant, if improbable."

The chief and I exchanged glances. I lifted one eyebrow and nodded slightly at the door. The chief shook his head vigorously and pointed to another guest chair — one that stood along the wall beside his desk rather than in front of it.

I deduced that the chief wanted a witness to his interview with his guest, and thought me more suitable than Kayla, so I took the chair and tried to make myself as unobtrusive as possible. The chief sat at his desk. Kayla's voice could still be heard over the intercom, repeating "Chief? Chief?"

The chief pressed the intercom button. "Yes, Kayla?" he said, all the while staring at Callie.

"There's a lay — um, a woman to see you. I told her to wait but she went back anyway."

"That's okay, Kayla," the chief said. "Thank you." Then he turned to his guest. "What can I do for you, Ms. Peebles?"

"I want my papers," she said. And then she sat there expectantly, as if that explained everything.

"Your papers," the chief repeated. "I'm afraid I don't know what papers you're talking about."

"Don't pretend you don't know who I am," Callie snarled.

"Ms. Callie Peebles," the chief said. "But I'm afraid I don't know what papers you're talking about."

"Oh, come off it," Callie said. "Or maybe you don't really know who I am — Mrs. Caligula Peebles Henson."

I couldn't help it — I started to guffaw,

and had to quickly pretend to be overcome with a coughing fit. The chief didn't say anything, and I could see his mouth twitching slightly. Evidently he, too, thought it was pretty funny that Callie's parents had decided to name her after one of the most infamously corrupt and perverse rulers in history.

"The late Mr. Shep Henson was your husband?" he asked, when he had recovered.

"Ex-husband," she said. "But I should still be on the insurance. It's not as if he had anyone else to leave it to. And when I talked to our sheriff, he said you'd taken all Shep's papers. I want them."

"I see," the chief said. "Sheriff Whicker is correct — I have taken custody of Mr. Henson's papers as part of my investigation into his murder. I'm afraid I can't release them at present. But if you'll give me your contact information, I'll see what we can do to expedite release of any insurance documents we find."

"I don't understand," Callie said. "Why can't you just give me my papers?"

Clearly, from the chief's expression, he thought he had already explained why. I decided to chime in.

"Insurance companies never pay a claim on a murder victim until the police figure

233

out who did it." I had no idea if this was correct, but if I said it with conviction, maybe I could help the chief get rid of Callie. "So your best bet is to do everything you can to help the chief solve it. The faster he does, the sooner you get your money."

"Really?" Callie looked astonished.

I nodded my head. She glanced over at the chief.

"Ms. Langslow is essentially correct. But I assure you, we'll do whatever we can to expedite — er, to get you what you need as soon as we can. We haven't actually found the papers in question — Mr. Henson's desk was rather disorganized."

"Yeah, that's Shep," Callie said. "Couldn't organize his way out of a wet tissue. But you'll get me the paperwork as soon as you can?"

She accompanied this request by simpering and batting her eyes at the chief. She was wearing false eyelashes so long and thick that it looked as if small black rodents were squirming on top of her cheeks.

"As soon as I can," the chief said. "And where can I contact you?"

Callie rattled off her address and phone number. The chief scribbled in his notebook.

"And just for the record, where were you

on Thursday night between ten p.m. and two a.m.," the chief said. "Just a formality," he added, seeing Callie shrink back at the question.

"I was down at the Pigeon," Callie said.

"The Clay Pigeon?"

"That's right, dearie." Callie clearly found the thought of her favorite watering hole reassuring. "You just ask them down at the Pigeon. They know me there. I was there all night — I'm there most nights. If you drop in, maybe I'll let you buy me a drink." The rodents squirmed again, and Callie leaned over in a way that caused even more of her décolletage to spill out of the hot pink bra or swimsuit top or whatever it was. The chief nodded solemnly, staring pointedly at her face.

"Thank you," he said. "I won't take any more of your time."

"That's okay, dearie," Callie said. "Any time."

She rose and sashayed out, with a lot of unnecessary hip swaying. The chief watched her departure with a slight frown on his face. Probably not the reaction she was aiming for. When she closed the door, he turned to me.

"Would you mind following her to the entrance?" he asked. "Make sure she doesn't give Kayla any trouble?"

"Can do," I said.

"And see if you can detain her for a little while by engaging her in conversation," he went on. "If you can manage to take away her keys, that would be excellent."

"You think she's too intoxicated to drive?"

"I would simply take her keys and administer a Breathalyzer, but I might need her cooperation for this investigation and I don't want to poison the well."

"But it won't hurt anything if she gets mad at me," I said. "Okay."

I stood up and headed for the door.

"If I can't find an officer who can get here in the next few minutes, I'll come out and arrest her myself, no matter how hard it makes things later," he said. "But if you can delay her . . ."

"Roger."

I exited and headed down the hall, trying to look nonchalant. Callie either didn't notice me behind her or paid no attention. She had dropped the exaggerated swaying gait in favor of a comfortable saunter. I found myself staring with fascination at her hair, which actually seemed to glow slightly in the dimmer light of the corridor. Was this a natural phenomenon, or had she added some kind of fluorescent ingredient to her hair dye? Probably not tactful to ask, but I filed away the phenomenon as something that might be interesting to investigate next Halloween.

For now, my job was to delay her. I rummaged in my purse and came up with a pack of gum.

"Callie?" I called, holding up the gum. "Did you drop this?"

As she turned she caught one of the spike heels on something and stumbled, catching herself on the front desk.

"I'm so sorry!" I said, rushing over to help her upright again. "I shouldn't have startled you."

" 'Sno problem, dearie," she said. "Not your fault, really. This slippery floor's a death trap."

She frowned at Kayla as if she were responsible for the glossy, well-buffed linoleum.

"Isn't that the truth," I said. "It's only safe for the officers in their heavy boots. Are you sure your ankle's okay? It looked as if you twisted it a little. Sit down for a second and let me check it out."

I steered her toward the nearest plastic guest chair, a purple one that looked particularly festive next to her lime-green and fuchsia outfit.

"Are you a doctor?" Callie asked.

"No, but my father is," I said. "And I've picked up a few things."

I fussed over Callie's ankle for a few minutes, and she seemed to enjoy the attention.

"Maybe I should go down to the ER," she said cheerfully. "Show my ankle to some nice young doctor and see what he thinks."

"Oh, good," Kayla said. "Vern's back."

"I think you're good to go," I told Callie. "Do you feel okay to drive?"

"I'm fine," she said. "Though maybe I will drop by the ER, just in case."

"Let me bring your car to the door," I suggested, holding out my hand for her keys. "Save you a walk across that rough parking lot."

"Not a problem," she said. "I'm parked right outside."

She pointed to a red truck parked in the handicapped spot just outside the front door — without benefit of handicapped plates or a sticker.

"Don't blame me when they throw you in the slammer," I muttered, as she stumbled out toward her truck.

CHAPTER 15

"There's no way she should be driving," Kayla exclaimed.

"That's why I was stalling her until Vern got here," I said.

And then, just in case Vern wasn't quite in time to spot the parking violation, I pulled out my cell phone and took a picture, taking care to get in not only the truck's license plate but also the handicapped parking sign. I also got a nice shot of the driver's door, which had CALLIE written on it in purple and gold cursive letters festooned with stars and flowers and way too much glitter. Was that actually painted on or was it some kind of vinyl decal?

"I'm sorry," Kayla was saying. "She just shoved her way past me."

"Not a problem," I said. "Turned out okay."

I went back to the chief's office. He was on the phone with someone.

"That's good," the chief said. "No, I don't know what she's driving, but there can't be that many other vehicles in the lot —"

I held up my phone.

"Yes, the red Ford Lariat," the chief said. He rattled off the license plate number. "That's right. Yes, the one in the handicapped zone. Yes, but the DUI is more important. Roger. Vern's here," he added to me as he hung up.

"I'm wondering if maybe I should wait a little while before I drive," I said. "Any chance I have a contact drunk from breathing too close to her?"

"Perhaps she's been drowning her sorrow over Mr. Henson's death," he said.

"More likely her sorrow over the tragic disappearance of the insurance papers."

Just then we heard a siren go off nearby. The chief nodded with satisfaction.

"Good," the chief said. "Vern will handle her. No way I want her driving the streets of my county in that condition."

"I bet she came straight from the Clay Pigeon," I said.

"The Clay Pigeon," he muttered. "It would be the Clay Pigeon."

" 'You will never find a more wretched hive of scum and villainy,' " I quoted.

"Which Holmes story is that from?" the

chief asked. "I don't recognize the reference."

"It's from *Star Wars,*" I said. "So does this mean some poor Caerphilly deputy has to brave the squalor of the Clay Pigeon to check her alibi?"

"I suppose." The chief sighed and shook his head. "Just to be thorough. Although frankly, I don't see the use. If she really is a regular at the Clay Pigeon, I'm sure the denizens of the place will back up any story she tells. 'Wretched hive of scum and villainy' — you have no idea how apt that quotation is."

"Still, she's a suspect, right?"

"And all the more suspicious thanks to her keen interest in Mr. Henson's insurance policy," the chief said. "Which would be ironic."

"Why?" I asked. "Does he not have life insurance?"

"He does," the chief said. "Through Brown Construction Company. And it appears that upon divorcing the former Mrs. Henson, he changed his beneficiary to his brother."

"Biff?" I asked.

"Yes, Biff," the chief said. "He only has the one brother."

"A large policy?" I asked.

"Depends on what you call large," the chief said. "A hundred thousand dollars."

"Large enough," I said. "Way more than pocket change. And as I already mentioned, I've begun to suspect that Mr. Brown is suffering from cash flow difficulties. A hundred thousand dollars would definitely be tempting to a man in that situation."

"No argument. But Ms. Peebles doesn't look particularly affluent, either, and if she thought she was still his beneficiary — ah, well." He straightened up, as if he'd suddenly remembered that he was talking to me, not Vern or Aida or another of his deputies. "We'll sort it out before too long."

"And I'll leave you to it." I'd noticed that his eyes had been straying toward a monitor in his credenza with increasing frequency. I wasn't sure whether this was unconscious or whether he was giving me a deliberate hint that I was overstaying my welcome. Either way, I figured it was time to go.

"Before you go," he said. "You've been studying Mr. Throckmorton's list of Brown Construction clients in Caerphilly County. Notice anything interesting about it?"

I thought about it for a few moments.

"I had a hard time finding someone I thought would talk to me," I said. "I think at least half the people on it were Pruitts,

242

and you can imagine how likely they'd be to confide in me.

"Or me," he said, grimacing. "Though I interviewed them anyway, for all the good it will do. And your report of the quarrel between Mr. Brown and one of the Pruitts only confirms something I had already observed — that the relationship between Mr. Brown and the Pruitts is not as warm as it once was."

"Any idea why?"

"None whatsoever," he said.

I thought about it for a few moments.

"I wonder if Biff's financial problems helped cause the demise of the Pruitts' bank," I said. "Or it could be the other way around and the bank failure caused his problems. Either way, I can imagine there would be ill-feeling on both sides."

"Very possible," the chief said. "Look, you're apt to have more chances to observe them than I will, and they're less apt to be wary in front of you. So if you see or hear anything that might have some bearing on the issue, please let me know."

"Will do," I said.

"And please note that this is a request to share information you might come across in the normal course of your work for the county and your participation in the Summerball League, not an encouragement to involve yourself in my investigation."

"I will strive to be the proverbial fly on the wall in their company," I said. "So you suspect the Pruitts?"

"Perhaps." He scowled slightly and stared into space for a few moments. Then he shook his head and sat up straighter. "Although perhaps we're a deal too ready to suspect the Pruitts here in town."

"We wouldn't suspect them so readily if they didn't have such a history of getting up to suspicious things," I pointed out.

"True." He was glancing at the monitor on his credenza again. "You might want to take the side door out," he said, pointing to it. "Ms. Peebles is not proving to be a model prisoner." I took a few steps closer and saw that the screen was filled with the pictures from half a dozen security cameras. All were serene and motionless except for one showing Kayla, apparently hiding behind the front desk, and one with a view of the parking lot, where we could see Callie's truck standing in the middle of the entrance. As we watched she began flailing at Deputy Vern with the giant leopard-print purse.

"I'm not sure she's actually aware that she's a prisoner," I said.

"Officer in need of assistance." Shaking

his head, the chief stood, pulled his gun out of the drawer again, and began buckling it onto his belt.

"I can see another patrol car arriving," I said.

He paused on his way to the door and glanced back at the monitor. The second patrol car had effectively blocked the exit from the parking lot. Deputy Sammy Wendell got out of the newly arrived car and stood behind it. Callie had stopped trying to whack Vern with the purse and was digging inside it.

"She's got a gun!" The chief and I said it in unison as Callie pulled her hand out of the purse. He took off running.

"Stay here," he called over his shoulder. "Kayla, run back there to my office and keep your head down!"

In the cameras, I could see Kayla rise from behind the front desk and disappear. A few seconds later she appeared at my side. Vern and Sammy had taken refuge behind their cars. I couldn't see Sammy, but I had a good view of Vern on one of the monitors. He had his gun out and trained on Callie. Was he really going to shoot her?

Callie looked around triumphantly, evidently thinking she'd vanquished the officers, then gave a rebel yell and fired a couple of shots in the air.

"Ms. Peebles." The chief's voice, amplified by a megaphone, carried easily all the way from the parking lot. "Drop the gun and put your hands in the air. I repeat —"

Callie turned and sprinted for her truck, but she tripped again and went sprawling. The gun went off and the front left tire of her truck began rapidly deflating. Vern ran out and grabbed something lying on the asphalt — Callie's gun. Then Sammy and the chief appeared. Sammy pulled out an evidence bag for the gun. Vern handcuffed Callie. Then he and the chief helped her to her feet and began escorting her to the station entrance. Or maybe dragging would have been a more apt term. Callie's ability to walk or even stand unsupported appeared to be disappearing.

"Wow," Kayla said. "I wonder if my mom will still let me stay at the front desk after this."

"Probably not," I said. "Do you really want to be at the front desk?"

"Not really," she said. "Never thought I'd say this, but I can't wait to be back in the file room."

"Why doesn't the chief call in a few volunteers, the way he usually does when they get swamped?" I asked.

"He did, but they all went out to round up Merle Shiffley's pigs."

I pulled out my phone and speed-dialed Mother.

"Mother," I said, when we'd finished with the usual amenities. "We just had a shooting incident down at the police station. No one's hurt, and I wasn't even close to it, but I wanted you to be the first to hear that I'm fine."

"Oh, dear! What happened?"

I told her, as succinctly as possible, but with enough detail that she could make it a truly spellbinding story when she hit the grapevine with it — as I knew she would about two seconds after we hung up.

"So with all this gunplay going on, I'm not sure the chief is going to want Kayla Butler minding the desk," I said in wrapping up. "Which she's been doing to help out, because the murder investigation has them short staffed. Any chance you could call around and recruit a couple of people to help out here? Preferably people not qualified to take part in the pig roundup."

"Of course, dear."

"The shooting incident won't be a deterrent?"

"Hmm, yes. They might be miffed to be invited after everything's all over. I'll find a way to suggest that there could be more excitement in the offing."

With that she signed off.

Kayla was watching the monitors, one of which showed the reception area where Sammy, Vern, and the chief were standing in a circle around Callie. She was hand-cuffed to an orange plastic chair and had fallen asleep — or passed out.

"Thanks," Kayla said. "Should I tell the chief about the volunteers?"

"Yes," I said. "Why don't they take her back to a cell and let her sleep it off?"

"They have to search her first," Kayla said. "And for that they need a female offi-cer, which means either Mom or Deputy Riddle, because Deputy Crowder is off on maternity leave."

I made a mental note that Kayla might be an excellent source to cultivate if I was curi-ous about what was going on down at the police station.

"So I guess they'll keep her there, clearly visible in the security cameras, until one of the female deputies arrives," I said.

"Yeah." Kayla nodded. "Oh, here comes your cousin Horace. He seems in a hurry."

"They're probably going to have him test the gun," I said. "Fire some bullets and do a comparison with the ones that killed Shep

Henson."

"Uh-huh." Kayla looked thoughtful. "Do you think she killed Mr. Henson?"

"No idea," I said, shaking my head.

"Mr. Henson wasn't such a bad guy," she said. "He was a rotten umpire, but I think that was Mr. Brown's fault. I remember sometime a year or two ago we were going home from one of my cousin Melvin's games, and he couldn't find his bat, and I said I'd go back to the dugout to look for it, and when I got close I could hear Mr. Brown really yelling at someone."

"Mr. Henson?"

"Yeah." She shook her head. "He was just laying into him — you wouldn't treat a dog like that. I figured out pretty fast what the problem was — Melvin's team had won the game six to five — should have been more like twenty or thirty to five, but even with Mr. Henson making a whole lot of really bogus calls in the Yankees' favor, we beat them. Mr. Brown was really put out. And then she came along and stuck up for Mr. Henson." She nodded at the monitor. "She was really mad at him. Mr. Brown, I mean. If it was Mr. Brown who got murdered instead of Mr. Henson, she'd be my prime suspect. But I don't think she'd kill her husband. She's kind of loud, but she seems nice enough."

Only he was her ex-husband now, I thought, as I went out the side door to avoid encountering Callie again. And Kayla probably had no idea what the breakup of a marriage could sometimes do to even the nicest of people.

At least a bad breakup could. But had Callie and Shep had a bad breakup? Surely if they had, she wouldn't be expecting to collect his insurance money?

And even if Biff was the intended victim, that didn't eliminate Callie as a suspect. Shep was at the ball field, where anyone who knew Biff would have predicted he'd be on the night before Opening Day. And while Callie, of all people, should be able to tell them apart if anyone could, the resemblance was uncanny, and who knew what a congenial night down at the Clay Pigeon might have done to her powers of perception?

Well, she was in custody now, and after her performance in the parking lot, the chief would be looking pretty closely at her.

When I got back to the Behemoth I decided to make one more call before heading home to enjoy whatever festivities Mother and Michael had arranged. Randall answered on the first ring.

"Meg! Just the person I need to talk to," Randall said. "I have a bit of good news."

"That's nice." I braced myself, because all too often Randall's bits of good news involved massive amounts of work for me.

CHAPTER 16

"I just talked to the chief a few minutes ago," Randall said. "He's releasing the field, and Jim's authorizing us to do a bit of maintenance on it tonight."

"Jim?"

"Jim Witherington." Evidently Randall had made progress ingratiating himself with the Summerball bigwig.

"That's great," I said. "Listen, I have a new theory — what if Biff is having cash flow problems?"

"He very well could be," Randall said. "But I'm not sure how that fits into the case. Killing Shep wouldn't help his cash flow problems — unless Shep had some insurance and Biff is the beneficiary."

"Shep did, and Biff is," I said. "Facts I'm sure the chief will take into account in his investigation of the murder. But forget the murder for a minute — I've been working on how to get the town square renovation project moving. What if Biff hasn't started because he has no cash and his credit's in the toilet and he can't get the materials?"

Randall was silent for a few moments, then —

"Damn. Yeah, I suppose it could be that simple. But if that's the case, why doesn't he just say so?"

"And admit to his hated business rival that all is not well in Brownsville?"

"You're right," he said. "That absolutely could be it and — okay, call me a paranoid son of a gun."

"Only if you insist."

"That break-in down at Biff's scrapyard last night — what if it wasn't a real break-in?"

"Aida said she and Vern couldn't find anything missing," I said. "Which doesn't surprise me, because I can't imagine there's much in there that any sane thief would bother hauling away. But that doesn't mean the break-in part wasn't real."

"And to hear Biff tell it, his quick action in calling the police warded off a burglary," Randall said. "Except you're right, I can't imagine anyone, even in Clay County, crazy enough to think Biff has anything worth stealing. So what if Biff staged the break-in to make it look less suspicious when someone breaks into the Shiffley Construction Company lumberyard a night or two later?"

"You think he'd do that?"

"In a heartbeat."

"And he would expect us not to notice when he shows up the next day, ready to work, hauling in a load of supplies that happen to be a precise match for what's missing from your inventory?"

"Not a deep thinker, Biff. I'm going to call my cousin Cephus and get him to put on some extra security for the time being."

"Good idea," I said. "And while we're talking about supplies — how about if you figure out what Biff needs to do the town square work, and for the time being we'll pretend we happened to have found all of it in some town or county storage facility. And I will talk to Biff and see if I can renegotiate the contract so he's only providing the labor."

"At a lower cost," Randall said.

"At the same labor costs stated in the contract," I said. "And I'll use the 'we know you have so much on your plate with your brother's death' tactic."

"Worth trying," he said.

"Then e-mail me some kind of document I can pretend is part of an inventory of county surplus supplies," I said. "And I'll tackle him as soon as I get it."

"I'll have it to you tonight. Good going! I knew you'd figure out a way to solve this Biff thing!"

Not solved yet, I thought, as I put my phone away. But I was feeling guardedly optimistic.

I was pulling out of the parking lot when my phone rang again. I saw it was Michael and pulled over to park so I could safely answer it.

"Where are you?" he asked.

"I'm sorry," I said. "I meant to be home by now, but I found out some information I thought I should tell the chief, and I'm just leaving the station."

"Actually, it's great that you're still in town," he said. "Can you pick your grandmother up at the college TV studio?"

"Sure, but what in the world is she doing there?"

"Giving them an interview about her life. Why didn't you tell me that she had played in a women's professional baseball league?"

"I only found out last night, and I haven't had time to get many details," I said. "She was pretty busy with the kids at the picnic."

"She's incredible," Michael said. "She's straightened out Mason's crazy batting stance, and is helping Adam time his swings better, and the whole team's starting to throw better. So if she's finished at the studio, we could use her here."

"I'll head right over. And once we get her home, let's twist her arm to tell Jamie and Josh about her baseball career. It would be so much fun if they heard about her professional baseball career from her, not the college TV station."

On my way to pick up Cordelia I found myself wondering how she felt about taping her interview in the new drama building. When I pulled up at the front door, I suspected I had my answer. Cordelia was chatting graciously with two obviously adoring drama students, but from time to time I saw her frown as she caught sight of the huge brass letters affixed to the brick front wall of the building, proclaiming it the DR. J. MONTGOMERY BLAKE DRAMATIC ARTS BUILDING. But she was all smiles as the students helped her climb up into the Behemoth. She saved her ire for me.

"What the devil has your grandfather ever done to deserve having the drama building named after him?" she demanded as soon as we drove away.

"He gave them the money to build it," I said.

"You mean they'll name a building after

256

anyone who gives them money?"

"Why do you think the college has so many buildings named after Pruitts?"

"Ridiculous," she muttered.

"Not so ridiculous," I said. "Grandfather's spent more time on camera than a lot of professional actors, and even he would have to admit that he owes his success in equal parts to his scientific ability and his flair for the theatrical."

"Well, that's certainly true," she said. "He always was a big ham. Bully for him, I suppose, finding a way to make it pay so well. Let's talk about something more interesting. Like baseball."

So we spent the trip home discussing the subtle differences between major league baseball and youth baseball rules.

Back at the house, we found not only all twelve Eagles in our backyard, but also at least a dozen of their older brothers who played on the league's minor and major league teams. No, make that several dozen non-Eagles, and I was pretty sure some of them weren't anyone's older brothers. In fact, the more I looked around, the more I suspected at least half the players in the league were practicing somewhere in our backyard or the adjoining pasture. Almost all of the teams in the league were represented — not only Eagles but also Flat-worms, Wombats, River Rats, Sandgnats, Muckdogs, Grasshoppers, Nats, Pirates, and Red Sox. And both the kids and their parents were wearing their team colors, so our yard swirled with brightly colored t-shirts.

No Stoats or Yankees, though, since those were the teams Biff coached.

And in addition to the Eagles' parents and Mother's family, I spotted a lot of friends and neighbors — presumably ones who had kids on one of the teams. And most of them, to judge by the overflowing picnic tables, had shown up bearing foodstuffs and were now happily milling about in the backyard, plates in hand.

Cordelia was immediately drafted to repeat her throwing drill for some of the younger players. I hoped Dad had warned Rufus, his farm manager, to keep the cows and sheep out of this particular pasture for the time being. The ground was so thickly littered with baseballs that even the sure-footed Black Welsh Mountain sheep would have had a hard time keeping from slipping, and I had no great confidence that we'd manage to pick them all up afterward.

In another part of the backyard, several technicians from Michael's film classes had set up cameras and laptops, and were videotaping batters in action so they could see what they were doing and work on improving their technique.

Tory Davis was running a pitching clinic over near the barn for a small group of minor and major league players.

And most of the older kids were in the makeshift ball field, holding a lively scrimmage that was subject to interruption every time one of the dozen assembled coaches or fathers spotted a teachable moment.

"This is great!" Vince Wong appeared at my side, with his catcher's mask pushed up on top of his head. Tory had called a halt and her aspiring pitchers were gathering all the balls that had gone so wild Vince couldn't catch them. "Let's just hope Biff doesn't show up again to spoil our fun."

"I rather hope he does," I said. "He needs to learn that the league isn't his personal fiefdom. And we all need to learn to stick together and stand up to him."

Vince looked startled for a moment, and then a smile crept over his face.

"Yeah." He threw back his shoulders and stuck out his chin. "Bring him on."

He marched back to the side of the barn, where Tory's troops had finished refilling their ball bucket.

"This is marvelous!"

I started slightly, and turned to see Randall and Mr. Witherington.

"We heard about the party and I didn't think you'd mind if we showed up," Randall said. "And I rode out with Jim, so if you're finished with the Behemoth, I can take it off your hands."

"Be my guest," I said, handing him the keys.

"But this isn't just your team," Mr. Witherington said, looking slightly puzzled. "You must have half the kids in the league here."

"More like three quarters," I said.

"We knew many of the families were planning to spend the day out at the fields, watching other teams when they weren't playing," Randall said. "So we put out the word that anyone who wanted to practice or scrimmage or get coaching should show up here for potluck and baseball. We appreciate you and Michael being willing to host," he added to me.

"Wonderful," Mr. Witherington exclaimed.

Randall and I trailed behind him as he darted around the yard, inspecting everything. Over by the barn, a Red Sox player was showing a Pirate and two Grasshoppers the finer points of pitching a slider. Out in the pasture, the Flatworms, Eagles, and

Wombats had taken a break from throwing and shagging flies with a cheerful competition to see who could gather up the most balls. At the video station, a mixed party of Muckdogs and River Rats were helping one of the Muckdogs improve his batting stance. And on the ball field, the scrimmage had given way to Pickle, a game in which one team tried to steal as many bases as possible while the other team tried to get them all out.

"Wpfher foo," Mr. Witherington said — at least that's what it sounded like thanks to the mouthful of food he was trying to talk around. Mother had brought him "just a little something" — her term for a plate piled high with samples of at least half the dishes on the buffet. He swallowed and tried again. "Wonderful," he said. "This is just the sort of thing I was hoping to see. The good, solid, down-to-earth, small-town values that Summerball stands for."

Mr. Witherington found a lawn chair with a good view of the practice field and sat down to enjoy the Pickle game. I could see Mother pointing him out to several of our younger cousins, and one of them scampered over to refill his lemonade glass.

"I'm not staying long," Randall said. "I'm going over to the field. Remember my telling you Jim Witherington's given us permission to do some fixing up?"

"Define fixing up," I said. "I don't suppose it includes installing flush toilets."

"No, just what we can get done tonight to make it look as good as possible tomorrow for Opening Day, take two. But who knows? Maybe if he likes what he sees he'll give us the go-ahead for a more complete renovation later on. Meanwhile, my workmen have already started, with orders to fix anything we have the time and materials to fix."

"I can't wait to see it," I said. "In fact, I may drop by and get a sneak preview, though not until after we get the boys to bed."

Suddenly we noticed that Mr. Witherington appeared to be choking on something. Randall rushed over to check him out, and I looked around for Dad.

To my relief, Mr. Witherington's problems only seemed to be some lemonade that had gone down the wrong way. Although he was clearly agitated about something. As soon as he could speak again, he croaked out a few hoarse and unintelligible words.

"Sorry," Randall said. "I didn't quite catch that. Maybe you should just rest for a few moments before trying to speak."

"I said, isn't that Tory Davis?"

Randall frowned slightly and glanced up at me.

"The baseball player?" I asked. "Yes it is."

"Who's Tory Davis?" the young cousin with the lemonade pitcher asked.

"Only the finest woman player ever to compete in the NCAA," Mr. Witherington said. "And for that matter, one of the best pitchers of either gender ever to come out of the UCLA baseball program. And she's one of your coaches?"

"Actually, her husband is," I said. "For some reason her application to coach got lost in the shuffle, but her husband's the head coach of the Eagles, and Tory's very generous about teaching the kids."

Mr. Witherington glanced up and frowned, and then grimaced slightly — no doubt as he parsed out what I meant by "lost in the shuffle." Then he turned back to the field and delight once more lit up his face.

"If only my girls could see this!" he exclaimed. "I must bring them down next time I visit."

"Yes, I think we're making progress," Randall murmured. "Before I head out, I'll bring Tory over and introduce her."

I left him to continue the subtle indoctrination of Mr. Witherington into the NAFOB point of view.

By nine, the party had begun thinning out, as more and more people remembered that the first games tomorrow were at eight. Michael and I took the boys upstairs, leaving Mother to say farewell to the departing guests and, if necessary, evict anyone under the delusion that this was a slumber party. It helped when Randall's workmen came to haul all the portable lights down to the real ball field.

And, of course, that fired up my curiosity to see what Randall and company were doing, so once the boys were settled — and Michael, whose full day of coaching and bonding with his sons had been pretty strenuous — I tiptoed out and headed for the field.

Chapter 17

About twenty workmen were at the ball field. Two of them were in the parking lot, dumping dirt in some of the worst ruts and depressions and raking smooth some of the mounds and accidental speed bumps. Half a dozen were hauling the huge portable lights into place and fine-tuning their arrangement to ensure that there would be no dark pockets on the field. Another half dozen were in the outfield, leveling bumps and filling holes. Two or three were improving the pitcher's mound, piling dirt here and removing dirt there, and then checking the results with a level. Several more were replacing the worn, badly splintered bleacher seats with well-sanded new boards. One workman was reshingling the Snack Shack roof. Randall and Mr. Witherington and one of the workers were wandering about with a giant tape measure, and it was probably as a result of their measurements that a workman was digging up the anchor that held the misaligned second base in place, in preparation to moving it to the spot where it really belonged.

Chief Burke was standing near the home dugout, observing. I strolled over to see him.

"Are you okay with what they're doing to your crime scene?" I asked.

"Apparently this isn't my crime scene," he said. "The state police brought in some dogs this afternoon — dogs who can detect blood in amounts invisible to the human eye."

"And they didn't find anything."

"Dead squirrel just outside the right-field fence," he said. "And a little mild interest in the area at the edge of the parking lot where the porta-potty was. Which would be consistent with someone bringing the body here in a vehicle and stuffing it into the porta-potty, shedding a little blood along the way."

"But not from very far away, according to what Dad said, right?" I asked.

"Correct," the chief said. "Apart from that one spot, nothing. You've never seen two more bored and discouraged cadaver dogs in your life."

"So if this isn't the crime scene, where is?"

"We're sending the dogs out into the woods in the morning," the chief said.

"They're resting now — they can only work for so long at a stretch. And while we're at it, we're going to turn them loose on our various suspects' cars."

"Hope none of the suspects are prone to nosebleeds," I said.

He chuckled at that.

Just then Randall spotted us and headed our way, with Mr. Witherington trailing behind him.

"Looks like progress," the chief said, nodding at the field.

"I just wish we'd been able to start this a week ago," Mr. Witherington fretted.

"We'll do what we can," Randall said. "I'm going to get my tool kit and pitch in."

"I can help if you like," I said. "I've got my own tool kit in the car."

"The metal parts of the bleachers and dugouts could use a lot of work," Randall said. "I've got a soldering iron and gear over in my truck, but everyone else I could ask to use it is already doing something slightly more important."

"Randall, you do realize that a soldering iron isn't a tool many people know how to use," Mr. Witherington said. "I, for example, wouldn't have the slightest idea what to do with one."

"Meg's a blacksmith," Randall said. "She's

probably better with a soldering iron than I am."

"I stand rebuked for doubting," Mr. Witherington said.

"I'm nowhere near as skilled as either of you," the chief said. "But I can use a shovel."

"So can I," Mr. Witherington said. "I'd be happy to help out with the field leveling."

"How about a paintbrush, chief?" Randall said. "And you, too, Jim, if you've got some old clothes you can change into. The Snack Shack and the concrete parts of the dugouts could really use a coat of paint. By the time my guys are finished with what we're already doing, it'll be too late for it to dry by morning, but if you can tackle it now —"

Both the chief and Mr. Witherington were already taking off their jackets and rolling up their sleeves.

"Start with the Snack Shack, so Meg can work on the dugouts," Randall said. "We may not be able to get everything done with the bodies we've got, but we can make a darned good start."

"How many bodies can you use?" I stopped halfway to Randall's truck to ask.

"If you can find them, we can find something for them to do," Randall said. "You thinking of calling Her Highness?"

"Calling who?" Mr. Witherington asked.

"Mother," I was already saying into the phone. "We could use volunteers to get the ball field ready. Can you see if anyone there's willing."

"Of course, dear."

"Excellent," Mr. Witherington said. "I do wish Mr. Brown would return my calls tonight. We could use the keys to the Snack Shack and the supply shed."

"Meg can probably pick the lock," Randall said.

"Useful skill for parents of small mischievous boys," I said, seeing Mr. Witherington's startled look. Though actually I owed my burglary skills to the long-ago summer when Dad — after reading too many of Lawrence Block's Bernie Rhodenbarr books and watching Cary Grant in *To Catch a Thief* one too many times — had decided he wanted to become a white hat burglar and tried to learn picking locks. After hours of painstaking effort, Dad still had trouble opening doors with a key, but I had become reasonably proficient at picking ordinary, uncomplicated locks.

And fortunately, ordinary, uncomplicated locks were all Biff had bothered to install on the Snack Shack and the supply shed. I got them open just in time for the arrival of a posse of volunteers carrying brooms, brushes, buckets, and bottles of bleach.

I collected my tools and Randall's soldering gear and tackled the dugouts. The Eagles were scheduled to be in the visitor's dugout for tomorrow morning's game, so just in case I only had the time to make one structurally sound, I started with that one. The dugout was really just a low concrete wall surrounding a bare wooden bench and topped by a ramshackle chain-link cage. It might protect the players from fly balls and help the coaches keep them more or less where they were supposed to be while the team was batting, but it offered no shade on a sunny day or shelter from a rainstorm. We could do better for our kids. And if I had anything to do with it, we would.

But for now, I set to work. Neither cage nor bench was well-built to begin with, and I could see no signs that anyone had ever bothered with any repairs or maintenance. I unbolted the bench and tossed it outside, trusting that Randall's crew could repair or replace it, and began hammering and soldering to repair first the frame that was supposed to support the bench, and then the chain-link cage.

As I was finishing up, Randall and one of his cousins arrived with a new, nicely sanded two-by-four for the bench.

"It's still not pretty," I said as we bolted the seat in place. "But it's a lot safer."

"I feel much better about putting the kids in this," Randall said, nodding with approval.

"I'd feel even better if we could get some kind of a roof on this thing," I said.

"Lipstick on a pig," Randall said. "I'm already drawing up plans for new dugouts."

"But for tomorrow, why not rig up some tarps to make a roof," I suggested. "And then the kids and coaches won't have to broil in the sun, so we'll see less sunburn and heat prostration —"

Randall was already pulling out his measuring tape to see what size tarp was needed.

As I was packing up my gear to start working on the other dugout, Mr. Witherington arrived carrying a paintbrush and a bucket of paint.

"I'll be out of your way in a minute," I said.

"No rush," he said. "I welcome the excuse to take a breather. Randall's a pretty stern taskmaster."

It didn't really sound like a complaint, and while he was paint-smeared and disheveled, he looked a lot more relaxed and happy than he had when I'd first seen him this morning.

"Nice to do something physical for a change," he went on. "And it's taking my mind off things. It's been an unsettling day."

"Murder tends to have that effect," I said.

"I wouldn't know," he said. "I've never had any previous experience with murder. Tell me — was Shep Henson well liked here?"

A good question.

"I wouldn't say well liked," I said. "But not really disliked, either — just not that well known. He lived over in Clay County and did most of his socializing there. People here in Caerphilly mainly saw him at baseball games."

"So people here only knew him as an umpire," he said. "Which means they probably disliked him."

"Probably," I agreed. "But only mildly. And in an impersonal kind of way. I mean, people say they hate the tax man, but that doesn't mean they'd take it out on a neighbor who happens to work for the IRS."

"I suppose you're right," he said. "Anyway, seeing that he wasn't exactly a popular man here, I thought it would be nice to notify some of his colleagues."

"Other umpires?"

"Yes," he said. "I thought I'd make a few calls, find out which of the regional umpire associations he belonged to. I thought perhaps they might want to do a wreath. Or perhaps even send a delegation to the funeral when that's held."

I has a sudden vision of a graveside delegation of umpires, clad in blue uniforms with black face masks and chest protectors, simultaneously raising their fists in the well-known "you're out" gesture. Probably not what Mr. Witherington had in mind.

"Sounds like a nice idea," I said aloud. "Did you have any luck?"

"None at all," he said. "Mr. Henson didn't belong to any umpire association that I've ever heard of."

"Well, that's — odd." I actually started out to say something like "that's about what I'd expect with Biff running things," but thought better of it. Biff bashing might make Mr. Witherington want to defend the man his organization had chosen to head our league. Much more effective to let Biff make our case for us.

"Very odd," Mr. Witherington said. "And disquieting. Mr. Henson appears to have had no association whatsoever with any of the organizations that provide umpire training and credentialing, which casts serious doubt on his qualifications."

"Maybe his brother could shed some light

on that," I suggested. "I mean, wouldn't he have checked out Shep's qualifications before hiring him?"

"One would assume so," Mr. Witherington said. From his tone I deduced that he and Biff had already had a conversation on the subject, and that he wasn't pleased with the results.

I kept a grave, worried look on my face, because I didn't think it would make a very good impression if I did a fist pump while yelling "Yes! He's getting it!"

"So, there's unlikely to be a delegation of umpires at Mr. Henson's funeral," Mr. Witherington went on.

"We'll spread the word and he'll have a good turnout," I said. "We owe him that much. Meanwhile, on a practical note, do we have an umpire for tomorrow's games?"

He looked at me and blinked in surprise.

"Do you know you're the first person who's asked that question?" he said.

"You mean we don't?" I exclaimed. "Is there someone we can call now? The college athletic department might have someone locally who's qualified. Or —"

"Relax," he said. "I took care of it this afternoon. I found a volunteer for tomorrow's games — he's coming up from Richmond, so there should be no question of partisanship. We can make do with one tomorrow, and I have almost certainly lined up two very seasoned and qualified professional umpires for the Sunday and Monday games. I know the league isn't accustomed to paying for two umpires, but it does make for a much better game experience, and if the treasury can't handle it I can talk to the home office and see if we can provide some financial assistance. We do that sometimes for leagues that are just getting started."

"You'll have to ask Biff about the treasury," I said. "Though if you ask me, if the treasury can't handle a few umpires, there's no reason we can't all pitch in and do some fund-raising to cover it. People around here are pretty good at volunteering for things." I nodded at the field.

"Then why wasn't all of this done before the start of the season?" Mr. Witherington made a sweeping gesture that took in the field, the bleachers, the Snack Shack, and the parking lot, all hotbeds of repair activity.

"Nobody asked us to," I said. "And I think a lot of people were afraid that volunteering to fix up things would be seen as a criticism of the job Biff has been doing. Thank goodness you were here to help make this possible."

We both stood for a few moments watching the hive of activity around us. In the outfield, a team of volunteers was disassembling the outfield fence, which we'd discovered was not according to Summerball regulations, being too deep in center field and too shallow along the sides. Someone had used the baseline chalker to mark the proper location, and a second team with fencepost-hole-digging tools was reinstalling the fence.

"No, we can't put down turf tonight," we overheard Randall saying as he strolled by with a couple of volunteers. "It takes time for the grass roots to grow into the ground — if we played on it tomorrow morning, it could slip out from under the kids' feet like a throw rug. But if you're still willing to donate some at the end of the season, I'll donate the labor to install it."

Chief Burke was supervising the installation of a tarp over the home dugout — I recognized one of the red, white, and blue tarps we used to shade the viewing stands on which the dignitaries sat to watch the parade every Fourth of July. A similar tarp was already draped over the fence beside the visitors' dugout, waiting until I finished making it structurally sound. I jotted a line in my notebook to remind me that we might need to arrange replacements for the viewing stand — unless Randall got busy and built those new dugouts in the next two months.

Plenty of time to worry about that.

One of Randall's workmen was hanging a new SNACK SHACK sign over the serving counter that ran the width of the front wall of the freshly painted little shack. Behind the counter half a dozen women in aprons and kitchen gloves were vigorously scrubbing every inch of the shack's interior, all the while muttering such things as "Who in the world leaves a food service area this filthy?" and "Lucky we haven't all been poisoned by now!" On the far side of the shack, more women were doing the same to the grill, the condiment table, and the picnic tables. I recognized a mix of women from the Baptist Ladies Auxiliary and the Episcopal Guild of St. Clotilda's, and deduced that both Mother and Minerva Burke had been recruiting volunteers.

The workers in the parking lot had finished leveling it, and were now using rakes and shovels to help level the loads of gravel now arriving in Shiffley Construction trucks.

"Well, that other dugout isn't going to repair itself," I said.

I repaired the other dugout. And then the bleachers. And some hinges and shelves in the Snack Shack. The fence needed a lot of work — in fact, it might have been less trouble to replace it altogether — but with the help of some of Randall's workmen, who had finished with the lights and the parking lot, I made sure it wasn't going to fall down and that there were no dangerous sharp edges and protruding wires that could shred small shins or poke out young eyes.

In the middle of our efforts on the outfield fence, I went back to my car to get another tool and spotted something in the parking lot that brought me to a halt. A pickup truck whose right rear taillight had been broken and then patched with strips of silver duct tape in a neat pattern like a giant asterisk. I'd seen that mended taillight before.

And then I remembered where I'd seen it, and forced myself to keep moving. That was the pickup I'd told Aida about, the one that had been parked at one end of a line of trucks in the parking lot of Biff's scrapyard, and then disappeared by the time Aida and I had returned from our hike to the other gate.

I fetched the tool I'd been looking for, and on my way back to the field I committed the truck's license plate to memory.

Then as soon as I got the chance, I took the chief aside and told him about it. I was afraid he'd think I was being overly imaginative, but he took me seriously enough to call Debbie Ann to ask her to run the license number.

"You're sure you saw it out there?" he said, as we stood waiting for Debbie Ann's computer to produce results.

"Reasonably sure," I said. "One truck looks pretty much like another to me, but the taillight repair was pretty distinctive."

He was opening his mouth to say something, then paused and listened. He frowned.

"Thank you," he said. "No, nothing else for now."

He put his phone back into his pocket and turned the frown on me.

"Keep this to yourself for now," he said.

I nodded and watched for a few moments as he thought. He looked up, saw me, and smiled slightly.

"This may have nothing to do with the murder," he said.

"Of course not," I said.

"But I will be asking Mr. Samuel Yoder the reason for his visit to Mr. Brown's place of business this afternoon."

He picked up the can of paint he'd been

using and headed back to the field. I followed more slowly and peered around as I walked to see if I could spot Mr. Yoder. Yes, there he was out in left field, using a posthole digger. Hard work, I knew, so maybe that accounted for the grim look on his face. Although everyone around him seemed cheerful enough. Mr. Yoder was the only one with an expression on his face like an Old Testament prophet. And in spite of his gray hair and thin frame, he was wielding the posthole digger with impressive ease. Yes, he'd have had the strength to hoist Shep's body and stow it in the porta-potty.

I wondered if the chief would be including Mr. Yoder's truck on tomorrow's to-do list for the blood sniffing dogs.

Not my problem. I shoved Mr. Yoder out of mind and focused back on my work.

By 1:00 A.M. we'd finished nearly everything we could think of to do, and except for Randall and a few of his workmen, everyone had straggled home. As I fell into bed, I couldn't decide which emotion was strongest — the intense satisfaction of finally getting my hands on the ball field and making it better — or my intense dread of the alarm clock that was going to wake me far too early.

CHAPTER 18

I was back on the baseball field, yelling at Biff. He was carrying a roll of sod out onto the field, and I kept telling him to stop, that it wasn't safe, that if he installed sod right before the game it wouldn't be stable. He ignored me. He set the sod down on the infield, on top of all the old grass and weeds, and began unrolling it. I realized it wasn't good sod — it was just a tangle of crabgrass, stinging nettles, and poison ivy. And then I heard the boys calling "Mommy! Mommy!" and turned to see that they were both sinking into the horrible Biff sod, as if along with the weeds he was unrolling quicksand.

"Mommy! Mommy!" I opened my eyes and found Josh and Jamie bouncing on the bed. Michael was already up and in the shower. "Mommy! Time to get up! It's Opening Day again!"

I forced a smile, and remembered that it had been my idea to start the games an hour earlier. Of course, when I had suggested an 8:00 A.M. starting time, I had no idea I'd be up past midnight doing manual labor.

"Mommy, where's my baseball pants?" Josh asked.

"I can't find my belt," Jamie countered.

"Can I have French toast for breakfast?" Josh asked. "While you find my baseball pants?"

"I don't want French toast," Jamie said. "And —"

"Go downstairs and see what Rose Noire is fixing for breakfast." Thank goodness for having a resident cousin who not only liked to cook but was an inveterately cheerful morning person. "If you do it nicely, you may ask her if she can fix French toast for those who want it and something else for those who don't. But if she says she's too busy, don't whine. And while you do that I will look for all of your baseball gear."

The herd stampeded downstairs. While Michael donned his baseball clothes, I took a quick shower and got dressed in jeans and my Caerphilly Eagles t-shirt, all the while playing with my new favorite fantasy — that I could find a way to tag all the boys' baseball gear the way Caroline had tagged Biff's coat and car. In fact, not just their baseball gear — all of their possessions. I could see myself calling the number Caroline had given me and saying, "Hey, can you give me a location on Jamie's right cleat? Great! How about Josh's math homework?"

Of course, that reminded me that I hadn't checked up on Biff lately. I paused in the middle of searching a laundry basket and called the zoo's security desk.

"Hi, Meg," said a cheerful young woman's voice. "You want a location on those tags?"

"Please."

"Just a sec. . . . Yes, they're both down at Percy Pruitt Park."

"Great. I was wondering . . . do you keep historical data on where the tags have been?"

"Of course," she said. "That's really the main purpose of the device — to study the animals' movements."

"So you could tell me, for example, where the devices went when they left my house Thursday night?"

"Of course. Here we go. They both went straight to Percy Pruitt field, and after half an hour there, to a location near the Clay County border." She rattled off a set of coordinates, then translated them to a street address on the Clay Swamp Road. I recognized the address of Biff's business. "Then yesterday they went to Percy Pruitt Park at seven forty-five a.m. After that they did quite a lot of wandering around yesterday — do you want the details?"

"Maybe later," I said. "Just let me know their present location."

"At Percy Pruitt Park," she said. "Since about seven a.m. So what is this special project of Caroline's? I'm assuming some kind of application of the device to companion animals instead of wildlife."

"Just out of curiosity, what makes you think that?"

"Because whatever these critters are, they occasionally travel at speeds in excess of sixty miles an hour. I assume they're traveling in someone's car at those times, because if we have some kind of wildlife here in Caerphilly capable of that kind of speed, I think I'd have heard about it."

"Good deductions," I said. "And thanks."

I'd let Caroline explain what her project was.

And it was a relief that the tracking devices confirmed Biff's alibi. Not that I'd really doubted it — after all, Aida and Vern were pretty reliable. But after seeing Biff's place of business, it had occurred to me to wonder if he could possibly have sneaked out while they were at one end of his scrap-

284

yard. If both our local police and the tracking devices thought Biff had stayed put, then Biff was very well-alibied for the time of the murder. I decided that on the whole this was a relief. However much I might wish that we could figure out a way to disentangle Biff from our local baseball organization, I didn't think the spectacle of having the league president arrested for murder was one we wanted to see.

And it was also a relief since I wasn't at all sure how the chief would feel if he found out about our belling the cat, as Caroline had called it. I needed to find out if what Caroline had done was legal, and if not, what kind of penalty she'd face if the chief found out about it. Fortunately, since the tracking device confirmed Vern's and Aida's evidence, this wasn't quite as urgent as it would have been if it had contradicted them, but still . . . I had the sneaking feeling it was illegal.

And that meant it could still come back to haunt us if an indiscreet zoo staff member gossiped about Caroline's special project. Or if Biff found the device. Or what if some new crime occurred — say that break-in at Shiffley Construction Randall more than half expected — and the tracking devices recorded data that either cleared or implicated Biff.

Festus. I could call him to tell him more about the Yoder farm, work the conversation around to the subject of Grandfather's tracking devices, and jokingly ask what would happen if I decided to tag a few human beings with them.

No, he'd see through that. Better to just ask him point-blank. I entered an item in my notebook to remind me to do that — but later, at what Mother would call a civilized time of day.

I returned to emptying out the laundry basket and found Josh's baseball socks near the bottom, rolled up in Jamie's damp swimsuit. Jamie's baseball pants were draped over the Ping-Pong table in the basement, and since there was a belt already threaded through the belt loops, I deduced that the belt Josh was carrying around actually belonged to Jamie. Although threading the belts through the loops was a major pain, in the interest of preserving harmony I removed the belt so I could pretend to have found it separately.

A good thing we lived so close to the field, because otherwise I'm not sure we could possibly have been among the first there. Michael took the boys to the outfield and started a little fielding practice. I took a stroll around the field, nodding happily at the results of our night's work.

It looked good. Not perfect. There were still more dirt and weeds than grass in the outfield, but at least the weeds and grass were cropped close enough that it was hard to tell them apart. And they'd actually dug up all the grass and weeds that had sparsely dotted the infield and done a fabulous job of leveling and smoothing it. A lush grass infield would have been optimal, but for now, a neat, smooth dirt infield would do just fine. The bleachers and dugouts weren't fancy, but they were structurally sound and as spruced up as they were going to get.

As I watched, a Brown Construction truck turned into the parking lot — a flatbed truck with a battered, mud-colored porta-potty on the back. The truck rattled over to the end of the parking lot where Biff's old porta-potty had stood and backed into position.

"Oh, give us a break," I muttered under my breath. "As if anyone with a sense of smell is going anywhere near that thing."

Biff was strolling over to meet the truck, and supervised as four of his workmen wrestled the porta-potty into place — not quite in the same place where the old one had been, but fifteen or twenty feet farther away from the field. It was as if even Biff realized that the odds of anyone using his porta-potty were low, but had brought it out to the field anyway as a gesture of defiance.

Biff stood for a few moments, gazing at his porta-potty in what appeared to be satisfaction. Not a sentiment apt to be shared by many of those who came close to it — I noticed a couple of the workmen, now that they were out of Biff's line of sight, were clowning around, holding their noses and pretending to be about to puke.

Biff turned around to bark an order at them and they all scrambled back onto the truck and vamoosed. Biff began rambling around the field, inspecting everything we'd done the night before and shaking his head as if he found it all sadly unsatisfactory.

Two women were waiting by the Snack Shack: the older woman in the sari who'd been at the Thursday night party — now identified as the elder Mrs. Patel, Sami Patel's grandmother — and Rose Noire. Biff noticed them waiting, but he took his own sweet time coming over to let them into the Snack Shack.

In fact, he kept them waiting at the door of the Snack Shack while he opened up the supply shed and strolled inside.

I could see Rose Noire taking some of the deep, calming breaths she was always telling me to try when things upset me.

Then Biff stormed out of the shed.

"Where the hell are my buns!" he shouted at the first person he saw — which unfortunately happened to be Mrs. Patel. She shrieked, whirled around, and ran away.

I took off running toward the shed.

"You big bully!" Rose Noire stepped into the space Mrs. Patel had vacated and shook her finger in Biff's face.

"We had a whole season's supply of hot dog and hamburger buns in here," Biff yelled.

"I have no idea where they are, and neither does Mrs. Patel," Rose Noire yelled back. "Now go over there and apologize to that poor woman!"

Rose Noire was actually shaking her fist at him. Considering that Rose Noire regularly escorted even noxious insects like stinkbugs and cockroaches out into the yard and had been known to apologize to furniture when she bumped into it, Biff had achieved the near impossible feat of making her lose her temper.

But before I could intervene, a tall man — probably a Shiffley — wearing a Caerphilly Flatworms t-shirt stepped to Rose

Noire's side and spoke up.

"If you're talking about those moldy old hot dog and hamburger buns on the top shelf, they had a 2013 expiration date," he said. "I threw them out."

"And who the hell are you?" Biff snarled, turning to the new arrival.

"Padgett Shiffley. County health inspector." Padgett opened up his wallet and held it out, obviously to show Biff an official ID of some sort.

Biff blinked for a few moments. Rose Noire stepped aside, though I noticed she was staying close enough to eavesdrop.

"Well, who the hell left those there anyway?" Biff muttered.

Padgett just stared impassively at him. Biff scowled fiercely and retreated.

"Good riddance," Padgett said.

"Except we still need him to open the Snack Shack door," Rose Noire said.

"Blast the man." Padgett took off after Biff.

Seeing that Biff had gone, Mrs. Patel timidly returned to Rose Noire's side. She looked anxious when Biff came storming back, waving his key ring.

"Do I have to do everything around here?" he muttered.

I could see Rose Noire pressing her lips

together, as if fighting not to point out that she and Mrs. Patel were the ones who'd be doing the work, if only he'd let them get on with it.

Biff unlocked the door, pulled it open, and was about to barge into the Snack Shack — no doubt to find something else to complain about.

"Something else, Mr. Brown," Padgett said.

Frowning, Biff turned to face him. With his back turned, Mrs. Patel ducked under his arm and scurried past him into the Snack Shack. Biff turned and yelled at her to keep out. A sudden sharp thunk! rang out, and Mrs. Patel began screaming hysterically.

Biff, who could see inside the door, turned pale, and his jaw fell in shock. Rose Noire, Padgett, and I leaped toward the door, shoving the frozen Biff aside.

Mrs. Patel appeared unharmed, although she was curled in a ball in the far corner, screaming. Over her head, a foot-long machete blade was buried in the wall on our right, about five feet up from the ground. On a shelf on the opposite wall was a complicated metal gadget that looked like a cross between a crossbow and a giant mousetrap.

"What the —" Padgett exclaimed.

"A booby trap," I said as I pulled out my phone. "I'm calling nine-one-one."

"You poor thing!" Rose Noire exclaimed, racing forward to comfort Mrs. Patel before I could shout out a warning about the possibility that there could be other booby traps. Fortunately there weren't.

The chief and several deputies were there in minutes. Rose Noire led Mrs. Patel away to the Eagles bleachers to be comforted by the rest of the team mothers and grandmothers.

Not surprisingly, the chief declared our newly repainted Snack Shack a crime scene. I dispatched a brace of burly cousins with a truck to haul several of the folding tables from our house to the field.

Biff stood rooted in place just outside the Snack Shack for fifteen or twenty minutes, staring through the doorway at the machete and muttering things like "that was meant for me," and "I could have been killed." After inspecting the machete and the device that had launched it, the chief went over to talk to him.

"You see," Biff said. "Someone is after me. I'm always the first one in the shack. If that woman hadn't barged past me, I'd have been killed."

The chief just frowned and nodded. Biff did have a point. He was incredibly lucky that Mrs. Patel had barged past him. And we were all incredibly lucky that tiny little Mrs. Patel was on Snack Shack duty. If Rose Noire or I or any of the other team parents had walked into that booby trap, we might be dead by now.

Eventually a couple of Stoat fathers came over and escorted Biff over to his team's dugout. I felt bad for Biff. Not as bad as I felt for poor Mrs. Patel — but still, he'd had a shock.

Dare we hope that he'd stay subdued once the game started? Probably not. Every time I glanced over at the Stoats' dugout, he seemed more himself. Pity.

The burly cousins returned with the tables and we set up a new outdoor Snack Shack about twenty feet from the old. Rose Noire recruited Janet Wong as a replacement for the still shaky Mrs. Patel, and the two of them began calmly selling chewing gum and bottles of water. Eagles fans in black and red dominated the crowd, but I could also see kids from other teams, especially the red-and-white uniforms of the Muckdogs and the River Rats in their yellow and gray, since they were playing right after the Eagles vs. Stoats game. And by the size of the crowd, I suspected half the town had come out to enjoy a day at the ballpark.

Just before the game started, my cell phone rang. I looked down as I pulled it out and checked the caller ID. Festus Hollingsworth. Aha! My chance to ask my cousin about the tracking device. As I answered it, I looked around for someplace reasonably private to talk. About the only place in sight not packed with people was the far end of the clearing, beyond where Biff's replacement porta-potty stood, so I headed that way.

"Meg, thank you!" Festus said. "The Yoder farm is perfect!"

"You've seen it already?"

"Only your pictures and the county property records, but I can tell it's exactly what I want, and although it's not actually on the market yet, Mr. Yoder's going to have to sell, which gives me the chance to make a deal with him. And you were absolutely right — Yoder's been in litigation with the Brown Construction Company for five years now. Mr. Brown began a major renovation of the Yoder barn and then abandoned all work on it at a point when it was completely unusable. That hasn't been Yoder's only financial problem, but it's probably the thing that drove him over the edge."

By this time I'd reached the general area of Biff's porta-potty and taken my seat on a nearby fallen log. My retreat had the added advantage of letting me keep an eye on the Snack Shack, where the chief and Deputy Vern Shiffley stood, apparently watching Horace doing forensics on the booby trap.

"Be nice to Mr. Yoder," I said to Festus. "If he's been in litigation with Biff for five years, he's been through hell already."

"Don't worry," Festus said. "I have every intention of being nice to him, by which I assume you mean giving him a fair price for his farm. I don't want every farmer in the county to hate me from the minute I arrive. Mr. Yoder is a very nice man, and I'm exactly what he's been looking for — someone who can afford to buy his farm and has no intention of turning it into condominiums or a golf club or anything like that. In fact, when he asked me what I intended to do with the land, I told him that I didn't intend to do anything except see if I could find someone to farm it for me. And he indicated he might be willing. And that's perfect! I can look out my window and see cows and sheep and corn and whatever else farmers grow around here and not have to feed or plow anything myself."

"That's great," I said. "Assuming he's still

around to do the farming."

"He wants to stay around," Festus said. "He's got grandkids in the area."

"I'm sure he does," I said. "But right now he's definitely one of Chief Burke's suspects in yesterday's murder." I explained about the uncanny resemblance between Biff and Shep and Mr. Yoder's odd, surreptitious visit to Brown Construction. Festus remained quiet for a few long moments after I'd finished.

"Troubling," he said finally. "I can certainly testify that he's angry enough at Mr. Brown."

"Angry enough to kill?" I asked.

"Angry enough to be a suspect. If he gets arrested, let me know. I will find him a very good defense attorney. I don't want to see anything get in the way of my — hmmm . . . buying the farm sounds a bit ominous. Purchasing it."

"Will do. By the way, in return for steering you to the farm, may I cadge a small bit of free legal advice. Not for me, actually."

"Absolutely." Suddenly his voice had reverted to Festus Hollingsworth, Esquire.

CHAPTER 19

"Grandfather has a new toy," I said. "His weasels have been regularly escaping from their habitat, so he's attached tiny little geolocator tags to them. It not only helps him recapture them, but he can record data from the tags in his computers and use it to track the weasels' movements and figure out how they're escaping."

"I have a sinking feeling I know where this is going," Festus said. "Please tell me your grandfather hasn't decided to tag some human being whose whereabouts he wants to investigate."

"No, he hasn't," I said. "And I can't imagine he ever would — when has Grandfather ever taken the slightest interest in the whereabouts of anything other than his beloved wildlife?"

"That's a relief," he said.

"But what if someone did?"

"Meg! You didn't!"

"No," I said. "I didn't, either. But what if someone did. Let's leave it at someone for now. And just so you know, we're not talking about anyone you're related to, in case you were suspicious of Dad. Stop trying to guess who the someone is and tell me exactly how much trouble the someone is in."

"Not my primary area of expertise, so I'd have to do some research, but I'm pretty sure it's illegal. Hang on, let me run a search."

I tapped my foot impatiently for what seemed like several hours, though it was probably only a few minutes that I stood there, listening to what sounded like the rattle of a keyboard.

"Yes," he said finally. " *'Any person who installs or places an electronic tracking device through intentionally deceptive means and without consent, or causes an electronic tracking device to be installed or placed through intentionally deceptive means and without consent, and uses such device to track the location of any person is guilty of a Class 3 misdemeanor.'* "

"What do they do to you for a Class 3 misdemeanor?"

"A fine of up to five hundred dollars," he said.

"No jail time?"

"Not if that's all she did."

"He or she," I corrected, but I also let out the breath I hadn't realized I'd been holding.

"But if someone did that to me and I resented it enough, I'd start looking to file a civil suit."

Not good. Still, as long as Caroline wasn't going to jail. Or me, for that matter, if getting data from the GPS counted as aiding and abetting her.

"So," I said aloud. "If my hypothetical someone had done this, what should I try to get them to do now?"

"Is there any chance they could retrieve the tracker without being detected?"

"I don't know," I said. "It's possible. Should I tell them to try?"

"Yes, but they should make sure they know a good criminal attorney in case they're caught."

"Got it," I said. "So as long as we're talking about my hypothetical someone's hypothetical felony — what if the data they got from the tracker was potential evidence in a criminal investigation? What if it proved or disproved someone's alibi?"

Silence. A rather long silence. So long I began to worry that we'd been cut off.

"Festus?" I said finally.

"Maybe I should rethink this moving to Caerphilly thing," he said. "Clearly it is not the peaceful bucolic refuge I was imagining. Did anyone on your police force encourage your friend to plant this device or know about it in advance?"

"No," I said. "I think planting it was a pretty spur-of-the-moment thing. And as far as I know, so far the police are unaware of its existence."

"Then the data from it would probably be admissible. Illegally obtained evidence is usually admissible as long as it wasn't illegally obtained by the government. The Fourth Amendment doesn't protect us from illegal searches by private individuals. Give me a little more information here. Who was the victim of this bugging, and what did the person doing the bugging hope to achieve by it, and why do you think the police would be interested in the data?"

"The victim was Biff Brown, who barged into Mother's party and accused us of having an illicit baseball practice — he seems to think he can keep the other teams from practicing except for the very limited times when he lets them use the official fields. The person who planted the bug wanted an Early Biff Warning System, so if Biff showed up, the team could pretend to be just having a picnic and go back to practicing when we were sure he wasn't lurking in the shrubbery. Because even if what we were doing was perfectly acceptable within the Summerball rules, we didn't want to waste time arguing with him about it. Shep Henson's murder happened a few hours later, and the data appears to confirm Biff's alibi — that he was with one or both of the deputies searching his construction yard for a possible prowler for the whole period during which the murder could have been committed."

"Well, that's good," Festus said. "If you — correction, your friend — had been sitting on evidence that would have sent the chief down a completely different investigatory path, he might be more than a little peeved. Look, I need to come down soon to inspect my future farm in person. I'll see if I can arrange to meet with Mr. Yoder this afternoon or maybe tomorrow. While I'm down there, I can talk with your friend, and if he, she, or it is comfortable being represented by me, I can try to set up a meeting with Chief Burke and the county commonwealth attorney to negotiate turning over the data."

"Does this mean he, she, or it shouldn't try to get back the devices?"

"I'd still go ahead with that. Better safe than sorry."

"Roger."

We hung up, and I stood, phone in hand, scanning the crowd around the field. No sign of Caroline. The Eagles were still in the outfield, warming up, but it was almost game time, so I was sure she'd be here somewhere.

I dialed her cell phone.

"Meg! Why aren't you here at the ball field?"

"I am," I said. "I need to talk to you — someplace reasonably private."

"Well, no place around here, then," she said. "It's a zoo. Want to meet in the parking lot and drive somewhere?"

"I'd rather stay here and keep an eye on things," I said. "Can you meet me near the Brown porta-potty?"

"Yuck. Why would anyone ever want to go anywhere near that thing?"

"Precisely," I said. "We don't have to go all that near, actually — just close enough to be sure we're the only ones within earshot."

"If you say so."

Within a couple of minutes I saw Caroline striding toward my fallen log.

"Well, you're right," she said. "Nobody

out here, and every reason for it to stay that way."

"Unless someone spots us and wants to talk to one of us for some reason," I said. "So let me cut to the chase. Remember the tracking devices you planted on Biff and his car?"

She nodded.

"Remember how I asked if they were even legal?"

She nodded again.

"Well, they're not." I outlined the gist of my conversation with Festus.

"So what's the big deal?" she asked. "Why not just pay the five hundred dollars if they catch me?"

"You could do that," I said. "But what if Biff finds out about them and tries to sue you? The longer they're there, the more you've invaded his privacy and caused him emotional distress and —"

"Okay, okay," she said. "Good point. I get why we need to retrieve them. We can work on that while he's here at the baseball field. But why not just get them back and shut up about it? It's not as if the data does anything but prove the alibi Vern and Aida gave him."

"As far as we know," I said. "And what if the data implicates him in some other crime?"

"There haven't been any other crimes here in the last few days," Caroline said.

"That we know of."

"For heaven's sake, this is Caerphilly!"

"Let's just worry about getting the bugs back first," I said. "And Festus is coming down tonight or tomorrow — talk to him. If he thinks the data is not worth taking to the police, I'll shut up about it."

"Okay," she said. "Let me go find that cousin of yours who helped me bug his car. I don't actually know where on the car he put the darned thing."

"Suggestion," I said. "May I tell Festus you're his new client?"

"Might as well." She stomped off, clearly annoyed with me.

"Don't shoot the messenger," I muttered.

I thought of pulling out my phone to tell Festus. And then I changed my mind and pulled out my notebook instead. I added a to-do item: "Tell Festus who his new client is." I could tell him when I saw him.

Maybe by that time Caroline would already have retrieved the bugs. Festus would probably be a lot happier if he was representing a client who had repented of her crime, or at least stopped committing it.

And besides — the game was getting started. I scrambled back to the field in time to see as well as hear as some fifty members of the New Life Baptist Choir delivered a rousing rendition of the national anthem.

"Play ball!" the announcer called at the end, though it was a couple of minutes before the maroon-clad choir members could finish their processing back off the field and into the crowd, where most of them shed the maroon robes and settled down in their multicolored t-shirts to watch the game.

And the game went well — for the Eagles, at least. Biff must have recovered from his earlier shock. He charged out of the dugout at every opportunity to contest the umpire's calls. I'd met the umpire in passing before the game — a slender man with thinning sandy hair and a ready smile. But on the field he was impassive, no-nonsense, and apparently unruffled by Biff's antics.

I did see him glance occasionally toward the spot right behind home plate where Mr. Witherington, with admirable impartiality, had set up his bright red folding chair. Maybe the umpire was under orders to ignore Biff's antics as far as possible. If so, was that giving Biff unfair treatment? Or just room to hang himself?

But nothing Biff said or did could change the fact that the Eagles were clearly dominating the Stoats. Most of the crowd had sprawled on the third-base side of the field and were rooting for the Eagles, but it was a generous crowd, cheering almost as loudly for a good play by the Stoats — on the infrequent occasions when they made one. At the end of the fourth inning, with the score at twenty-two to three, the umpire announced that he was invoking the mercy rule and the game was over.

Both sets of coaches collected their teams in the outfield for a postgame team meeting. Michael and Chuck were clearly passing out a lot of praise, to judge by the smiling faces and high fives in left field. In right field, the Stoats slumped in morose silence while Biff paced up and down in front of them. Fortunately the sound system came on and John Fogerty's "Centerfield" drowned out whatever Biff was saying.

I went over to take my turn in the Snack Shack — the real Snack Shack again. After Horace finished processing it, the chief gave us permission to resume operations. We had no shortage of volunteers, thanks to Mother's recruitment efforts, but I wanted to be seen doing my fair share of the scut work. Maybe it was the new impressively clean state of the Snack Shack or maybe Randall was right about the salutary effect of knowing clean porta-potties were at hand, but for whatever reason, business was booming, pouring floods of coffee, soda, Gatorade, bottled water, gum, and snack chips into the milling crowd. And I could tell they were eyeing the still-cold grills with interest. At this rate, maybe we'd manage to raise the funds for those permanent lights and flush toilets by the end of the season.

The Eagles mobbed the Snack Shack, and from the conversations I overheard, it was clear that most of them were dying to stay to watch the rest of the day's games — and those parents who weren't also planning to stay were making arrangements with those who were.

None of the Stoats had showed up at the counter by the time my half-hour shift ended. Were they still out in right field being lectured? No, but apparently they weren't eager to stay around and watch more baseball. The right-field bleachers were filling up with fans wearing Muckdog t-shirts. No Stoats in sight.

And come to think of it, there hadn't been any Stoat parents on the Snack Shack roster. Was this a minor schedule aberration, or did being in Biff's camp provide immunity from work details?

I took a picture of the Snack Shack duty

schedule that hung just inside the door, noticing that there were also no Yankee parents scheduled to work during their 1:00 P.M. game with the Nats. Interesting.

The Muckdogs beat the River Rats five to four in a lively and good-natured game. The Eagles fans left over from the first game distributed themselves impartially between the two sets of bleachers, and any really good play generally got cheers from both sides of the field.

And then the right-side bleachers mostly emptied out again as the one o'clock start time of the Yankees/Nats game approached and the Yankees parents began claiming their spots.

"I've been wondering," I asked Michael. "How come all the Pruitts are on Biff's team, and all the Shiffleys on the Flatworms, while your team is mostly children of college staff and faculty? Wasn't there some kind of tryout, or did everyone just pick their friends' kids?"

"According to Chuck, there was a tryout, but then he was supposed to submit his choices to Biff, and a week later Biff told him who he'd gotten. And yeah, you're right about the teams being mostly people who already know each other. We figure Biff stacks the teams that way for some reason."

"Maybe to keep people from getting to know too many other parents in the league," I said. "Reduce the chances they'll join forces and rebel."

Michael frowned and nodded slightly. As we watched, Biff strutted out onto the field, barking orders at his players.

"Maybe we should take a break," I suggested to Michael over the heads of Josh, Jamie, and the several other Eagles who were staying with us to watch the games.

"No!" "But we want to stay!" "You said we could watch all the games!" the Eagles protested in loud chorus.

"No one wants to go get lunch?" I asked. "There's nothing to eat here but hot dogs and hamburgers from the Snack Shack."

"But we like hot dogs and hamburgers from the Snack Shack," Josh protested. Jamie, Mason, Sami, and Adam chimed in their agreement.

"I think it will be all right," Michael said. "We'll be here to . . . explain things."

And we couldn't protect them from the rough edges of life forever, I thought, with a sigh. It started off much like the Eagles/Stoats game, with Biff challenging the umpire at every turn. Although the umpire, spoiled by the tranquil congeniality of the Muckdogs/River Rats game, seemed just a little less patient and impassive.

Or maybe it was Mr. Witherington who had lost patience. I could see the umpire glancing back at him from time to time. Was Mr. Witherington giving him some signal so subtle I couldn't pick up on it? A signal that usually said "patience; just let him hang himself" — and sometimes "go for it!"

The Yankees were doing even worse than their younger siblings on the Stoats. By the top of the third inning, the Nats were winning, seven to two. And the farther behind the Yankees fell, the more Biff demonstrated his dire need for an anger management class. If I were the umpire, I'd have tossed him out at least an inning ago. As it was, the umpire was looking at Mr. Witherington a lot more often.

Intrigued by this phenomenon, I left Michael to wrangle the Eagles and took up a position behind the backstop, closer to Mr. Witherington. Randall was already there.

"One of my nephews," Randall said, nodding at the current Nats batter. "Good little hitter."

"Ball three."

"Good eye!" Randall called out.

"Are you kidding, Blue?" Biff groaned. "Bring your Seeing Eye dog next time."

The umpire ignored him.

The Yankee pitcher, after a few nervous glances at his dugout, wound up and threw again. This time the ball hit the backstop about four feet to the right of the plate. Surely even Biff couldn't argue with the call on that one.

"Ball four!" The umpire waved the Nats batter toward first base.

Biff came boiling out of the dugout, and I saw the umpire stiffen, until he realized that Biff was heading for the mound, not the plate. The entire ballpark went silent — so silent that we could hear most of what Biff was saying to his pitcher. Not a word of helpful advice about how to correct what he was doing wrong — just verbal abuse.

I felt sorry for the poor kid on the mound. Did Biff really think that yelling at an eleven- or twelve-year-old kid was going to improve his pitching? From where I stood, it looked as if the kid had been doing a pretty good job at the start of the inning, but then he'd walked a batter, and Biff had gone charging out to the mound, red-faced and scowling, and berated the kid for what seemed like an eternity. The poor kid had walked the next batter — probably because he was so shaken from being browbeaten — and Biff had repeated the process. And now the kid had walked a third batter, loading the bases, and there went Biff again. Did he really think the third time was a charm, and yelling at the kid would work this time? Or —

Wait a minute. Third time's a charm.

Biff was stomping back toward the dugout. The pitcher was hunched as if fending off blows. The catcher was standing halfway to the mound, as if he wanted to go out and comfort his teammate but didn't dare for fear of Biff.

"He has to pull the pitcher," I called out. Everyone was still silent, cringing as they watched Biff in action, so my voice carried even better than usual.

People turned to stare at me in shock. Didn't anyone else read the rule book? Or maybe the question was, didn't anyone else dare to call Biff when he broke the rules? Even the umpire was still staring dumbfounded at Biff. Surely he'd seen bad behavior before.

"Play ball!" Biff bellowed from the dugout.

"Third time to the mound in a single inning." I turned to face Mr. Witherington, but made sure I was loud enough for the umpire — and Biff — to hear. "He has to pull the pitcher. Rule 5.18 in the Summerball Official Rule Book: 'A manager or coach may visit the mound twice in one inning, but after the third visit, the player must be removed as pitcher.' Have I got it right?"

Mr. Witherington glanced over at the umpire and nodded almost imperceptibly.

"The lady is correct, sir," the umpire said to Biff. "Send in your new pitcher so he can start warming up."

"Play ball," Biff bellowed.

"We play ball when I say so," the umpire said. "Either get a new pitcher out to the mound to warm up or forfeit the game."

Biff swarmed out of the dugout and ran over to the umpire, ending up so close to him that I think their noses bumped. I had to give the umpire credit for not flinching or backing up an inch.

"You idiot!" Biff began, and then he began to berate the umpire, dropping the F-bomb twice in his first sentence.

"Coach," the umpire broke in. "Take a step back and lose that language."

Biff paid no attention and continued his tirade.

"Take a hike," the umpire said, jerking his thumb in the direction of the parking lot.

Biff uttered an incoherent howl and lurched at the umpire, both hands outstretched as if to grab him by the throat.

CHAPTER 20

Apparently Biff's assistant coach had an inkling that something like this could happen, because he was already halfway to the plate when Biff lost it. For that matter, the two Nats coaches were already running in from their base coach spots at first and third. The umpire managed to escape throttling by setting a new world record for the standing backward broad jump, and then the three sane coaches grabbed Biff and kept him from doing any physical damage. The three of them half-led, half-dragged Biff back to the dugout. Several men from the Yankees bleachers raced into the dugout and hustled Biff through it and out into the parking lot.

Mr. Witherington was still standing just behind home plate, fingers twined into the chain-link fence as if he needed to hold onto something. He glanced back and saw me looking at him.

"Is this customary in your league?" he asked.

"Lord, I hope not," I said. "I think I'd have heard about it before now if it was."

He nodded and looked back at the field. We could still hear Biff's angry voice ranting out in the parking lot.

"I guess he's under a lot of strain right now," I said. Why was I making excuses for Biff? Perhaps because I didn't want Mr. Witherington to think too badly of us. "With his brother's death and all."

"Yes," Mr. Witherington said. "His brother's death. It would be nice to feel certain he wasn't in any way responsible for that. 'Summerball League President Arrested for Killing Brother' would be such an unfortunate headline."

"He's alibied," I said.

"I see. Still, 'Summerball League President Hires Contract Killer' isn't much better."

I made a mental note of his words so I could repeat them to Randall, along with the satisfying news that, just as I had predicted, Biff was doing a fine job of making our case against him to Mr. Witherington.

I glanced over at the Nats bleachers, where Chief Burke was sitting. I noticed that he had his little notebook out and appeared to be writing in it. And glancing over at the Yankees bleachers. Taking note of Biff's known associates, perhaps? Because, yeah, the idea that Biff had found someone else to kill Shep was definitely on the table, and if I were the chief I'd definitely start checking out the small band of stalwarts sitting on the Yankees bleachers, glaring daggers at the rest of us.

And I noticed that the Pruitts weren't among the fathers who'd gone out to the parking lot to help calm Biff down. All three of them were sitting in a small clump on the side of the bleachers farthest from the dugout. Two of them looked untroubled, and the third was actually grinning.

The chief also seemed to be studying them with a thoughtful look on his face.

"Looks like the cat who ate the canary, doesn't he?" Randall said, returning to lean against the fence beside me.

"Would that happen to be Adolph Pruitt?" I asked.

"Ah, so you've met the newly paroled jailbird?" Randall said.

"No," I said. "Just a lucky guess."

As I watched, a fourth Pruitt strolled over and showed a piece of paper to the three sitting on the bleachers. Two of them burst into laughter as soon as they glanced at the paper. Adolph had to stick his nose a couple of inches from the paper and stare at it for several seconds with his eyes scrunched up before he burst into chuckles.

I glanced over to make sure the chief had seen that one of his prime suspects — well, one of mine, anyway — was incredibly nearsighted and could easily have mistaken Shep for his brother.

"I'd have pegged Adolph for just a loud-mouth myself," Randall said, as if reading my thoughts. "Just trying to cause trouble for Biff. Cephus says he's been stirring up the two Pruitts who have kids on the team. Convincing them that their little darlings aren't getting their fair share of playing time. Which they're not, but if Biff did give them equal playing time, the Pruitts would be the first to complain that the team wasn't winning."

I looked back at the field. The stocky left fielder, who hadn't moved his feet since plodding out to his position at the start of the inning — almost certainly a young Pruitt. As I scanned the rest of the players, the remaining Yankees coach went out from the mound and took the ball from the pitcher. The three Yankees on the bench — one of them, by the shape of him, probably the other juvenile Pruitt — looked up expectantly, then slumped again when the coach gestured to the right fielder. The pitcher and the right fielder jogged to exchange places.

The new pitcher began warming up. He started off a little wild, probably because he was paying as much attention to what was going on in the parking lot as what was happening on the field. But then so was everyone else, including the umpire, who let the pitcher have a few more practice throws than usual. Someone turned on the sound system and the opening bars of Bruce Springsteen's "Glory Days" succeeded in drowning out Biff, which probably helped the new pitcher find his rhythm.

Still, "Glory Days" had given way to the first pounding chords of "Don't Stop Believin' " by the time the umpire finally shouted "Play ball!" The fans sent up a rousing cheer — well, except for the parents on the Yankees bleachers, who were huddled together with shell-shocked looks on their faces, as if not quite sure how to cope with this strange new order of things. And Adolph Pruitt was still whispering to the other two Pruitts. Neither of them appeared very happy, but Adolph, looking like a cross between Machiavelli and an overgrown frog, seemed to be having the time of his life.

The rest of the game went smoothly. The new pitcher gave up three runs in his first inning, putting the Nats ahead ten to two, but after the first inning without Biff, the Yankees rallied — in fact, they actually seemed to be having fun out on the field — and the lead shifted back and forth in what turned out to be an exciting and surprisingly unacrimonious game. Either the Yankees' assistant coach was a nicer guy than he'd allowed us to see with Biff around or he'd accurately read the prevailing mood and was feigning niceness.

During the bottom of the fourth inning, one of the Yankee fathers appeared and talked to Mr. Witherington in an undertone. I didn't catch most of what they said, only a couple of sentences.

"He is still the league president," Mr. Witherington said. "I see no problem with him performing tasks appropriate for that job. But he stays off the field until the game is over and he doesn't communicate with anyone on the field."

Having overheard that, I was probably one of the few people not surprised to see Biff appear behind the outfield fence at the start of the fifth inning, carrying a black plastic garbage bag and one of those trash pickup sticks with a sharp point on the end. I didn't exactly find it reassuring to see someone with Biff's anger management issues toting a tool that could so easily be used as a weapon, but at least he was far away from the crowd — the few people hanging around behind the fence made themselves scarce as soon as he appeared. And while he definitely did more watching and muttering than trash collection, at least he was staying to the letter of his exile.

During the bottom of the fifth, I realized I needed to use the bathroom. After a scornful glance at Biff's porta-potty, which was as deserted as if someone had put an invisible fence around it, I headed for the other end of the field, where Randall's superior porta-potties stood. He'd even put a couple of benches nearby so people could wait in greater comfort, although having three porta-potties meant that there usually wasn't much of a wait.

On my way there, I spotted Gina, Biff's soon-to-be-ex-wife. She was sitting in a folding camping chair on the Yankees' side of the field, but far out along the first baseline, so she wasn't near any of the other team parents. Not surprising, if many of them were Biff cronies. A kid about Josh and Jamie's age was sitting at her feet, almost clinging to them. Neither of them seemed to be paying any attention to Biff, who was standing behind the centerfield portion of the fence, staring at the game and rhythmically stabbing the ground at his feet with his litter stick.

Had the chief talked to Gina yet? Obviously she was a potential gold mine of information about both Biff and Shep — their relationship to each other, their cronies, their enemies. But he'd need to sift what she had to say carefully. She'd said some pretty negative things about Biff — how much of that was accurate and how much was driven by her anger against him? Or would she soft-pedal the truth to protect her children? And how much had Biff even let her know about his business or the way he ran the league? He didn't strike me as the type of guy who came home and shared his deepest thoughts and aspirations and worries with the wife. But you never knew.

The chief's problem, not mine — thank goodness.

"Meg! There you are!"

I turned around to see Caroline Willner.

"Any progress in your project?" I asked.

"Not so much," she said. "He didn't wear the jacket with the tag in the pocket today — it's back at his scrapyard. And my minions have been lurking in the parking lot for the last couple of hours, trying to find an unguarded moment to slip under Biff's car."

Her minions. Why was I picturing the Artful Dodger and the rest of Fagin's juvenile gang?

"Have you considered the possibility that the longer they lurk, the more people will notice them?" I asked aloud. "And that the more people notice them, the less likely they'll be to leave their cars unguarded?"

"It's just Thor and Eric," Caroline said. "They're pretending to be bored with the game and killing time until they can leave, and you'd have to be pretty paranoid to find them suspicious."

I glanced over to the parking lot. Yes, there was Thor, the college student who served as chauffeur and general factotum to my grandmother during summers and school breaks, doing something on his iPad. Eric, my teenaged nephew, was looking over his shoulder. Whatever they were doing didn't seem to hold their attention very well. Both of them kept stealing glances across the parking lot at a battered brown pickup with BROWN CONSTRUCTION painted on the door. And also glances at a nearby station wagon which seemed to serve as the head-quarters for a mixed party of Yankee and

Stoat families who were having some kind of morose little tailgate party. As I watched, two Yankee fathers arrived holding Coca-Cola cans. They handed them to a Stoat father, who pried empty Bud Light cans out of what were obviously only Coke-can shells, popped the tops of new beer cans, and sent them on their way with their new beers camouflaged.

"The park's supposed to be an alcohol-free zone," I said. "County ordinance. Not necessarily one I'm all that keen on myself, although I suppose it's a small price to pay to keep beer out of the hands of people with anger management issues — Biff, for example. But —"

"Eric and Thor have plenty of videos of the illegal drinking," Caroline said. "I suppose we could have reported them to Chief Burke, but that would interfere with our retrieval mission. We almost got a chance a little while back — something exciting must have been happening on the field, because they even left the beer cooler unguarded, but just as Eric was about to nip under the car, they all came back dragging Biff, and it's been pretty busy ever since."

Just then Thor and Eric both glanced over, with apologetic expressions on their faces.

"I think I know a way to help them," I

said. "Back in a sec."

I strolled over to the Twinmobile and fished in the back for a couple of the tennis balls Michael always kept back there. We often used them to entertain the boys when we were stuck in boring circumstances — waiting for a tow, for example, or enduring a family gathering with few other kids, or even just killing time in the parking lot of the Caerphilly Market while one of us did the grocery shopping. I wasn't sure if it was premeditated on Michael's part or just a happy by-product of his scheme for keeping the boys amused, but all those games of catch had definitely honed their baseball skills.

"Hey, Eric," I said. "You still thinking of trying out for your high school baseball team?"

Eric looked up, startled. He shook his head slightly and indicated the tailgate party with his eyes as if to remind me that he was on duty.

"Here," I said. "Catch this."

I fired a tennis ball at him. Thor leaped away and hugged the iPad protectively to his chest. Eric caught the tennis ball.

"Not bad," Caroline called. "But let's see how you throw."

Eric lobbed the ball back to me. I caught

it and fired it back. Eric started to look annoyed, and threw it back harder. I caught it, then fumbled it — deliberately — and had to reach slightly under the bumper of the car behind me to retrieve it. I could see Eric's eyes open wide as enlightenment struck. Thor, too, caught on. He stowed his iPad in a knapsack and stepped forward as if to join the game.

"Not bad," I said as I fielded Eric's latest throw. I moved a little until I was standing in front of the car next to Biff's truck and lobbed it back to him again.

Eric, Thor, and I threw the ball around a few more times until I saw my chance. I deliberately bobbled the ball again, and then managed to kick it under the car next to Biff's truck in a way that I was pretty sure looked accidental.

"Sorry," Eric called. "Bad throw."

"Blast!" I leaned down and peered under the car, and then under Biff's truck. "Can you see which one it's under?"

"The car," Thor said.

"Looked like the truck to me," Eric said. "Or maybe that car on the other side."

"Well, can one of you crawl under there and look?" I asked. "I am not in the mood to grovel on gravel today, and by the looks of it you've already been doing that."

Eric started by looking under the car and then crawled under the truck. Thor made a big show of crawling under several nearby cars. All the while, they kept up a running dialogue.

"Yuck! There's chewing gum under here."

"Aunt Meg, are oil stains hard to get out?"

"I found a toad!"

"Hey, I think I found that foul ball no one could find."

"Maybe after this we should find a better place to play catch."

Eventually Eric crawled out from under the car.

"Give me a hand up?" he asked.

I did, and was delighted to see the little geotracking device in my palm when Eric took his away.

"That was probably a good idea, playing catch someplace else," I said.

"And if you want to hit the Snack Shack on your way to that someplace else, it's on me," Caroline said, handing each of the boys a folded bill.

Thor retrieved his backpack, and the two ambled off toward the Snack Shack. Caroline and I followed more slowly.

"Thanks," she said.

"No problem," I said. "Mind if I keep the you-know-what for a little while? I want to show it to someone who might have a chance to pick Biff's pocket."

"Be my guest," she said.

Back at the bleachers, Caroline and I took a seat in what had been the Nats bleachers. I wasn't sure which team we'd be rooting for next — the Flatworms were playing the Wombats at three thirty, but I couldn't tell from the gear in the dugouts which team was which. Not a problem. The boys had friends on both teams. If we wanted to be nonpartisan, we could play musical bleachers halfway through the game.

But meanwhile, we were relaxing. Family members were catching up on news while watching the Flatworms and Wombats warm up. Even Grandfather was here, though he didn't exactly look all that interested. More likely he was just trying to make sure Cordelia didn't monopolize too much of the boys' time.

"Mommy, can I have some gum?" Josh asked.

"I'll buy you some gum," Grandfather said. "On two conditions."

"O-kay." Josh sounded slightly dubious.

"First, you have to get a pack for your brother as well," Grandfather said.

"Okay," Josh said, more cheerfully.

"And second, you have to bring me a

hamburger and a Coke." Grandfather pulled out his wallet and handed Josh a bill.

"We're all going to have a picnic right after the game," I said. "Mother and Rose Noire are on their way with the food."

"And if they bring anything more substantial than cucumber sandwiches, I'll join you," Grandfather said. "But I'm in the mood for a burger, and I want it now. Ketchup and onions," he added to Josh.

Josh scurried off. Jamie was watching a Grasshoppers pitcher warming up in the bullpen — their game wasn't till six, but the bullpen wasn't needed for the coach-pitch Flatworm/Wombat game. Jamie was drinking it all in, and making little arm movements as if mimicking the Grasshopper. Grandfather's eyes were flicking back and forth between the two. I suspected that by dinner time he'd have some new observations on the similarity between what Josh and Jamie had been doing all day and the learning behaviors of other immature primates, but as long as he didn't make any comments too insulting to the boys, he was welcome to observe them all he liked.

I surreptitiously fished the little tracking device out of my jacket pocket and studied it, with my fingers carefully curled so no one else could see it. Yes, it did look like a random bit of mechanical junk. I tucked it back in my pocket again. I pondered the notion that if Biff actually did find it in his pocket, he might not recognize what it was. And if he did find it, who was to say that he hadn't accidentally picked it up out at our house? In fact, what if I started showing the little device to everyone who'd been at our picnic and asking them if they'd picked up one just like it by mistake? I could say that Caroline had brought me two to try out with Spike and the llamas, and we'd dropped one somewhere.

I turned the idea over in my mind. I liked it. But maybe I should run it by Michael to see what he thought.

"Back by game time," I said to Caroline. I stood up and looked around for Michael, spotted him over in the parking lot, and headed that way. I wasn't making much progress, thanks to the vast number of friends and relatives who kept accosting me, but then I wasn't in any particular hurry. In fact, I was feeling relaxed and downright cheerful.

Until I heard a distant cry of "Mommy!"

Distant, but all too clear to me. I glanced over my shoulder to see that Jamie was still sitting on the bleachers beside Grandfather, completely focused on baseball. But his brother —

"Where's Josh?" I snapped.

I held up my hand for quiet and the two cousins I'd been talking to stopped in mid-sentence. I stood on tiptoes and whirled about, scanning everywhere until I spotted it.

Biff Brown was holding Josh by his shoulders, almost lifting him off the ground, yelling at him and shaking him.

I think I knocked down one of the cousins on my way there.

"You no good, miserable little thief!" Biff was yelling. "I'll show you what happens to —"

"Mommy! Mommy!" Josh was wailing.

"Get your hands off my son," I shouted as I drew near.

Biff ignored me.

"Lying, thieving juvenile delinquents," he was screeching.

"I said get your hands off my son." I grabbed his elbow, and instead of paying any attention to me, he jabbed back. I wasn't sure whether he was merely trying to dislodge my hand or if he was actually trying to whack me with the point of his elbow. Josh had stopped uttering coherent sounds and was simply wailing in terror and possibly even pain and Biff showed no signs of

letting go —
  I punched Biff in the nose.

CHAPTER 21

Biff keeled over. As he fell, I managed to retrieve Josh, who latched onto me like a small, snot-smeared limpet.

"Mommy's here," I said, wrapping him tightly in my left arm. I kept my right free, in case Biff showed signs of retaliating. He had landed hard on his rear, and stared up at me in astonishment for a few seconds. Then his face flushed with blood and he began gathering himself as if to get up.

"Stay down," I said. "If you come one inch closer to us, I'll really hurt you."

Biff scowled, and seemed to be trying to struggle to his feet.

I drew back my right foot and was ready to kick him in the crotch. He turned pale, clutched himself protectively, and stayed down.

By now, some of the other parents nearby recovered enough from their astonishment to take action and hurried over to help.

Vince Wong, Evan Thornton, and Luis Espinoza hovered behind me as if ready to intervene if Biff tried to retaliate.

"Are you okay?" Vince asked me.

"Did he hurt the kid?" Luis asked.

"The lady told you to stay down," Evan was telling Biff. "I think you should follow orders."

"What's going on here?"

Chief Burke.

"She attacked me," Biff bellowed.

"He was abusing my son," I said. "I intervened."

"She punched me in the nose!"

"Mommy, he hurted me," Josh wailed.

"Hurt, not hurted," I said. "Show me where it hurts."

Josh held up one arm and pointed to several angry red marks on his forearm. They looked like finger impressions.

"I had to stop him," Biff said. "The kid stole two packs of gum from the Snack Shack."

He pointed to the ground, where you could just barely make out the end of a pack of gum that had been ground into the mud during our struggles.

"The hell he did," came a voice from behind me.

We looked up to see Anisha, the younger

Mrs. Patel.

"I saw him walk up to the Snack Shack and take two packs," Biff said.

"The boy came up and paid for a hamburger, a Coke, and two packages of gum — one for himself and one for his brother." Anisha's low, musical voice sounded perfectly calm, but the hint of a British accent had grown stronger. "He couldn't carry it all, so he asked if he could take the hamburger and the soda to his grandfather and come back for the gum. I told him it was fine. And that's what he was doing when you came up and manhandled him — collecting two packs of gum that were already bought and paid for."

"That's true," said another mother. "I was there, too."

"Well, I thought he was stealing," Biff said. "How was I supposed to know?"

"You could have asked," Anisha said.

"She still punched me in the nose." Biff turned to the chief. "I want to press charges. Assault and battery."

"I'll see your assault and battery and raise you child endangerment," I said. "Do you have any idea how dangerous it is to shake a child —"

"Child endangerment!" Biff bellowed. "If your little —"

"Enough!" Chief Burke wasn't all that loud, but somehow even Biff got the idea that shutting up was advisable. The chief studied Biff for a few moments, then lifted his eyes to examine the circle of people around us. He ended up with me. No, actually with Josh. His jaw clenched slightly. Then he looked over his shoulder, where Deputy Sammy Wendell was standing.

"I am still rather busy with the murder investigation," he said. "To say nothing of this morning's attempted murder in the Snack Shack. So Deputy Wendell will be taking statements from Mr. Brown, Mrs. Langslow, and anyone who was a witness to their altercation."

"Oh, great, so all her buddies can lie for her," Biff said.

Many of the onlookers gasped or murmured at his words, then fell silent when the chief said nothing. He just stared at Biff who, after a few moments, began to squirm slightly.

Then someone stepped forward out of the crowd. Mr. Witherington.

"I beg your pardon, but since I'm a relative stranger to town — and to both of the participants in the altercation — I wanted to make sure Deputy Wendell knows how to reach me for my statement. James Wither-

335

ington, Regional Vice President of Summerball. My cell number is on the card."

He handed a business card to Sammy.

Restless murmurs from the crowd, who were, perhaps, aware that Witherington was here at Biff's invitation, and might not realize how much progress Randall and I were making in winning him over from the dark side.

"I was originally only supposed to be here for the Opening Day," Witherington went on. "But given the unfortunate events that occurred yesterday, I'm staying on to resolve a few issues I've found in our local league."

A few murmurs at that.

"Assuming I can find a hotel that actually provides at least a token amount of hot water," Witherington continued. "Meanwhile, may I suggest that someone photograph the young gentleman's bruises while they are still fresh? I would hate for there to be any uncertainty later about when and how he received them."

As he spoke he looked at Biff with an expression so fierce that I felt a sudden surge of optimism about the future of the Caerphilly Summerball league. And from the approving murmurs coming from the crowd, I wasn't the only one.

"Here." Vince Wong handed Mr. Witherington a card. "I'm the assistant manager of the Caerphilly Inn. We would be happy to accommodate you for as long as you choose to stay."

"Thank you," Mr Witherington began. "Is there —"

"The league can't afford the Caerphilly Inn!" Biff bellowed.

"Please tell me you didn't actually stick him in the Whispering Pines!" I exclaimed. Although the Pines was no longer technically a hot sheets motel, it still seemed to exude the noxious atmosphere of its unseemly past.

"The Clay County Motor Lodge," Biff said.

"Oh, like that's soooo much better," muttered someone in the crowd.

"We're on a budget," Biff growled.

"The Inn will be happy to offer Summerball a competitive rate," Vince said. "Would you like me to drive you over now to collect your luggage? Or if you're very busy, I could send over a staff member to do it for you."

"Whatever's easiest for you," Mr. Witherington said. "Is there any chance the Inn has a large conference room I could rent for a general league meeting?"

"Rent a room?" Biff exclaimed. "I never waste money on renting rooms — several of

337

my board members have free spaces that they make available for my meetings."

"How very kind of them," Mr. Witherington said. "But this is *my* meeting."

No one said anything for what seemed like a really long time as Witherington and Biff glared at each other. Then Vince spoke up.

"I'm sure I can arrange for the hotel to provide a suitable room at no charge, as a gesture of goodwill to the community," he said.

"Thank you," Mr. Witherington said. "We can discuss the financial arrangements later. The important thing is that we can have a large room. Now why don't we all get back to the reason we're all here? We have a ball game to play!" He glanced around the crowd with a tight little smile on his lips and then slowly walked off.

The crowd began breaking up. Biff stormed off in the opposite direction from that Mr. Witherington had taken.

"A meeting about what, do you suppose?" Vince asked.

"Whatever it is, we need to pack it with sane people," Evan said. "Because you know Biff's crew will turn out."

"Maybe it's wishful thinking on my part," I said. "But from my reading of the Summerball rule book, the main thing you do at a general membership meeting is elect officers."

"I thought election time was before the season started."

"It is," I said. "But any time is impeachment time."

They all looked startled and maybe even a little anxious for a few moments. Then big grins began to spread over their faces.

"But Biff won't take it lying down," I said. "We have to pack the house with NAFOBs."

"NAFOBs?" Evan echoed.

"Not a Friend of Biff," Vince explained. "We're on it."

"Come on, Josh," I said. "I bet you're hungry by now."

"I'm too upset to eat," he announced.

"Not even ice cream?"

He thought about that for a few moments. "I'm not really in the mood for ice cream." His tone was an uncanny imitation of the languid tone in which his Uncle Rob often declared himself not in the mood for something — although I couldn't ever remember Rob refusing ice cream. "But if it would make you feel better, I could probably eat some."

It did, indeed, make me feel much better to watch him eat his ice cream. Also two hot dogs, two chocolate milks, a handful of

339

hot potato samosas from Mrs. Patel, some organic raspberries from Rose Noire, and a chocolate milk shake that Rob brought back from town. And although Jamie had not undergone any particularly traumatic experiences during the day, he valiantly did his share of comfort eating.

We stayed to watch the Flatworms and Wombats battle to a fourteen-fourteen tie before they had to cede the field to the Grasshoppers and Sandgnats. We stayed to watch that game, too. Michael and the boys — and for that matter, most of the rest of the Eagles and their fathers — were completely absorbed in the games.

I spent most of my time organizing for the league meeting. Making sure every single Eagle family would be represented. Liaising with the team moms from the Flatworms, Wombats, Grasshoppers, Sandgnats, Muckdogs, River Rats, Pirates, Red Sox, and Nats, to make sure those teams also turned out in force.

We didn't worry about the Stoats and the Yankees. Biff would make sure they showed up.

As soon as the last game was over, Michael and I sent the boys home with Rose Noire, since she was the only family member not fired up to attend the league meeting.

"There will be so much negative energy there," she said, with a shudder. "The boys and I will have a lovely, quiet evening at home."

"The boys would probably love watching the Nats game," Michael said. "The grown-up Nats, that is, on TV."

"I'm not sure I could even figure out what channel it was on."

"Don't worry," I said. "The boys can."

With that Michael and I set out for the league meeting.

CHAPTER 22

Luckily we were early enough to get a parking spot fairly close to the Caerphilly Inn's door. Latecomers would end up parking along the mile-long tree-shaded entrance road, unless they decided to spring for the Inn's stunningly overpriced valet parking.

In spite of the short notice, the Inn had posted a sign at the entrance saying, in elegant calligraphy, *Welcome, Caerphilly Summerball League.* And I found myself suspecting that this was not the first time the Caerphilly Inn had hosted a baseball-related event. Or if it was, they'd certainly risen to the occasion in their usual fashion. The hotel's sound system was playing a lush if rather muted solo piano version of "Take Me Out to the Ball Park," and the placards directing us to the room were decorated with drawings of bats, balls, and gloves. Along the back wall, the tables containing pitchers of water and rows of glasses were also festooned with pyramids of baseballs topped by little American flags, and the hotel staff attending the room wore their usual black-and-gold uniforms with plain black baseball caps.

Michael and I snagged seats in the front row, and were enjoying watching the other attendees enter — some confidently, as if a conference room in a five-star hotel was an everyday sight for them, and others timidly, as if more than half convinced they'd be thrown out.

And then there were the ones like Biff who seemed almost too confident, as if determined to carry through on bluster. He'd snagged a seat in the front row on the other side of the room, and seemed to be surrounded by a posse of friends and supporters, to judge by the way they were patting him on the shoulder or giving him a thumbs-up sign. Okay, a relatively small posse. And made even smaller by the fact that the Pruitts, who would normally have been a part of it, were sitting in their own scowling clump not far behind Michael and me — definitely apart from the Biff forces. Adolph was among them, and seemed to be having an intense discussion with one of his cousins. Thinking it might be a good idea to learn about any strategy they were pursuing, I turned slightly and pretended to be scanning the room while trying to eavesdrop. But after a few minutes, I realized that any strategy the Pruitts might pursue wouldn't be coming from Adolph. He seemed to be giving his cousin a blow-by-blow account of his latest session of playing a particularly violent video game, punctuated frequently with a loud, braying laugh.

I also spotted Ms. Nondescript — Edna, that was her name — seated toward the back of the room, very far from Biff's contingent. She appeared to be clinging close to Ideen for protection, though I noticed she was paying close attention to the conversations around her. And since most of the people around her were Red Sox or Flatworm parents, she probably wasn't hearing any complimentary remarks about Biff. Well, let her lurk and spy all she wanted. No one outside of Biff's camp was plotting anything sneaky or underhanded, so she was welcome to repeat anything she heard.

And speaking of Biff's camp . . .

"Lot of faces over there that I don't recognize," I murmured to Michael as the meeting's start time drew near. "Are they college people, do you think?"

"I don't think we have that many college

faces that I wouldn't recognize." He was frowning, and I could see he was looking at some of the same people I'd been studying. "This is going to sound paranoid, but could they be Clay County people?"

"The logical question would be why a bunch of Clay County people would show up at a Caerphilly County Summerball meeting," I said. "But I think you're right. I recognize those two in the plaid shirts — they were two of the guys who delivered Biff's replacement porta-potty this afternoon. And according to Aida, almost all of his employees live in Clay County."

"So it's a fair assumption that Biff's trying to pack the house," Michael said. "It will be interesting to see how Mr. Witherington handles this. On the whole, he seems —"

"Ladies and gentlemen." Mr. Witherington was standing at a podium in the front of the room. He tapped on the microphone a couple of times to make sure it was on. "Please take your seats."

It was standing room only by now, with some of the hotel staff setting up extra chairs in the back, while one, with a worried look on his face, was slowly walking down one side of the room, making counting gestures with his forefinger. Worried about the fire marshal, no doubt. I wondered if it would reassure him if I pointed out that the fire marshal, whose son was on the Red Sox, was seated in the second row, arms crossed, staring straight ahead as if determined not to see any potential occupancy violation.

"Ladies and gentlemen." Mr. Witherington rapped on the podium for order, and the crowd quickly fell silent. "I'd like to call this meeting of the Caerphilly Summerball League to order. At the last league meeting, held" — he glanced down at a piece of paper on the podium, frowned slightly, and looked back out at us — "held on March eleven, it was announced that, due to illness, Mr. Lemuel Shiffley would be unable to continue in his position as league president, and Mr. Biff Brown was elected to fill the vacancy."

At that, the crowd erupted in loud murmurs, because apart from Biff's crew none of us remembered attending or even being invited to the March eleven meeting — or for that matter, any other league meetings.

"League meeting, my eye!" came a voice from the back of the crowd. "Biff and a couple of his lackeys, that's all!"

Scattered applause greeted these words. I craned my neck and spotted Callie Peebles near the back of the room, perched on one of the tables beside the water pitchers. I was pretty sure she didn't have a kid in Caerphilly Summerball, but apparently word about the meeting had gone out over the grapevine in both counties.

Samuel Yoder stood not far away, arms folded, looking more than ever like an Old Testament prophet in a wrathful mood. Moses, maybe, getting ready to call down another plague on the Egyptians.

Biff might have brought all his supporters, but he also had a lot of enemies here. If I were him, I'd make sure I had someone walk me to my car when the meeting was over.

Mr. Witherington had been waiting for the crowd to grow quiet again.

"However," he went on, "due to the unfortunate events of the last few days, it appears that Mr. Brown will no longer be able to continue as league president —"

"That's a lie!" Biff leaped to his feet and turned to face the crowd. "I never resigned and I'm not going to! They're trying to railroad me!"

The people immediately around Biff jumped to their feet and began shouting things like "fraud!" and "unfair!" and waving their arms around wildly. From where Mr. Witherington sat, they probably looked like a frenzied mob, but if you were a little distanced from it, as Michael and I were at the other end of the row, you could tell that it was a tempest in a teapot. In fact, it looked rather like one of those moments at a political convention when a dark horse candidate with next to no chance of winning has been nominated and his supporters are trying to make up with enthusiasm what they lack in strength.

Then Ms. Ellie, the town librarian, who was sitting a few seats down from us, stood up, turned to face the audience, and began to clap rhythmically in the "One! Two! One-two-three!" pattern she always used when story hour and other library events grew too boisterous. Seeing what she was doing, Michael and I joined in immediately, as did a few others. In fact, since several generations of Caerphillians had been trained to respond to that particular rhythm, before long the entire room was clapping along — and many of us stomping as well — completely drowning out the feeble noise that Biff and his cronies were making. One by one the cronies shut up and sat back down, until only Biff was left standing at the head of the room, with his mouth hanging open.

When the last crony had sat down, Ms. Ellie held up her right hand and the clapping and stomping stopped instantly, as if we'd rehearsed the maneuver for hours. She turned to Mr. Witherington, nodded, and sat down.

"As I was saying." Mr. Witherington glared at Biff for a moment before continuing. "Mr. Brown will no longer be able to continue as league president because I, as the duly authorized representative of Summerball National, have removed him for cause."

Wild applause from most of the crowd greeted that statement.

"Good going, four-eyes!" Callie shouted.

"We will need to elect a new league president," Mr. Witherington said, when the room had grown quiet again. "In fact, we'll also be electing a new vice president and treasurer."

"Point of order, Mr. Chairman," Biff said. "Am I correct in assuming that only Caerphilly Summerball League members in good standing will be allowed to vote?"

Mr. Witherington stared over his glasses at Biff for a few moments.

"Mr. Brown is correct," he said finally. "Only members in good standing will be allowed to vote."

At these words, many of the people seated near Biff began waving little cards in the

349

air. No doubt these were cards declaring them league members in good standing.

"Where do we go to get a card?" Michael muttered. And from the sound of the muttering behind us, he wasn't the only one thinking this.

"However," Mr. Witherington went on, "since under the previous management there does not appear to have been a good faith effort to enable prospective members to join, we will postpone the voting until all those present who aspire to membership have been given a chance to pay their annual dues."

"No fair!" Biff leaped to his feet, already shouting.

"Stow it, beef brain!" Callie called out. "Four-eyes has your number."

Even Mr. Yoder was smiling now, though it was as stern and forbidding as a smile could be and still qualify for the name.

Meanwhile, before Mr. Witherington had even finished speaking, the non-Biff portion of the audience had already begun forming an orderly line leading up to the podium.

Ms. Ellie, Mother, and I pitched in to organize the dues-paying. We recruited several volunteers to work their way down the line, taking cash or checks and writing out receipts, which Ms. Ellie and I then carried up to Mr. Witherington in batches for his official signature.

The only sour note was that Biff's supporters were shouting protests and waving their arms to be recognized. Mr. Witherington was ignoring them, but I could tell they were wearing on his nerves.

"While you do that, I will suppress the opposition," Mother murmured to me. I was looking forward to seeing how she did it — I was rather hoping that, like the guinea pigs in *Alice in Wonderland,* this would involve stuffing them into bags and sitting on them. Mother's more civilized solution was to organize entertainment to amuse the crowd while the dues collection went forward, and to chide Biff's cronies for their bad manners if they interrupted the entertainment.

They sat still for Dad's dramatic recitation of "Casey at the Bat." I was a little worried that Mother would let him recite other, less baseball-oriented poems — his repertoire leaned to long, nineteenth-century narrative poems like "The Midnight Ride of Paul Revere," "The Rime of the Ancient Mariner," or "The Highwayman." But after Mighty Casey struck out in the last stanza, Mother called upon Michael to do a dramatic reading — and, to my surprise, he obliged with a touching rendition of Lou Gehrig's Farewell Address.

But the line was still going, and some of Biff's cronies were beginning to mutter about calling the question. Did Mother have other aces up her sleeve? Even Dad reciting "The Hunting of the Snark" might be preferable to letting the forces of Biff prevail.

"And now," Mother said, "I would like to introduce you to a figure out of baseball history. My mother-in-law, Mrs. Cordelia Lee Mason — who played in the All-American Girls Professional Baseball League under her maiden name of Delia Lee."

"Delia Lee?" Mr. Witherington's head snapped up, and he almost stabbed me with the pen he'd been using to sign the latest batch of receipts. He looked up at me. "She's Delia Lee? I must bring my girls down here to meet her," he muttered as he dived back into signing receipts.

Cordelia entertained the crowd with anecdotes about her days on the diamond, interspersed with bits of general baseball humor, all the while keeping her eye on the progress of the line. And as Mr. Witherington signed the last few receipts, she brought her remarks to a graceful close and handed the podium back to him.

"Thank you, Mrs. Mason," he said. "And now we will proceed to the heart of our meeting — the election of a new league president. Would anyone like to make a nomination?"

The Biff contingent had been muttering together busily all during the entertainment. From the little bits I'd overheard, they were debating whether there was any chance Mr. Witherington would let them nominate Biff or whether they should just put up a puppet candidate who would let Biff run things from behind the scenes. And I was a little worried, because while we'd all just expended a lot of energy making sure we could outvote them, the forces of good hadn't had any time to discuss who we wanted to vote for. Could we elect Lem Shiffley, and figure out later how much help he needed and who could provide it? Was there anyone else capable of running the league — even without the roadblocks Biff could be expected to throw his way? But while both the pro- and anti-Biff forces were still murmuring in clusters, Mr. Witherington called on someone who'd raised his hand — Will Entwhistle.

"This is the first league meeting I've managed to attend," Will began. "Mainly because it's the first one anyone bothered to tell me about."

Cheers and scattered applause from various parts of the room; glares from the Biff precincts.

"Preach it, kiddo!" Callie called from the back.

"I think better communications should be one of the goals of whoever we elect as the new president," Will went on. More cheers. "Also better field maintenance and at least a status report on how much longer it's going to be before we get some of those improvements we've been promised for the last five or six years. I think we could get a lot of these things done if we had a president who was good at organizing things and communicating with people and getting them to do stuff. I think Lem Shiffley was going a great job till he took sick, and I hear he'd be willing to come back when he's better."

"If he gets better," one of the Biff supporters called out. "And we need a president now."

"That we do," Will said. "So I nominate Lem for president, and Meg Langslow for vice president, and that way I think we'll be pretty well covered no matter what happens." With that he sat down.

"Hang on," I was starting to say, but I was drowned out by calls of "I second that!" from various parts of the room.

"Don't worry," Michael whispered. "We can get you lots of minions."

"Don't worry," Mother was whispering in my other ear. "Lem finishes his chemo in two weeks, and in the meantime I'm sure everyone in the family will be delighted to help out."

So I gave up the idea of protesting and let them nominate me. After several hurried conferences, the Biff contingent nominated Adolph Pruitt, but Lem and I were elected by a landslide. Vince Wong was elected treasurer by an equally overwhelming margin.

Mr. Witherington congratulated the new officers, instructed the outgoing league officers to hand over all relevant files, records, equipment, and account information within the next twenty-four hours, and adjourned the meeting.

Not surprisingly, the defeated Biff supporters fled before either Vince or I could make arrangements for the handing over.

"Don't worry," Mr. Witherington said, with a thin-lipped smile. "Summerball has dealt with this situation before." Including the complication that the outgoing league president might end up either a victim of murder or on trial for it before the end of the season? "Meanwhile, we have a more pressing problem. It's raining outside."

"Don't worry," Randall said. "We've got a plan for the rain."

We were standing under the awning in front of the Caerphilly Inn. Michael had dashed out in the rain to fetch the Twinmobile, scorning the bellhop's offer of an umbrella. Randall was about to do the same. Mr. Witherington, now ensconced in a room here at the Inn instead of the beastly Clay County Motor Lodge, wasn't going anywhere, but appeared to want to continue our discussion of how to deal with the rain.

And apart from waiting it out, how in the world does a baseball league deal with rain? Unless Randall had workmen already unfolding a giant economy-sized tarp to cover the entire field, tomorrow's games were probably going to be postponed. Maybe even Monday's games, given how badly our local red clay mud drained. Or was Randall planning to build a giant pipeline to channel the water elsewhere? California would probably love to have it, but I didn't think even Randall could pull that off by morning.

Randall must have noticed that I looked puzzled. Or maybe "alarmed" was the proper word.

"We can use big wet/dry vacs," he said. "We literally suck the water up and dump it someplace where it will drain."

"And there are several brands of absorbent clays that can be used to increase the drying," Mr. Witherington said. "We can try to find some in the morning. Unless, of course, your league has laid in a supply, although that seems rather unlikely under the circumstances."

"I'm pretty sure the league hasn't," Randall said. "But the county has, so we're good. I'll line up some workmen who can get started at first light and send both of you an e-mail once I've got a plan."

At first light. Nothing like hitting the ground running in my new job.

CHAPTER 23

I awoke to the dreaded sound of continuing rain. Only a drizzle, but a steady drizzle. And while it was still dark outside, someone had left the driveway light on, so when I peeked out the window I could see enough puddles to tell that it had been drizzling for some time. Or maybe pouring for part of the night.

I sighed, and pulled out my phone.

"Relax," Michael mumbled from the bed. "No baseball this morning. Too wet."

"You coaches and players can relax," I said. "We acting league presidents have to worry about how much longer it's going to be raining, and whether there's any chance we can rescue tonight's games or at least tomorrow's." Not to mention whether our predecessors were going to do anything to make the transition even more difficult.

"Don't fret; it's just for the time being," Michael said. "I'm sure Lem will be back on the job before too long."

Or if he wasn't, I had a couple of other ideas about people I could draft to take over for me. But for now . . .

"Can you take care of the boys today while I focus on baseball?" I asked.

"Sure thing."

I threw on some old clothes and headed downstairs. To my surprise, no one else was up — not even Rose Noire, who usually had breakfast ready long before I came downstairs.

Of course, I didn't usually come downstairs at a little before six.

"Good grief," I muttered. "The sun isn't even up yet."

And wouldn't be for another half hour, according to the weather app on my phone. Which also predicted scattered showers off and on all day.

I stuck a slice of bread in the toaster, grabbed some leftover fruit salad, and used my phone to check my e-mail. Apparently Randall Shiffley and Jim Witherington were also already up and planning to meet at the field at dawn. And I was invited if I wanted to come.

"Meet you there," I replied.

I had other e-mails from various parents and coaches. I glanced through them as I wolfed down my fruit and toast. Nothing that couldn't wait until after I inspected the field.

And no reason not to head there immediately, I decided.

The road was slick, and in a few places puddles spread most of the way across its surface. I was pleased to see that the baseball field's parking lot was in good shape — it would have been a sea of mud if Randall's crew and the volunteers hadn't spread all that gravel Friday night.

Unfortunately the field *was* a sea of mud. A sea of mud with ambitions of becoming a pond.

And there was someone standing by the backstop staring out at it. Biff.

He didn't look up when I drove up — just stood there, fingers twined in the chain link, staring. He was wearing an industrial gray rain poncho over jeans. The poncho had a hood, but it was pushed back, and his Yankees cap looked sodden, as if he'd been standing there in the rain for some time.

He wasn't wearing the wretched windbreaker with the tracker in its pocket, or if he was, it was well hidden under the poncho. Probably just as well. The sight of the windbreaker might have tempted me to get out and see if I could pick his pocket. A temptation I hoped I'd have resisted, since he was still very much a murder suspect. Instead, I turned my car engine off and sat there, watching him, until a truck pulled into the parking lot.

Two tall forms in rain slickers got out and began unloading equipment from the bed of the truck. The men looked familiar — in fact, they looked like two of Randall's many cousins — so I got out and sloshed over to greet them.

"We're here to work on the field," one of them said.

"Work on it how?" I asked.

"Wet/dry vac," he said. "The more water we can suck up, the faster the field will dry. Is he going to hassle us about doing it?"

He was pointing to Biff.

"I doubt it." I shook my head. "He's not in charge anymore. And if he tries, I'm here. Tell him to talk to me about it."

He nodded. Both of them hefted their wet/ dry vacs — enormous black-and-yellow objects that looked like giant mutant vac-uum cleaners — and trudged out onto the field.

Biff didn't try to interfere with them, just stood there staring. I strolled over to see him. Not that I was eager to talk with Biff, but we had things to discuss, and I figured this might be one of my best chances to do so.

He didn't turn around, but I suspected he knew I was there. He hunched his shoulders a little higher and pulled his cap a little farther over his eyes, but he didn't leave.

"Morning," I said, when I reached his side.

"Come to gloat?" he asked.

"No." I leaned against the fence in a pose that echoed his, watching the Shiffleys vacuuming up puddles. A seemingly thankless task, since the drizzle still continued. Already one Shiffley had stopped to carry a bag full of water off the field and through the parking lot so he could empty it into a drainage ditch that ran along the road.

Biff and I stood there for a few minutes, side by side, in what with anyone else would have felt like companionable silence. If I glanced to my left, I could see him, hunched a little away from me.

"I don't want to bother you in the middle of the holiday weekend," I began.

"Then don't," he said.

"I'd be happy not to, provided you make an appointment to see me on Tuesday and promise to show up. It's been six weeks since Randall assigned me to be the contact between your company and the county government, and so far you've ducked every call and visit I've made."

"Didn't have anything to report."

"You don't have any progress to report," I said. "I can see that every time I drive through the town square. But that doesn't mean you don't need to talk to me."

"Look," he said, whirling around to face me, "I've had labor problems and materials problems and weather problems, so I haven't started the job yet. But it won't take more than a week to do the work, and there's still four weeks till Memorial Day, so why don't you quit badgering me?"

"Now was that so hard?" I said, keeping my tone as mild as possible. "If you'd called me back that first Monday morning I left a message, and said that — well, said it in a slightly less combative tone — I'd have left you alone for the rest of the week. Think of how much more relaxing your week would have been without me calling every day. And then if the next Monday you'd called to say that you still hadn't been able to start the job, but it was on your schedule — and even better, given me the tentative start date — I'd probably have left you alone for the rest of that week, too. It's not just about getting the work done, it's also about keeping the customer happy."

"We all have our own ways of doing business," he said.

"Yours doesn't get many repeat customers," I said.

"Is that a threat?"

"Call it a helpful observation."

"Bet you'll take the ball field away from me, too," he said.

I glanced down at the field in front of us. Under the puddles, the outfield was still a patchwork of crabgrass and bare red clay — more red clay than yesterday, thanks to all the hole filling and hill leveling. The infield was now all red clay — well, red clay and water at the moment — though at least it, too, was now a lot more level. The only thing that really made me feel better about how the field looked was that Randall had already calculated how much sod would be needed to replace the clay and crabgrass with lush green turf and penciled the work in on the Shiffley Construction Company's calendar to start the day after the playoffs. And if Biff tried to claim the work for his company — well, once the county attorney finished her study of the contract, then yes, we probably were going to take the ball field away from him.

"It could use some work from somebody," I said aloud.

"Well, you can do what you want," he said. "It's your league now."

"No, it's not," I said.

"It's not?" He looked at me with a curious expression on his face, hope visible through the gloomy scowl.

"It's not my league," I said. "It's our league. It belongs to you and me and everyone who has a kid in the league or maybe just loves baseball and wants to help make the league as great as possible."

"You'll see," he said. "They'll drive you crazy. They've all got their own damn fool ideas about how things should run."

"Maybe some of those ideas are good," I suggested. "Or maybe they're not, but if nobody tries them or even listens to them, how will we know?"

He shook his head and snorted slightly.

"So the league's not your personal fiefdom anymore," I said. "Never was, for that matter — but you still have a voice. What do you want for the league? What's your vision?"

I expected bluster and bombast, a passionate defense of how much better equipped he was to run the league. Instead he sighed and swept his gaze around the field.

"I want it to be the way it was," he said.

Did he mean with him at the helm?

"When I was growing up," he added, as if answering my question. "We didn't have fancy fields and uniforms. No electronic scoreboards — if you wanted to know what the score was, you paid attention to the game. You wanted a seat, you brought a lawn chair. Parents didn't have to spend a month's salary on fancy equipment for eight-year-olds. The snack shack sold Cokes and hot dogs and bubble gum — you wanted crêpes suzette and quiche, you could bring your own in a picnic basket. Baseball was simpler back then."

"A lot of things were simpler back then," I said. "Simpler isn't necessarily better. Kids get fewer injuries thanks to some of that fancy equipment. And hot dogs, Coke, and bubble gum don't exactly make up the healthiest diet."

"We had more fun then," he said.

"You were a kid then," I said. "Of course you had more fun. All you did was show up and play ball. It was your parents who had to buy your equipment and haul it and you to practices and games. Not to mention packing the picnic basket and the folding chairs and the bug spray and the sunscreen and the water bottles. And then there's figuring out how to get the red clay mud stains out of those blindingly white baseball pants all the teams seem to pick."

"You don't like the white pants?" From the look on his face, I suspected this was some kind of baseball heresy.

"I like the white pants," I said. "I don't like the work it takes to keep them spotless, but when the boys walk out on the field, so proud of their uniforms, I like it. It's fun to watch them. Fun that requires a lot of grown-up work to make it happen, but maybe that makes it all the sweeter."

"I'm not sure I get your point."

"I probably won't do everything the way you've been doing it," I said. "Heck, maybe I won't do anything the way you've been doing it, and maybe I'll make some really stupid mistakes. It'd be nice to know that you'll do what you can to make the transition easier."

"You want me to resign from coaching my teams, I expect," he said.

Part of me wanted to cheer, and say, "Yes, of course." But I found myself wondering if that really was the best idea. It would certainly alienate some if not all of the Yankee and Stoat families. We might have trouble getting a new coach, or even keeping enough players for the teams to continue, and that would mean only three teams instead of four in our already tiny coach-pitch and majors divisions.

"Not necessarily," I said.

He turned to look at me, with a startled expression.

"You'd have to play by the rules," I said.

"Your rules," he said.

"Summerball rules," I said. "Plus any local rules approved in a general meeting, though offhand I can't think of any we need. But if I do think of any, they'll be voted on publicly and disseminated to everyone."

"Okay."

"I'm going to be particularly fierce about the rule against profanity and abusive language," I said. "And if I ever hear you belittling one of your players the way you did during yesterday's games, you will be out on your ear. I know it's part of the coaches' job to make sure the kids learn from their mistakes, but raised voices should never be part of that learning process."

He scowled and nodded.

Another idea came to me.

"And I'm not going to argue with Mr. Witherington's requirement that you attend some anger management counseling as a condition of your continuing."

"Anger management?" From his tone of

voice, I could tell the very idea ticked him off.

"If you fight that, he's going to fight having you continue as a coach."

"Whatever." He sounded defeated.

"I'll talk to Witherington, then." And warn him not to act surprised when Biff announced his willingness to undergo anger management counseling. "Getting back to the town square — have you been having trouble getting the materials?"

"Trouble? What do you mean, trouble?" He sounded more like the old Biff. "What business is it of yours how I run my business?"

"It's just that Randall has been complaining that some of Shiffley Construction's suppliers haven't been very reliable lately." I hoped this sounded plausible, because I was making it up as I went along. "So much so that we did an inventory of the county warehouse to see if we had any materials we could repurpose for one of the contracts his company is working on. And it seemed to me that some of the stuff on that inventory might be usable for the town square project."

"So you're taking that away from me, too?"

"I'm suggesting we renegotiate the terms

369

of your contract," I said. "You supply the labor and the county provides the materials out of surplus from our warehouse. The county gets back much-needed warehouse space, and you don't have to deal with those unreliable suppliers."

"I also don't get the usual markup on the materials," he said. Definitely more like the old Biff.

"No," I said. "So if your suppliers are more reliable than Randall's and you're having no problem ordering the supplies and don't care about having to have all that money tied up in materials until the work's done, fine."

"No, no," he said, quickly. "If it will help out the county, fine."

"So I'll have the county attorney draw up a revised contract," I said. "How about if we meet Tuesday to sign it. What time's good for you?"

"Whenever," he said.

"Ten a.m."

He nodded. If I had just made an appointment, I'd have pulled out my notebook and jotted it on my calendar. He just kept staring at the field. And at the Shiffleys who were methodically vacuuming up puddles and hauling the water to the ditch.

Was he really planning to meet with me?

Or just planning to blow me off?

"So does that work for you?" I asked.

"Assuming I'm still out of jail on Tuesday," he said, with a grimace. "Half the county seems to think I killed my own brother. And the chief seems to be in that half."

I wished I could say something reassuring. But about the best thing I could have managed was to say that I wasn't in the half who thought he'd killed Shep. I was in the half who wasn't sure who'd done it and just hoped the chief caught the killer before too long.

"Well, if you're in jail you're off the hook," I said. "Assuming you're not, I'll see you Tuesday at your office at ten a.m."

He nodded. I scribbled the appointment in my notebook, and added an item to figure out at least one person I could take along with me so I wouldn't be venturing alone in the lair of someone who, even if he was out of jail by then, could still be a killer. Someone other than Randall, who would only irritate Biff. Maybe —

"Look, I'm sorry about your kid," he said suddenly. "I shouldn't have jumped on him. It was just yesterday — this whole weekend — had been pretty tough, and thinking someone was stealing from the Snack Shack was kind of a last straw. Maybe Witherington's right. Maybe I do need this anger management thing."

He dug into his pocket and held something out to me. A key ring.

"Big one's for the Snack Shack," he said. "Small one's for the padlock on the equipment shed."

"Thanks." As I was pocketing the keys I saw headlights turning into the parking lot.

"Probably Mr. Witherington," I said. "I should go and see him."

Biff didn't seem to notice that I was leaving.

Actually it was Mr. Witherington and Randall. They had climbed out of their vehicles and were standing side by side, wearing nearly identical navy-blue hooded rain jackets.

"It works surprisingly well," Mr. Witherington was saying. "I'll send you the information when I get back to the office."

"Morning, Meg," Randall said, spying me. "Jim's going to give us some info on ways we can get the field to drain better."

"If you can afford to spend the money," Mr. Witherington said.

"I have my eye on a couple of potential donors," Randall said. "How's your morning going, Meg?"

"Biff agreed to the idea of using supplies

from the county warehouse to fix the town square," I said. "So order whatever you think he should be using and let's get the project moving."

"Will do," Randall said. "Of course, it's going to be a little hard to explain how we happened to have half an acre of fresh sod in the warehouse. Then again, who knows if Biff will even be around to wonder, and as long as his workmen are expecting a paycheck, they won't care."

"And Biff has agreed to attend anger management counseling as a condition of continuing as coach of the Stoats and the Yankees," I said to Mr. Witherington.

"An excellent idea," he said.

"I'm glad you think so," I said. "Because we're pretending it's your idea and that you'll insist he resign if he doesn't cooperate."

"Aha!" he said. "So we're playing good cop, bad cop."

"More like bad cop, worse cop," I said. "I think Biff would run roughshod over good cop. And of course, all of this is assuming Biff isn't in jail by the end of the weekend, which seems to be what he's expecting to happen."

"Oh, dear." Mr. Witherington looked anxious. "Do you suppose that constitutes an admission of guilt?"

"More likely an admission that he realizes half the county loathes and distrusts him and thinks he's a killer," Randall said.

"And that half of the county could very well be right," Mr. Witherington said. "If he's arrested, I'm going to ask him to resign his coaching posts for the good of the league. I already have our PR people working on how we'd handle it in the media. By the way, did he give you the league files yet?"

"Not yet," I said. "He did turn over the keys. I forgot to remind him about the files."

"I can remind him," Mr. Witherington said. "If you can tell me where to find him."

"He should be right over — never mind," I said. "He was right over there behind home plate, watching the Shiffleys work on the field, but I guess he decided not to stick around. He can't have gone far, though."

"His car's not here," Randall said. "Must have driven off while we were talking."

"I'll track him down," Mr. Witherington said. "Talk to you later."

He returned to his rental car and drove carefully off.

"I think I'll help the boys for a while," Randall said, nodding at the field.

"I'm going in to the courthouse to work on that revised town square renovation contract," I said. "If I can give the county attorney a draft to review, I suspect we can get that done a lot sooner than if we ask her to draft it."

"Like as not," Randall agreed. "Well, that field isn't going to dry itself."

Actually, given time, it would, I found myself thinking. But probably not until the holiday weekend was over.

I climbed into my car and headed out of the parking lot. But just as I was about to make the left turn onto the main road, I spotted Horace trudging along on the shoulder as if coming from town, looking wet and miserable. He was lugging something heavy — was that his forensic kit? He seemed excited when he spotted my car, and began running toward me, kicking up a great deal of mud and road spray in the process. I unrolled my window.

"What's wrong?" I shouted.

"Thank goodness!" he called out. "The chief's going to kill me! Can you give me a ride to town?"

CHAPTER 24

"Sure — I was just heading there myself." I popped open the passenger-side door, and Horace scrambled in, bringing a great deal of water with him.

"Hurry," he said. "The chief is waiting for me, and my car slid into the ditch and my cell phone's dead and —"

"Relax," I said. "I can drop you off wherever you like. Why is the chief waiting for you?"

He frowned and tightened his lips as if to indicate that it was police business and wild horses couldn't drag the answer out of him. And then he smiled rather ruefully and shook his head.

"I guess there's no harm telling you," he said. "You'd have heard as soon as you got home — your father figured it out from listening to the police band radio. Vern Shiffley just found Callie Peebles limping along the side of the Clay Swamp Road.

She claims while she was driving home from the Summerball meeting last night Biff Brown ran her off the road."

"Seriously?"

"Seriously. So I need to go out and do forensics on her car, so when we catch Biff we can see if there's any evidence to prove her story."

"When you catch him?" I echoed. We were passing Horace's car, which was probably going to need not only towing but also body work.

"Yeah. There's been a BOLO out on him for the last hour, but no luck yet."

"Wish I'd known that half an hour ago when I saw him at the baseball field."

"Half an hour ago? May I use your phone?"

I handed over the phone and listened in on his conversation.

"Chief . . . I know, I know. My car's in a ditch, but Meg's bringing me in — listen, she just saw Brown down at the ball field half an hour ago. . . . Okay, I'll put you on speaker."

"Meg, are you sure it was Mr. Brown you saw?"

"I didn't just see him," I said. "I spoke to him."

A few moments of silence on the other

end. No, not quite silence. I could hear the chief talking to someone.

"Any chance you could take Horace out to where Ms. Peebles' car was found?" the chief asked. "All my officers are out trying to apprehend Mr. Brown."

"Sure," I said. "Just tell me where."

"Take the Clay Swamp Road," the chief said. "Keep going till you're almost at the Clay County line, and then look for Vern's patrol car. He's guarding the scene. Horace, let me know when you get there. Meg, after you drop him off, could you come back and see me?"

"Can do," I said.

"Roger." Horace handed me back my phone.

"The Clay Swamp Road," I said. "That's out near Biff Brown's scrapyard."

"Sounds like," Horace said. "Mind if I plug my phone in to charge it?"

"Knock your socks off."

I focused on driving. And on resisting the temptation to race to the scene of the crime. The roads were horribly slippery, and it wouldn't help matters if I followed Horace's example and ended up in a ditch.

We finally spotted Vern's car parked on the shoulder with its blue lights flashing.

"Pull over here," Horace said when we

were still a quarter of a mile from Vern. "Rain's probably washed away any evidence that would have been on the road, but better safe than sorry."

I watched as he sloshed down the road toward Vern's car. Vern got out to meet him. Horace waved good-bye to me — okay, I can take a hint. I took my time making a three-point turn on the roadway and managed to get a glimpse of Callie's red truck off in the woods on the left side of the road.

Then I headed back to town. After all, the chief had said he wanted to see me. Odds were he only wanted to cross-examine me on exactly when I'd talked to Biff, or maybe whether I'd noticed any telltale damage to his car. I had a feeling he'd be disappointed by how little I had to tell him. Ah, well.

When I pulled into the station parking lot, I saw an SUV that had seen better days sitting just inside the entrance, with a familiar face behind the wheel — Gina. Formerly Gina Brown, though I couldn't recall the maiden name she was now using instead. I waved, but she just sat there, staring, with an expression of frozen distress, as if she'd spotted a scorpion crawling on her dashboard.

I parked a couple of spaces down from her, grabbed my umbrella, and walked down to her SUV. When I knocked on her door, she started and hit the horn, then jerked back, took a couple of deep breaths, and rolled the window down.

"Are you okay?" I asked.

"I'm —" she began, and then stopped herself, as if realizing that "I'm fine" would be not only inaccurate but completely unbelievable. "I can't go in there," she finally said.

"Do you need to?" I asked.

"Yes." She nodded decisively — no, convulsively — half a dozen times. And continued sitting.

"Why do you need to go in there?" I asked.

She closed her eyes and shook her head as if the notion of explaining was overwhelming. We stayed there for several long minutes, her sitting with her eyes closed, me standing outside the driver's window.

"Would you like me to go in with you?" I asked finally.

She didn't say anything for a few moments. Then she rolled up the window — that didn't feel like progress. Neither did seeing her bend over — to hide from me, or merely to get something from the floor of the passenger side of the SUV? I was relieved when she opened the door and stepped out, hauling two canvas Caerphilly

Market tote bags full of papers and file folders.

"Want me to carry one of those?" I asked.

She shook her head and pulled them closer to her body. I settled for holding the umbrella over her and her file collection and walking by her side across the parking lot, at a pace so slow an arthritic turtle could have lapped us. She stopped at the station door and looked as if she was thinking of bolting, but I held it open and smiled encouragingly. She stepped inside and eyed her surroundings as anxiously as if she had just entered a medieval torture chamber with racks and thumbscrews, rather than a clean, well-lit lobby with vintage molded plastic chairs in festive purple and orange, and an unusually random collection of aging magazines.

I spotted Caroline Willner behind the desk — evidently Mother had drafted her as one of the volunteers.

"May I help you?" Caroline asked.

Gina just stood there.

"I think she wants to see the chief," I said. "Isn't that right, Gina?"

Gina nodded.

"Maybe you could tell the chief she's here?"

"Can do," Caroline said. "But she can't

go in with those bags. Not unless we search them. Can you bring them over here so I can do it?"

Gina hugged the bags to her chest and shook her head slightly.

"It's okay," I said to Gina. "She's not going to take anything."

"It's just routine," Caroline said.

Was it? I didn't remember ever having my purse or tote searched when I visited the chief. Then again, I was known to everyone on the force and presumably considered reasonably trustworthy. Routine might be different when it came to the wife of a murder suspect, and someone whose ex-sister-in-law had already instigated gunfire here at the station. Especially since, when you came down to it, Gina herself looked a little wild-eyed and unpredictable.

"Just put them down here for a minute," Caroline said.

Gina shook her head again. I glanced at Caroline. She rolled her eyes.

"How about if I take a quick look," I said to Gina. "I won't even have to touch anything — you can take things out and show me. What's in there, anyway?"

"Evidence."

"Evidence of what?" We all looked up to see Chief Burke standing in the archway that separated the reception area from the hallway — evidently he'd overheard our conversation and come out to see what was wrong.

Gina was frozen again.

"Gina?" I said, as gently as I could. "You know Chief Burke, don't you? He's the one who needs to see your evidence. But — evidence of what?"

She closed her eyes and took a deep breath, and for a few moments I thought she was about to faint — I actually took a step closer so I could try to catch her if that happened. But then a determined expression spread over her face. She opened her eyes, lifted her chin, and threw her shoulders back.

"Evidence that my future ex-husband is a lying, cheating, conniving son of a — gun," she said.

She set the totes down on the floor in front of her, shoved her hand in one, pulled out a fat file folder, and slapped it down on the front desk in front of Caroline.

"Evidence on how badly he cheated the college when he did that big plumbing project for them three years ago." She reached down and pulled up another file. "Evidence of how he paid off the building inspector to approve his substandard work on the Clay County High School Annex." Another file. "Evidence on how he paid off Tolliver Pruitt to keep quiet about his roof caving in." Another file. "Evidence on where he buys the phony green cards for his undocumented workers." She picked up both totes, turned them upside down on top of the reception desk, and shook them, spilling another dozen or so fat files onto the pile. "You'll even find a file about how he cooks the Snack Shack books so no one will figure out that he's been stealing all the profits for years."

CHAPTER 25

Caroline and I were staring at the files. You'd think the chief would have pounced on them with glee, but he was also staring at them with a slight frown on his face.

"May I ask how you came by these documents?" he asked.

Uh-oh. The answer was probably that she'd stolen them from her husband. Did that mean the chief couldn't use them? Not even if they contained evidence that could convict Biff of crimes?

"Shep brought them to me," she said. "A couple of weeks ago, when he heard I'd filed for divorce. He'd been making copies of anything he thought was hinky for some time now. He called all this his life insurance policy, and said he was afraid Biff was onto the fact that he'd been collecting it and would come to his house and steal it. So he asked me to hide it."

"In Biff's own house?" I asked.

"Which I'd kicked him out of," she said. "Shep carried the box up to the attic, and I moved the files into another box that had been there forever, one of a bunch full of old letters and photos from my side of the family — not something Biff would ever have any reason to look at even if I let him back into the house long enough to go up to the attic. And we knew Biff knew that Shep and I never could stand each other, so he'd never expect Shep to give them to me to hide. And Biff is looking for them — ask the Clay County sheriff. Shep and his ex-wife both had break-ins two weeks ago, and last week Shep's old fishing buddy had one. I'd bet anything it was Biff, or someone helping him, looking for those." She gestured to the files. "And Shep told me if anything happened to him, to make sure they got to the sheriff. I figured he actually meant in Clay County, but since Sheriff Whicker is as crooked as a dog's hind leg and in Biff's pocket to boot, I brought them to you."

By the time she got all that out, she looked more than a little wobbly, so I pulled over an orange plastic chair and eased her into it. Caroline brought her a glass of water which she gulped gratefully.

The chief had stepped over to the counter

and was examining the files.

"Some of these, if they contain evidence of crimes that took place in Clay County, may be out of my jurisdiction," he said. "But I will review all the files carefully with the county attorney before sending copies to my counterpart there. And Mr. Brown may find that defrauding the college was a particularly bad idea."

"Caerphilly College carries a lot of weight here," I said.

"And I believe their recent plumbing project was at least partially paid for with federal grant money," the chief said. "Never a good idea to rile the Feds. Mrs. Brown—"

"Ms. Crocker," she said. "I'm going back to my maiden name."

"Ms. Crocker," the chief said, with a nod. "May I suggest that you could recover yourself more easily in my office? I have more comfortable chairs, and you would not be subjected to the prying eyes of anyone who happens to walk through the station."

She nodded. I gave her a hand up from the chair, but once up she seemed steady on her feet.

"Meg, if you could help me with some of these files," the chief said. "Before you go," he added, no doubt to make sure I didn't misinterpret the request as an invitation to take another of those comfy chairs and kibbitz on his conversation with Gina.

"Happy to," I said.

I helped get Gina settled and deposited my share of the files on the chief's desk.

"You just relax," he said to Gina. "Let me refill your water." He took her glass, then followed me out into the hall.

"It would be better for Mrs. — Ms. Crocker if this matter of the files were kept discreet for now," he said as we strolled down the hall toward the lobby, where the water cooler was.

"I understand," I said. "But someone may have seen her. She seems to have spent quite a while dithering out there in the parking lot before I came along and helped her get up the nerve to come in."

"And I will be advising her to tell people that she came down at my request for a routine interview about her brother-in-law's death," he said. "I actually was planning to talk to her today anyway. I'm relieved that we were able to get her out of the reception area before Ms. Peebles came back out. I get the distinct impression the two ladies aren't on the warmest terms."

"Callie's here?" I asked. "And you're letting her go again?"

"Well, she is the victim today," he said, with a ghost of a smile. "Alleged victim, at least. She does seem to have it in for Mr. Brown, so we'll be considering the possibility that she invented the story of being run off the road to cause trouble for him."

"I was surprised to see her at the meeting last night," I said. "Wasn't she in jail?"

"Once she sobered up we let her out on bail," he said. "And as expected, over a dozen hard-core denizens of the Clay Pigeon will swear that she didn't leave the premises until nearly dawn the night of the murder."

"And you believe them?"

"I'm keeping an open mind." He had grabbed a paper cup from the dispenser by the cooler and was filling it. "If the gun she pulled on Sammy and Vern should turn out to be the same one that killed Mr. Henson — well, I don't think the testimony of a few barflies would be that hard to impeach. Especially since it could turn out that half of her alibi witnesses were already in the Clay County drunk tank by midnight. On the whole, though, I don't think she's a very plausible suspect."

"You don't think she's capable of shooting someone?" I asked.

"Oh, yes," he said. "No question. I can absolutely see her shooting him. But I think if she'd done it she'd have left him lying wherever she shot him. I have a hard time figuring out how she could possibly have transported him from the crime scene — wherever that was — without getting a speck of blood on herself or her vehicle. And he's a big man, and she's — well, not tiny, but not exactly very athletic — do you really think she's capable of lifting over two hundred and fifty pounds of dead weight? And the same applies to Ms. Crocker, incidentally. Although however dubious I am of her ability to have hefted her brother-in-law's corpse into the porta-potty, the fact remains that she is not alibied for the murder and I don't discount the possibility that in the dark she could have mistaken Mr. Henson for the husband she is so eager to be rid of."

"Or maybe it wasn't a mistake," I said. "She did say Shep had collected those files she's turning over to you. What if she found out he was collecting information that might implicate her along with Biff? She could have killed him, stolen his files, taken out anything that pointed to her involvement, and then turned over the files to you to ensure that you knew Biff had a motive to kill Shep."

"It's a thought." And not one that made him happy, to judge from the look on his face. "I will keep my eyes open for any suggestion that she might be more involved in her husband's business than she admits. But in the meantime, the evidence she brought in could shed a very fascinating light on the crime."

"Yeah," I said. "First time anyone's suggested a reason for Shep to be the real target instead of just a sad victim of mistaken identity. That I know of," I added hastily. "You probably already thought of it."

"Actually, I hadn't," he said. "I've been pretty busy investigating the dozen or so people Mr. Brown has either sued or been sued by over the last several years, here or in Clay County. Some of them could well have benefited from Biff's demise. But if Shep was planning to inform on his brother — this should be interesting."

"And I'll leave you to it," I said, turning to go.

"One more thing," he said. "Is there anything you can tell me about your meeting with Mr. Brown that would help us track him down?"

"No," I said. "But I might know someone who does know something about his whereabouts — let me check."

He frowned slightly, then nodded.

"I'd appreciate knowing anything you find out."

Then he took a deep breath and walked back toward his office, carefully carrying the cup of water.

I hurried back out to my car, waving in passing to Caroline, and pulled out my cell phone. Then I called the number Caroline had given me when I wanted to check on Biff's whereabouts. The same perky young woman answered — or maybe being perky was a job requirement in Zoo Security.

"Hey, Meg — you want the location on those two tracking devices?"

Two? I'd almost forgotten the device we'd removed from Biff's car — only yesterday afternoon, though it seemed ages ago.

"Yes, please," I said aloud.

"Hang on."

As I waited, I felt around in my tote and retrieved the tracker, thinking what a shame it was that I'd been so ingenious about retrieving it. Having it still on Biff's car would have made short work of this morning's manhunt.

"Got them," the cheerful young voice said. She rattled off the locations. One was, of course, my location — nice to know the trackers were so accurate. And the other was more or less where it had been spending most of its time since Thursday night — out at Biff's scrapyard. Evidently the windbreaker had not made the cut when Biff packed for his great escape.

"Thanks," I said, as cheerfully as I could manage.

I hung up the phone and looked back at the front door of the police station, feeling a distinct sense of being let down and left out. Inside, the chief was sifting through the files Gina had brought, learning everything possible about Biff's misdeeds — including misdeeds against the baseball league I was supposed to be running. Inside, Callie had already made her hit-and-run accusation against Biff, and the chief was already trying to sort out how much of her story was true and how much was the result of her patronage of the Clay Pigeon. Even now, the chief might be getting word back from the crime lab in Richmond on whether the test bullets from Callie's gun matched the one they had taken from Shep's body. Or news that Biff had been spotted or even apprehended. For all I knew, the chief was already investigating the alibis of Samuel Yoder, Adolph Pruitt, and the rest of those dozen people who'd been in legal battles with Biff.

And here I was on the outside looking in. Of course, as a civilian this was exactly where I belonged, but that didn't make it feel any less frustrating.

As I reached to start my car, I realized my original goal in coming to town — working on the revised town square renovation project — might be entirely useless. If Biff was on the run, what were the odds he'd show up for that Tuesday morning meeting?

Of course, I could still pick up the contract and work on it at home, just in case.

Or I could avoid the creepy, deserted halls of the courthouse and go home to spend time with my family.

I pulled out my phone and sent a quick text to the county attorney about the need to revise the contract.

And then another thought hit me and I called Cousin Festus.

"You're going to hate me," I said, when we'd finished the usual greetings.

"Probably not," he said. "But why would you think so?"

"I got you all excited about buying Mr. Yoder's farm, and now it's all tangled up in a murder case — well, you knew that going in — but what if Biff killed Shep Henson because Shep was going to blow the whistle on his brother's financial crimes, and what if one of those crimes involved cheating Mr. Yoder? I mean, I don't wish Mr. Yoder ill, but I know you want the farm, and if he gets his money back from Biff —"

"It's okay," Festus said. "I already knew Biff Brown had cheated Mr. Yoder. And frankly, even if Biff hadn't come along, Mr. Yoder would have lost the farm eventually. His wife died last year after a decade of debilitating and expensive illness. Biff was just the last straw. Although Mr. Yoder's plenty angry with Biff — not just for cheating him, but also for making his wife's last days even more stressful than they had to be. To tell you the truth, Mr. Yoder's so over-the-top angry with Biff that I've been a little worried."

"That he might be the killer?" I asked.

"Not really," Festus said. "Okay, maybe a little bit, but more worried that people will start to think he's the killer even if he isn't. Because he really isn't rational on the subject of Biff."

"Do you know if he's alibied?" I asked.

"No idea. And speaking of alibis, I thought Biff had one."

"The theory is that he subcontracted out the actual murder," I said. "If he's responsible. Even if he's not the murderer, he's probably going to have some legal entanglements before too long."

"He already does." Festus chuckled slightly. "Though I gather you're referring to the criminal side of our justice system. He's already neck deep in the civil side. I did my due diligence before starting to bargain with Mr. Yoder. I not only checked him out, I checked out Biff. Pretty amazing — the man is either suing or being sued by twelve different people in Caerphilly and Clay Counties."

"Who?" I asked, getting out my notebook. I heard more clicking and key rattling — presumably Festus had done his searching electronically. And then I scribbled rapidly as Festus read out the names.

I didn't know any of the Clay County litigants, though I recognized most of the last names. Two Dingles, two Whickers, a Peebles, a Plunkett, and a Smith. Not surprising, since at least two thirds of the Clay County phone book was made up of people named Dingle, Peebles, Plunkett, or Whicker. I jotted the names down anyway. On the Caerphilly side, Will Entwhistle was on the list, along with the Fluglemans, who owned the feed and garden store, one of Randall's Shiffley cousins, and two Pruitts, Adolph and Herbert.

"That's twelve," I said. "But you left out Mr. Yoder."

"He can't afford to sue Biff," Festus said. "I'd take on the case myself if I thought there was any point to it, but I have a feeling my fellow attorneys are the only ones who'll make any money out of suing Biff."

"So what is Adolph Pruitt suing Biff about?"

I heard more clicking and keyboard rattling.

"Adolph claims Biff owes him three thousand dollars in return for personal services."

"What kind of personal services?"

"Doesn't say. Though I have heard rumors that Mr. Pruitt assists Biff in his cash flow management."

"Are we talking about the same Adolph Pruitt here?" I asked. "I'm not sure the one I've met could count to eleven without taking his shoes off."

"Cash flow management was actually my diplomatic way of saying that Biff used to send Adolph to encourage reluctant debtors to settle their accounts."

"Adolph's his enforcer?" I said. "Do we know if Adolph's alibied for the time of Shep's murder?"

"We do not, but the odds are the chief has already thought of that," Festus said. "Although I'm sure if Adolph was responsible for Shep's death he has already arranged for a suitable alibi. An alibi the chief will know to be fiction, but which will need to be disproved by solid forensic evidence. Let's hope our cousin Horace can save the day. Look, don't worry about me and the farm. I'm very well qualified to navigate whatever tangled legal waters may be involved. But you — take care of yourself. Don't go around accusing any of those litigants of killing Shep. They're not all nice people."

With that we said our good-byes and hung up. I headed home — a good thing I could do the drive on autopilot, because my brain was still turning over what I'd learned from Festus and at the police station.

I got home just as Mother was organizing the family to go with her to Trinity Episcopal for the eleven o'clock service. Hard to believe it wasn't even eleven yet — it already felt as if I'd put in a full day's work. In the interest of setting a good example, I decided to go along with the rest of the family and postpone my much-needed nap until afternoon.

No doubt the Reverend Robyn appreciated having a somewhat larger congregation than she would have had if baseball had been in session. The boys seemed a great deal more attentive than I would have expected them to be, though about halfway through the proceedings I figured out that they were less interested in the service than in an intense discussion of whether the sanctuary was large enough to play baseball in.

Damn the weather, anyway. I could already tell that, deprived of the opportunity to pursue their new obsession with baseball, the boys would be cranky and bored. For that matter, Michael wasn't quite his usual self.

Inspiration struck. Risking the stern and withering stare Robyn would give me if she caught me using my cell phone during church, I quickly sent out an e-mail to the Eagle families, inviting all the players to an impromptu batting practice in our barn.

"What a great idea!" Michael exclaimed when I told him about it. "Even if no one else comes, Cordelia and I can work with Josh and Jamie."

But to everyone's delight, all twelve of the Eagles showed up. Chuck and Tory Davis arrived with a carload, and the rest were dropped off by parents who were delighted to find something to amuse their kids on a rainy afternoon.

Which eventually became merely a cloudy afternoon, thank goodness, meaning that we'd have at least a fighting chance of playing baseball in the morning.

At around six, we fed the assembled Eagles with leftovers from the various picnics. Then Chuck and Tory and I divided the ten nonresident players between their SUV and the Twinmobile and set off to take them home. It was dusk by the time I dropped off the last player, Sami Patel, made sure he had his bag, and set out for home.

As I was helping Sami with his baseball bag, I noted a litter of unfamiliar objects left behind. Miguel's glove. Jake's left shoe. Someone's left batting glove.

If I were a better person, I'd deliver the stray items. Or at least the shoe.

But I was tired. When I got home, I could send out a group e-mail with an inventory of stray items I'd be bringing to the game tomorrow.

As I was heading out of town, I noticed a familiar car approaching from the direction of our house. It was Caroline. Then she took a left turn, onto the Clay Swamp Road.

Odd. What reason could Caroline possibly have for taking the Clay Swamp Road? Especially at this time of night. Most people who wanted to get to Clayville took the Clayville Road, which at least had the virtue of being more or less direct and containing about as much pavement as pothole.

About the only thing of interest on the Clay Swamp Road was the Brown Construction Company scrapyard.

I turned to follow.

CHAPTER 26

I followed Caroline as she passed the last few houses on the edge of town. She was definitely heading to Biff's. Considering how spooky the place was in the daylight, I didn't much like the idea of anyone going there at this time of night. I pulled out my cell phone and called her.

No answer.

And she was going pretty fast. Not a smart thing to do. Between the vast number of deer that lived in the surrounding woods and the vast number of deputies scouring the roads for Biff, following the speed limit seemed advisable. So I did. I soon lost sight of Caroline. But I wasn't too worried. If she was going where I thought she was going, I could still catch up with her before she got into too much trouble.

Sure enough, when I came to the end of the long, scantly graveled road through the swamp and pulled into the junk-infested clearing in front of Biff's front gates, I heard frenzied barking and saw Caroline's car parked by the fence. Caroline herself was dangling near the top of the fence, gazing at two dogs who appeared to be trying to hurl themselves over the fence at her.

I stopped my car a little way short of the gate and rolled down my window.

"Evening," I said.

"Don't just stand there," she said. "Get me down from here."

"And how were you planning to get down if I hadn't showed up?"

"I wasn't planning on getting stuck. Hurry!"

I carefully maneuvered my car until it was jammed up against the fence directly below Caroline. Not that I couldn't have climbed the fence under ordinary circumstances, but I didn't much like my odds of losing a few fingers or toes to the frenzied watchdogs. From the car's roof I was able to climb up at a level past where the dogs could easily reach. I untangled Caroline's sweater from a broken end of one of the chain links and then lowered her to the roof of my car. Then I jumped down myself and helped her from the car roof to the ground.

She stood a few feet from the fence while I moved the car to a safe distance.

"What a dump," she exclaimed, when I strolled back to join her.

"Bette Davis," I said. "In both *Beyond the Forest* and *Dead Ringer.*"

"I'm serious," she said. "How are we ever going to find that tracking device in this dump?"

"If I'd known you were planning on burgling Biff's business for the tracking device, I'd have told you what a bad idea it was."

"Just getting in there's going to be murder."

"More like suicide," I said. "I don't like the look of those dogs."

"Now, now," she said. "Just because they seem to have some pit bull in their ancestry, that doesn't mean they're vicious."

"I don't care what their ancestry is," I said. "I'm talking about their behavior. I wouldn't climb into a yard with a cocker spaniel who was acting like that."

Just to demonstrate, I reached out and rattled the fence a little, pulling my hand back quickly as both dogs hurled themselves at the spot where my fingers had been.

"So how did you get in there before?"

"I didn't," I said. "I looked at the outside and realized it was pretty foolish to try. And that was before seeing the dogs in action."

"Some detective you are."

"What's so all-fired urgent all of a sudden about getting the tracking device back?" I asked.

"I figured it wasn't important when all it did was confirm his alibi for Shep's murder," Caroline said. "But when I heard about the hit-and-run I got them to run the data from the tracker for that time period. He was there."

"At the scene of Callie's accident?"

"Yes," Caroline said. "I went out there with another tracking device to be sure. He stopped right where her accident was — some accident! — stayed twenty minutes, then came back here. We need to get that device."

"What we need to do is tell the chief about the device," I said. "If we go in and find it, we might just destroy any value it has as evidence. It would be our word against his that he ever had it. Make the call. Get Festus involved."

She continued staring at Biff's ramshackle building for what seemed like a couple of hours. Finally she sighed and looked down at her shoes.

"Fine," she said. "I'll call Festus when I get home."

"Let's call him now."

She grimaced, but she didn't protest when I took out my phone, dialed Festus, and put it on speaker.

"Meg?" Festus answered. "Something wrong?"

"Caroline Willner's ready to tell the chief about the tracking devices she planted on Biff," I said. "Can you arrange to have that happen as soon as possible?"

"I'll make the call now," he said. "Have her plan to meet me at the police station at eight a.m. tomorrow. If the chief wants to talk tonight, I'll call her."

"That work for you?" I said to Caroline.

She rolled her eyes and nodded.

"Meg?" Festus sounded impatient.

"She's nodding," I said. "She'll be there."

And so would I, to make sure she didn't weasel out. I wished Festus a good night and signed off. Caroline was still scowling at Biff's fence.

"Go home and get some rest," I said.

She didn't answer.

"Or if you're not in the mood to sleep, talk to the zoo security people and have them start gathering up all the data on where Biff's been over the last few days."

"Might as well," she said. "No sense standing around here all night." She stomped back to her car, got in, and took off, going way too fast for the rugged, pot-holed road.

I took a long look around. The place was even creepier by night. I couldn't get over the notion that eyes were watching me. Eyes other than the dogs'. I went back to my car and got in, calmly and deliberately, so at least any hidden human eyes wouldn't know how spooked I was.

And I breathed a sigh of relief when I got back to the Clay Swamp Road.

I was almost back at the main road to our house when Michael called.

"Are you still delivering Eagles?" he asked.

"I finished that about half an hour ago," I said. "I stopped to help Caroline with something. Fill you in when I get there."

"See you soon then."

"Soon," I echoed. "I just have one more stop on the way."

"Be careful," he said. "They're still look-ing for Biff."

"I will be."

I didn't tell Michael where my planned stop was because I was afraid he'd try to talk me out of dropping by the ball field, even though I had no intention of getting out of the car unless there was someone else nearby. Someone trustworthy. And prefer-ably several trustworthy someones. I wasn't that keen myself on visiting the field, but as the new acting league president, I needed to know how close it was to being ready for tomorrow morning's games. And however much we might associate the ball field with Biff, given all the activity that had been going on there this afternoon and evening, wasn't it really the last place in the county he'd be? Odds were he was miles away by now. So however creeped out I was at going to the ball field by night, I wanted to get over the feeling. It wasn't Biff's field, dammit — it was *our* field. Our field, for which I was responsible. Was I going to let Biff stand between me and my responsibility?

Chill, I told myself. The Shiffleys were probably still there in force. If they weren't, I could fulfill my responsibilities from the safety of my car.

And as I approached the field, it looked as if I'd be staying in the car. I should have seen the glow of the big work lights about the time I turned off the main road, but the skies were inky black. I pulled into the freshly graveled lot and parked right behind home plate, where I could look out over the field.

The completely and utterly dark field. With my headlights on, I couldn't see a thing for the glare reflected back by the fog and mists, and with the headlights out it was like sticking a pillowcase over my head.

"Damn Biff, anyway," I muttered. At any other time I wouldn't have felt the least bit nervous about getting out of my car to inspect the field. But until they caught Biff . . . No.

Maybe if I let my eyes adjust for a minute or two I could see something from here. I fished under the seat, pulled out my binoculars, and trained them on the field. They didn't help much. Instead of utter darkness I saw a few blurry, utterly dark shapes against the almost-as-dark background.

"I give up," I muttered.

I pulled out my cell phone and called Randall.

"There's no one here at the field," I said. "Is everything ready for tomorrow?"

"As ready as we can get it," Randall said. "We've gone over the whole field with wet/dry vacs and used a ton of that infield drying compound. Now we just need to keep our fingers crossed that we don't get any more rain. The boys and I will be going out there in the morning to run the wet/dry vacs again and pile on more drying compound if it's needed, but I don't think there's anything more we can do tonight. How does it look to you?"

"It looks dark," I said. "I could probably figure out how to turn on those portable lights to get a better look, but that would require getting out of the car and wandering around by myself in the dark. And quite apart from the fact that we've had enough rain to turn any really low-lying places into quicksand, there's still a murderer on the loose."

"A murderer who's looking a whole lot more like Biff every minute," Randall said. "Because even if he hired someone to do the actual deed, which sounds more and more plausible, that still makes him a murderer. Did you hear that after reading those files Mrs. Brown brought in the chief put out a statewide BOLO on Biff?"

"Then if they haven't found him by now it probably means Biff's long gone from here," I said. "But just in case he isn't, instead of stumbling around a pitch-black baseball field at well past midnight I'm going to go home to get some sleep."

"Probably wise," Randall said. "Even if Biff's long gone, the chief's still keeping an eye on the seventy jillion people who had it in for Biff and might have offed Shep by mistake. They're all still in town. Don't worry about the field. It'll be as perfect as we can make it. I'll be there at five in the morning to make sure of that."

"A whole five hours from now," I said.

"My apologies for waking you."

"Wasn't sleeping anyway," he said. "Been lying in bed listening to the police band radio, hoping to hear that they've caught Biff. Unfortunately it's been a quiet night. See you in the a.m."

"Later in the a.m.," I added, and we both chuckled before signing off.

I put away my binoculars and started the car. But as I was backing out of my parking space my headlights fell on something — the Brown porta-potty, standing in solitary splendor at the far end of the field, a location that would have been massively inconvenient if anyone had actually wanted to use it. And the words *Brown stinks!* were still scrawled across the door, in slightly luminescent paint. If I were Biff, I would certainly have cleaned that off before hauling the new porta-potty over. And —

Wait a minute. The porta-potty with *Brown stinks!* scrawled on it was the one that had been here at practice Thursday night. And so it should have been the one in which I found Shep's body Friday morning — the one that was now gracing the locked lot at the police station. Unless someone had defaced more than one of Biff's porta-

411

potties in an identical fashion.

I drove over as close as I could to the porta-potty and turned the car off, leaving the headlights on and pointed at the porta-potty. I pulled out my phone, turned it on, and began flipping through the photos I'd taken Thursday night and Friday morning. Surely some of them would show the porta-potty, if only in the background. Then again, I'd probably been doing my best to take my shots against pretty backgrounds, like the woods that surrounded the field. Aha! Here was one from Thursday evening of Josh, Jamie, and Adam with their arms around each other — and the porta-potty in the background. I used the phone's zoom feature and confirmed that the words *Brown stinks!* were clearly visible on the side. But what about Friday morning? I flipped on through my photos. Of course, Horace would have taken dozens of photos of the porta-potty from every conceivable angle, so what I really should do was let the chief know about this. But it would be nice to have confirmation that I wasn't imagining things — after all, it was possible that someone with a grudge against Biff went around scrawling graffiti on all his porta-potties, and maybe even his trucks and trac-tors to boot. Although I didn't remember seeing any similar graffiti at his scrapyard. And it was hard to imagine that the unknown graffiti artist always made that little extra line at the top of the second *S,* as if he'd started out to write "stinkz" and then changed his mind and opted for the more conventional spelling. And — aha! My picture of Dad and Horace squatting in front of the porta-potty door with grave expressions on their faces. Enough of the porta-potty's side was visible to show that it was bare of graffiti.

"Someone swapped the porta-potties," I muttered. "And I bet that someone is Biff." I knew from Caroline's tracking devices that after leaving our house Thursday night he'd made a brief visit to the ball field and then gone back to his scrapyard and, supposedly, stayed there all night — which made sense if he was currently living in a room there. Vern and Aida had seen way too much of him between ten and two for him to have been over at the ball field killing someone.

But what if the murder hadn't happened at the field — but at the scrapyard? What if Biff had run into Shep there and had an argument. Perhaps he'd caught Shep in the act of copying incriminating documents like the ones Gina had delivered to the chief.

"What if he killed Shep, stuffed him in

the porta-potty, and called nine-one-one to give himself an alibi." I said it aloud to see if it sounded completely ridiculous. It didn't. It sounded like the kind of brazen thing Biff would try to get away with. He'd have to hide the blood somehow — according to Dad there would be a lot of it. But given how huge and cluttered the scrapyard was, there were plenty of things he could put over it, and Aida and Vern would be looking for a live intruder, not a crime scene. Always a risk that they'd find the body while looking for the supposed intruder, but he'd be sticking to them like glue, making sure of his alibi, so in the unlikely event one of them was about to check inside the fateful porta-potty, he could find a way to warn them off or distract them.

And at some point he'd come up with the idea of swapping the porta-potties. A crazy idea, because if anyone spotted him rattling along the back roads of the county at three or four in the morning in a truck with a porta-potty on the back, the odds were they'd remember it the next day when his own half brother's body was found in a porta-potty. But he'd gambled, and it had worked. And the tracking device in his car had stayed put because he'd hauled the porta-potty in his truck — along with Shep's Harley, no doubt, the one that had been found abandoned in the woods near the field. And he'd probably shed the jacket with the other tracking device in the pocket before tackling the strenuous job of loading and unloading the porta-potty singlehandedly.

After all, it was a *porta*-potty. How had we all forgotten that?

Maybe the chief hadn't. Maybe he'd already figured all this out and was playing it close to the vest. Maybe that was the reason he was so convinced that Biff was involved in the murder. But just in case . . .

I dialed the chief's number. And got his voice mail. I wasn't keen on trying to explain this whole thing to the official police answering service. I always imagined that it was waiting impatiently for me to leave a succinct, businesslike message. "Just the facts, ma'am."

"Hi," I said. "It's Meg. I just stumbled over something that might be an important clue to the murder. Give me a call, no matter how late." And I rattled off my cell phone number just in case he was collecting his messages on a phone that didn't already have a few dozen messages from me in its call history.

I sat there for a few moments, hoping he'd call right back. And then told myself it was stupid.

"A watched kettle never boils," I remarked to nobody in particular. "And a watched porta-potty . . ." Invention failed me. "Anyway, I will wait for the chief's call at home. I have already spent enough of my evening staring at a glorified outhouse."

I started the car and backed out of my parking spot in front of the porta-potty. But as I was turning around to head for the road, my headlights revealed another vehicle that I hadn't seen when I'd first driven in, because it was parked at the far end of the parking lot, near the three Shiffley Construction porta-potties. A big pickup. My headlights bleached the color out of things, so maybe it was only my imagination that it was a bright red pickup. A pickup, at any rate, and one with visible damage to the left front side.

The driver's door was open and there was something falling out of it. Something that looked like a body.

My first instinct was to slam on the brakes, leap out of the car, and run over to see what was the matter. I suppressed the impulse. Instead, I clicked the button to make sure my doors were locked, got my cell phone out so I'd be able to call 911 if the situation warranted, and drove over toward the truck.

Yes, it was Callie's truck. As I got closer, I could see the the glitter-covered CALLIE logo on her door sparkling in the beam of my headlights. And I was pretty sure it was Callie hanging head-down out of the truck door, her long, slightly luminescent mane almost touching the ground.

I dialed 911, and while it was ringing, I parked my car about ten feet from Callie's truck, with the headlights aimed at her, and hopped out, phone in hand, to check on her.

She was still warm and yes, she had a pulse. The reason she hadn't fallen all the way to the ground was that her neck had caught in the V made by the lap and shoulder straps of her unfastened seat belt. I couldn't spot any injuries. But she reeked of alcohol. And from the way the seat belt was cutting into her neck, I was concerned that it might be interfering with her breathing. Probably a good idea to untangle her and ease her to the ground before it strangled her, but I didn't think I could do it with one hand still holding my cell phone. And speaking of the cell phone, what was taking Debbie Ann so long to answer? I lifted the cell phone and saw that it was still searching for a signal. Damned rainstorm! But then a couple of signal bars appeared. I looked back at Callie, knowing that at any second I would hear Debbie Ann's voice apologizing for the wait and asking me what was wrong, and —

Someone grabbed at my cell phone and, at the same time, hit me hard in the back. I didn't fall down but I stumbled, lost my grip on the cell phone, and had to scramble to avoid whacking Callie's dangling head.

When I turned around to see who had attacked me, I found myself staring down the barrel of the gun Biff Brown was holding.

CHAPTER 27

"Sorry, but I can't let you report seeing me," Biff said.

"I wasn't going to report seeing you," I said. "Because until you jumped me, I didn't even know you were here. I was going to report finding Callie either dead or unconscious here in the parking lot. Why don't you go away, and I'll get back to doing that?"

"And blame me for killing her? Then sorry, that won't work, because she's not dead. Just dead drunk. Get over there and drag her out of the truck."

He jerked his head in the direction of Callie, but kept his eyes — and the gun — on me.

"Why?" I inched a little closer to Callie, still keeping my eyes on him.

"Just do it," he said.

"I'm doing it." I had reached Callie, and put my fingers on her wrist. Her pulse was steady. "But why am I doing it? If you want me to drag her out of the front seat, throw her in the back of the truck, and drive her to the hospital, just say the word."

"I want you to drag her out of the front seat so I can use her truck to make my getaway," Biff said. "I'm pretty sure they've put out a lookout for my car, but her truck should be okay. Drag her out. If you're so worried about her comfort, you can put her in your own backseat."

He circled warily closer to my car, reached around to push the button that would unlock the backseat, and opened the door. He also grabbed my keys from the ignition before backing away a safe distance from me. I carefully untangled Callie from the seat belt's stranglehold and managed to hoist her over my shoulders in my best approximation of a fireman's carry. As I was staggering over to my car with her I realized that the boys' car seats were going to make putting her in my backseat a little difficult.

"I don't suppose you could move my car seats while you're at it?" I asked. "If I have to put her down on the ground, I might not be able to lift her again."

"Then she can lie on the ground for a while," Biff said. "Won't be the first time. It's a warm night — neither of you will freeze by morning."

I decided not to push it. Biff might be rude and self-centered as usual, but he also seemed calm and focused on his getaway. And that bit about not freezing by morning was reassuring. Either he was doing a masterful job of covering up his homicidal intentions or he genuinely didn't have any. Not that I was going to drop my guard. I had always found "hope for the best, expect the worst" a very sensible motto.

I draped Callie across the trunk. I reached in to unfasten the car seats and moved them to the front seat. Then I heaved Callie up again and deposited her in the backseat. I couldn't exactly say I was gentle — the angle was awkward, and Callie was no lightweight. But I managed to avoid banging her head on anything hard.

"You got any rope in your trunk?" Biff asked.

"Rope?" I echoed.

"Rope, or duct tape. Something to keep the two of you from siccing the cops on me two seconds after I drive off."

"Sorry," I said. "Hostage taking wasn't on my agenda today. We're out in the middle of nowhere — why not just take my keys and leave us here?"

"Because I happen to know you live out

here in the middle of nowhere," he said. "What is it — four, maybe five miles down the road?"

Actually, more like two, and I wouldn't even have to walk that far if he left me untied — not unless he found and confiscated both the spare car key I kept hidden in my purse and the one in the magnetic case sticking to the car's frame. So if I could just convince him not to tie us up, I could get help — and sic the police on him — fairly quickly.

Then again, maybe I should just concentrate on staying alive. If Biff took Callie's truck, he'd be pretty easy to track once the chief put out a BOLO for a red Ford Lariat with visible front end damage and the name Callie painted in glitter on the driver's side door. Maybe I should help him take off before it occurred to him that my blue Toyota was far less conspicuous.

"Search Callie's truck," he ordered. "Maybe she has some rope."

"So why are you running?" I asked as I headed for the truck. "Are you still afraid they'll suspect you of the murder?"

"No, I'm alibied on that, you know." Biff sounded smug. "I was there at my scrapyard from nine p.m. until two a.m. I've got two deputies who can swear to that."

Maybe it would have been wiser to keep my mouth shut, but that smug tone irked me.

"Yeah, you were there at the scrapyard," I said. "And so was the porta-potty you hid the body in. I'll hand it to you, it was quick thinking. You stuffed the body in the porta-potty and then called nine-one-one."

He was shaking his head.

"Quick thinking and nerve," I went on. "And it also took nerve for you to haul the porta-potty with Shep's body over to the field sometime between when Vern and Aida left and dawn. You almost pulled it off. But sooner or later Chief Burke will realize that it doesn't really take three or four workmen to shove a porta-potty onto and off that truck with the little elevator in the back and he'll come looking for you."

Biff had seemed to deflate as I was speaking.

"Yeah, I moved the body," Biff said. "You're right about that. But I didn't kill him. I can see by your face you don't believe me, but it's the truth. I've threatened to a time or two — only in the heat of an argument — and if I'd known he was planning to turn over a whole bunch of incriminating documents to the cops, maybe I'd have lost my temper and made good on those threats.

But you have to believe me, I didn't kill him."

"Then what happened?"

He scowled, and I was fully expecting him to say "what the hell do you care?" But then his face changed, and he seemed to be making an effort to speak calmly and civilly.

"I was in a rotten mood when I came home after finding your team having an illegal practice. Illegal by my rules," he added, forestalling my protest. "See how you feel when you make some new rules and people break them. I got back to my scrapyard, and I was about to go to bed when I heard Shep and Callie going at it, hammer and tongs."

"Do you mean arguing, or was there a physical struggle?"

"Just arguing as far as I could tell, but it always starts that way, and usually he whacks her or she whacks him, and then they start throwing stuff around, and I didn't want them breaking stuff in my office. Or worse, sometimes after they've trashed a joint they get it out of their system and start making up, just as loud. I damn sure didn't want to hear *that* going on outside when I was trying to get some sleep the night before Opening Day. So I went out and yelled at them to shut up and told

Callie to beat it. And I thought she did. I told Shep to close up and go home, and as far as I knew he was doing that. And then a little while after I got in bed, I heard more yelling, and then a couple of shots. I thought Callie had come back and was firing off that damned peashooter of hers again, so I called nine-one-one to report a disturbance and went out to tell Shep and Callie that the cops were on the way. I found Shep lying just inside the back gate with his brains blown out, and Callie was nowhere to be seen."

"Why not just tell the cops that?" I asked.

"Didn't figure they'd believe me," he said. "So I shoved Shep's body into a porta-potty and then I scattered a whole bag full of infield drying agent over the blood, to hide it and soak it up. Got that done just before the Caerphilly County deputies arrived at the front gate. And except for the part about finding the body and hiding it, I told the cops exactly what happened — even though I knew it might get Callie in trouble. Although I figured she was less apt to get in trouble if they found the body someplace else. Somewhere she didn't have much reason to go. Like the baseball field."

"And that mattered to you?" I asked. "Not getting Callie in trouble?"

"I don't know." He shrugged. "I guess. I wasn't thinking real straight. Shep was no angel. She put up with a lot from him. Plus I kind of already figured she was doing me a favor, in a way. Shep had been hinting that he knew some stuff I might not want the cops to know, stuff he could keep under his hat if I made it worth his while."

"He was blackmailing you."

"No, I wouldn't call it blackmail." Biff shook his head firmly. "Not really. Just trying to get a leg up in that old sibling rivalry, you know?"

He was smiling, but he wasn't selling it very well. Sibling rivalry or blackmail — no matter what you called it, I had a hard time imagining Biff sitting still for it.

"So Callie killed Shep and did you a favor by doing so," I said. "And all you did was hide the body in a place that would make it less likely that either you or she would be suspected of the murder."

"You got it," he said.

"And that machete that almost decapitated Mrs. Patel. You rigged that, didn't you?"

"I didn't mean for anyone to get hurt," he protested. "But I figured the chief would be less likely to try to blame me if I could convince him I was the target. I'm always the one who unlocks the Snack Shack, so everyone would assume it was meant to kill me. I figured I could pretend to spot it before I walked in, and then the chief would have more proof that someone was after me. How was I supposed to know that damned midget would duck under my arm and try to get herself killed?"

"So why are you telling me all this?" I asked. Always possible that he was in the throes of an irresistible urge to brag about what he'd done and figured telling me was harmless because he planned to kill me in a few minutes. In the mysteries Dad was so fond of reading, murderers seemed particularly fond of doing this, even though any sensible person would figure out that the longer you hang around bragging about your crimes, the greater the odds that your intended next victim will manage to escape and tattle on you to law enforcement. And while I wouldn't exactly call Biff sensible — even sane might be a stretch — there was something curiously nonthreatening about his manner.

"I want you to tell my kids," he said.

"Can't you just tell them yourself?" I asked.

"No." He shook his head, and his expression was sad. "Won't be around. The cops have it in for me. They'll probably think I helped Callie do it, or put her up to it, or maybe did it myself after she left. I could stay around and fight it, but what for? You've taken away my league. Randall's going to take away my business. My wife's poisoning my kids' minds against me. What have I got to stick around for?"

"So I should tell your kids you didn't kill their uncle Shep?"

"Yeah, pretty much." He looked a little sheepish, and his gun drooped slightly. "If you can, try not to tell them that their auntie Callie killed their uncle Shep."

"You jerk!"

Biff and I both jumped and whirled around to see Callie staggering to her feet behind us. Her upswept hairdo had completely fallen down in glittering Medusa-like coils and she was standing lopsidedly because one of her six-inch spike heels had broken off, but she was upright, and lurching our way.

Make that lurching Biff's way. I started slowly edging farther away from him.

"You lying sack of — how dare you accuse me of killing my own husband." Even before she got within range, Callie had started flailing at him with the leopard-print purse.

428

"Ex-husband." Biff was pointing the gun at her now instead of me, but he was also holding up a hand as if to ward her off. "And I didn't say I blamed you."

"You just did blame me," she said. "After you kicked me out I went down to the Clay Pigeon. I was there most of the night. Ask anyone who was there; they all saw me."

"And I bet a lot of them saw two of you," Biff said.

"Liar!" Callie was starting to land blows with the purse. "And where the hell do you get off running me off the road last night?"

"I didn't run you off the road — I was on my way home when I spotted your car lying in a ditch."

"Then why didn't you do something you son of a —"

"I came over to see if you were okay," Biff bellowed. "And I offered you a ride, and you just threw that damned leopard-skin suitcase at me and passed out. So I left you there to sleep it off."

"Why you —" Callie was scrambling in her purse. Remembering her in action at the police station, I ducked behind her truck — neither of them was really paying much attention to me at the moment.

"Don't do anything stupid," Biff said.

"They took my gun!" Callie shrieked, and

429

began flailing at Biff again with the purse, as if her weaponless plight was entirely his fault.

"Stop that!" Biff snarled. "I'm warning you." He sounded fierce, but he was backing away from her, covering his head with his left hand and holding the gun, pointed at the sky, in his right. I began to think maybe I'd misjudged Biff. Not the part about him being a jerk and a blowhard, but the picture that had built up in my mind of Biff the homicidal maniac, callously blowing his own brother's brains out and dumping him in a porta-potty. But if not Biff, who?

Of course, he still was a suspect. They both were. So while they were going at it hammer and tongs, to borrow Biff's description of Callie's fights with her late husband, surely I could manage to slip into the woods. I was only a few miles from home, and I knew these woods — well, not exactly like the back of my hand. Still, I'd spent a fair amount of time hiking in the area, accompanying Dad and Grandfather on nature walks and bird counts, helping Rose Noire with herb harvests, or journeying with the boys through The Forbidden Forest, Jurassic Park, Neverland, Lothlórien, Oz, and the Hundred Acre Wood. Maybe I couldn't find my way unerringly home, but I had a reasonable amount of confidence that I wouldn't run into anything really dangerous there, and would eventually stumble across a familiar location.

I stepped back until I was beside my car, and then crouched behind it — out of the two cones of light from my headlights in which Biff and Callie were circling. I was about to slip quietly back toward the tree line when I felt something hard pressing against the base of my skull.

"Don't move," a voice whispered in my ear.

Something about that voice chilled me in a way that Biff's and Callie's noisy antics never could.

"Stand up," the voice whispered.

I followed orders, with my brain working frantically, trying to figure out who had the gun on me.

"Hands up. Move."

Judging from where his voice was coming from, and the fact that the gun tilted slightly down from my neck, he was at least an inch or two shorter than me.

I stepped forward, moving carefully, because the only light came from my car headlights.

"Keep going," the voice said — still softly,

but no longer whispering.

And now I could tell that it wasn't a he. She poked me in the back again with her gun and I stumbled forward. And I was almost sure I knew who she was — Ms. Nondescript. Ideen's migraine-ridden guest. Edna something.

Just then Biff spotted us.

"Edna?" He sounded puzzled. "What are you doing here? And why are you holding that . . ." His voice trailed off, as if saying the word "gun" might cause the weapon to fire all by itself.

"Drop the gun," Edna said. "Or she gets it."

"I wish you could find some other way to threaten him," I said. "Considering how Biff feels about me, that might be a risk he could live with."

"I'm not a killer," Biff said. "Whatever you might think. I might be a lot of things, but not a killer." He threw the gun down. Threw it at Callie's feet, actually — was he hoping she could get away with grabbing it and using it? And yeah, Callie probably was brave enough or crazy enough to do it, but unfortunately she was now staring openmouthed at Edna, oblivious to the weapon at her feet.

"Edna?" Callie sounded surprised. "What are you doing here?"

"Finishing what I started," she said.

"You killed Shep?" Biff sounded surprised.

"See!" Callie said. "I told you it wasn't me."

"You mistook Shep for Biff in the dark," I said. "But why were you trying to kill Biff?"

"He ruined my son's arm," Edna said.

"You can't blame me for —" Biff began.

"Yes I can," Edna said. "My Billy was a pitcher — a good one. But now he needs Tommy John surgery. You know what that is?"

"Ulnar collateral ligament reconstruction," I said. "Dozens of baseball players have had it — mostly pitchers. My father's a doctor," I explained, seeing the surprised looks on Biff's and Callie's faces.

"It happens sometimes," Biff said. "Not anyone's fault."

"It happened because you overpitched him," Edna said. "I was a single mom. What did I know about baseball? When Bobby complained that his arm hurt, Biff said it was normal. No pain, no gain. When I found out about the league's pitch count rules, he told me those were recommendations, not rules, and there wasn't any problem for a pitcher as strong as Bobby. He was always on the All-Star team for his age. Every single year. We stayed on here in Caerphilly for six months even after those nasty Pruitts fired me, so he could finish out his last season in the league. I managed to get enough part-time work to keep us afloat. And we thought it was worth it — they came in second in the district playoffs. Then I got a new job and we had to move. We were really sad to leave all our friends on the team behind, but Caerphilly didn't have a league for thirteen-year-olds, just school teams, and his new middle school in Richmond had a great team, and of course I couldn't find a job here. But the first day of tryouts at his school the coach said don't bring him back till you've seen an orthopedist. That's when we found out how bad it was. Thirteen years old and his arm was ruined."

"The Tommy John surgery didn't help?" I asked.

"It might, when he can have it," she said. "We can't go ahead with it until I scrape together enough to cover the gap between what it costs and what my stupid insurance company will pay. I've only just finished paying off the orthopedist. Meanwhile, do you have any idea what happens to a kid who loves sports when you take that away from him? He doesn't study. He's starting to get in trouble. He was such a good kid."

The hand holding the gun was shaking, and her voice sounded as if she was choking back tears.

"Have you tried taking legal action?" I asked.

"Won't work," she said. "I tried. According to the official records Biff turned over to the league, Bobby didn't pitch all those innings. According to them, he never pitched more than the pitch limits."

"Our records are accurate," Biff said. "Ask the scorekeepers."

"What's the use?" Edna said. "They'd only lie for you again. Shep and all those miserable Pruitts."

"I believe you," I said. I did, actually; it wasn't just a ploy to get her to point the gun at Biff instead of me. "And I know a lawyer who'd be glad to take on your case. Even if he can't prove what Biff did, he can threaten to make such a stink that the league will be happy to pay for Billy's surgery to avoid the bad publicity."

I meant it. It was the sort of thing Festus would love. But maybe Edna was past believing in the system.

"Move over there," Edna said, giving me a hard shove toward Biff and Callie. I stumbled slightly but managed to keep from falling in the mud. Edna backed away until she was about twenty feet from us, then stopped. No doubt she thought she was far enough away that she'd have time to shoot us all if we tried to join forces and rush her. I had to agree with her, and even if she was wrong about the distance, I didn't see much chance of the joining forces part.

"I can't believe it," Biff said. "You killed my brother!"

"My husband!" Callie exclaimed.

"Ex-husband," Biff corrected.

"Yeah, well, half brother," Callie countered.

"If you —"

"Shut up, both of you," Edna said. "I didn't mean to kill Shep, but I'm not sorry I did. He could have done something to help me, but he didn't. And Callie, you could have helped, and you didn't."

She was shaking her head as if to deny some protest Biff and Callie were making. They just stood there, staring at her for a few moments. Then Callie spoke up.

"Meg hasn't done anything wrong," she shouted, ducking behind me as she spoke.

"Yeah," Biff said. "You can't just shoot her."

He ducked behind me as well.

I could hear a car in the distance. It seemed to be coming closer. One of the deputies, perhaps? I needed to keep stalling Edna.

"Look, I know you were wronged," I said. "But this isn't the way to handle it. What's more important to you — revenge? Or getting your son the medical help he needs. Besides —"

Just then a car going at least sixty miles an hour careened into the parking lot and braked to a halt, sending up a spray of gravel on either side. Its arrival startled Edna, who whirled to take a quick look at it. Seeing that, Callie and Biff both broke in opposite directions. I hit the mud and started rolling.

"No!" Edna shrieked. Several shots rang out. I heard the car start up again, and then brake again. I scrambled to my feet just in time to see Cordelia hop out of the car's passenger side brandishing a baseball bat.

"Be careful!" I shouted, as I took off running toward Cordelia.

"Stop or I'll shoot!" Edna was screaming. She was pointing the gun in Biff's direction, but he was making surprisingly good speed for someone of his age and size, and she was finding it hard to get him in her sights.

Then Cordelia swung her bat at Edna's gun hand and connected with a solid thud. Edna shrieked and dropped the gun. Caroline scrambled out of the driver's seat of her car, felled Edna with a flying tackle, and sat on her while Cordelia stooped to pick up the gun.

By the time I reached them it was all over.

"Here you go, Meg." Cordelia handed me Edna's gun.

"Maybe you should chase after those other two," Caroline suggested, waving in the general direction of where Biff and Callie had disappeared.

"I think we should let the police handle that," I said. "Let me call them."

"I already did on the way here," Cordelia said. "In fact — shhh!"

We all fell silent — well, except for Edna, who was sobbing quietly. And yes, I could hear a siren in the distance. Several sirens.

"I hope this doesn't mean the field's going to be a crime scene again," Cordelia said after a few moments. "I was looking forward to seeing some baseball tomorrow."

CHAPTER 28

"What a beautiful morning for a ball game!" Cordelia exclaimed as we got out of the car.

"A whole day of ball games!" Caroline added.

The operative word was morning. I tried not to resent how energetic they were. Of course, the chief hadn't kept them up nearly as late answering questions. And I did probably owe them my life. Still. Morning.

"There you are." Rob came running up to my car, but it seemed to be Cordelia he was talking to. "So far nobody's explained to me how you guys managed to show up at the ball field last night just when the bad guys got the drop on Meg."

"It was those tracking devices Caroline used on Biff," Cordelia explained.

"I thought Meg had gotten those back," Rob said.

"Only one of them," Caroline said. "The one on his car. And she was carrying it around in case she needed to show it to anyone who might be able to help us get the other one back — the one I dropped in his jacket pocket. Then when I heard the news that someone had run Biff's ex-wife off the road, I checked the data from the bug in his jacket, and that put him right there at the scene of the hit-and-run. So I called Festus and made arrangements to meet him at the courthouse this morning to turn myself in for the illegal bugging. But in the meantime, I told the zoo security desk to call me any time, day or night, if the bug in Biff's pocket ever got anywhere near the one in Meg's pocket. And a lucky thing for Meg that I did!"

"And a lucky thing for Biff and Callie, too," Cordelia added.

"Yeah, how about that?" Rob said. "Biff wasn't the bad guy after all."

"He's a bad guy," I said. "Just not the killer."

"He's been stealing money from the Snack Shack for years," Caroline exclaimed. "Can you imagine anything that low? Stealing money from kids!"

When the chief's investigation was over, I expected we'd also find that he'd been systematically cheating his clients, defrauding the federal government, hiring and exploiting undocumented immigrants, and abusing his wife and children, psychologically and perhaps even physically. But given that the amounts were probably relatively small, stealing money first from the Little League and then from Summerball did seem like some kind of ultimate slimeball move.

On the bright side, during a lull in last night's events down at the police station, the county attorney had made a point of telling me that after reviewing the town square renovation contract, she felt confident that Biff had already given us ample cause for termination.

"Nothing to do with his arrest tonight," she'd said. "Since under law he hasn't been convicted of anything." But apparently the contract contained a small clause requiring the contractor to keep the county apprised of his progress at appropriate intervals, and the detailed records I'd kept of my calls, letters, and e-mails to Biff were more than sufficient to prove he'd violated that clause. Once again, my notebook-that-tells-me-when-to-breathe saved the day. Although the timing made me suspect the county attorney was a lot more willing to act now that she knew Biff was likely to be so involved in multiple criminal investigations that he wouldn't have the time — or funds — to fight us. But no matter the reason, it made my morning just a little brighter, knowing that Randall's trucks were already on their way to the town square, laden with tools and sod.

Caroline and Cordelia headed over to the bleachers, with Rob carrying their gear. I pulled out my phone and checked my e-mail. Aha! An e-mail I had been awaiting very eagerly had come in while I was driving the ladies to the ball field. I looked around for someone to share the news with. Michael and the boys should be here, since they'd insisted on watching every minute of baseball practice available, including the Pirates and Red Sox practices at 7:00 A.M. But where were they?

"Mrs. Waterston?"

I turned to find the gaunt figure of Samuel Yoder looming over me.

"Mr. Yoder," I said. "Come to see your grandson play?"

"Yes," he said. "I understand you're the one who suggested that Mr. Festus Hollingsworth get in touch with me about buying my farm."

"I am," I said. "I hope that's okay." I wasn't sure, from his scowling expression, that it was.

"It's more than okay." His voice trembled, and I realized what I thought was a scowl was probably his way of fighting back tears. "It's a blessing. I get to keep doing what I love — working on the land and with the animals — and your cousin says he'll worry about the financial side. A blessing."

"I'm glad," I said. I held out my hand, and he took it in both of his and shook it gently before turning and striding off toward the ball field.

"Meg! There you are." I turned around to see Chief Burke approaching me, with Mr. Witherington in his wake. I strolled over to meet them.

"Do you have the key to the Snack Shack?" the chief asked.

"Or could you pick the lock again?" Mr. Witherington suggested.

"I have the key," I said. "We weren't going to open quite this early."

"Mr. Brown claims that the reason he was here at the ball field yesterday morning was to deposit the Caerphilly Summerball League files there so you would find them later," the chief said. "If you don't mind?"

I led the way over to the shed and unlocked the door. Two black plastic file totes sat just inside the door, marked SUMMERBALL 1 and SUMMERBALL 2. The chief opened them both and flipped through the files for a few moments before nodding and stepping back.

"Seems to be just what he told us," the chief said. "Though if you don't mind, I'd like to take them with me for the time being. Mr. Witherington's going to file embezzlement charges against Mr. Brown, and we might need these for evidence. I'll have Kayla make you copies of everything."

"Why not have her make an inventory, and I'll tell you what I need copies of?" I said. "No sense killing more trees than necessary, and I have a feeling Biff's records might be a lot more useful to you than they ever will to me."

"Good plan," the chief said, with an approving nod.

"I've accepted Mr. Brown's resignation as coach of the Yankees and the Stoats," Mr. Witherington said. "I'm afraid you're going to have to scramble to find replacements."

"Already taken care of," I said. "My grandmother has volunteered to coach one of the teams, and just now I got an e-mail from Lem Shiffley. He doesn't feel up to running the league yet, but he'd be delighted to coach a team. I'll let the two of them settle who gets the Yankees and who gets the Stoats. Oh, and unless you have an objection, Tory Davis will be taking over as head coach of the Eagles. Chuck and Michael are fine with it."

"As am I," said Mr. Witherington. "In fact, I'm delighted with all three appointments."

"And I hope you're all as pleased as I am to know that Mr. Adolph Pruitt is once again behind bars," the chief announced.

"What for?" I asked.

"Horace matched some flakes of paint on Callie's truck to his truck," the chief said. "A hit-and-run that results in more than a thousand dollars in damage is a class five felony, punishable by up to ten years in prison. And that's assuming we don't decide to go for attempted murder."

"I assume this means we can all feel a little safer today," I said.

"Absolutely," the chief said.

I decided to take advantage of his visible good humor.

"By the way," I said. "Have we figured out how Edna fooled Ideen Shiffley into giving her an alibi?"

"By staging a completely plausible attack of migraine," the chief said, shaking his head. "Apparently Edna does actually suffer from migraines — so does Ideen, and they compared prescriptions before Edna retired to the guest room, drew the shades, and begged her hostess to make sure she wasn't disturbed till morning. Ideen was so busy tiptoeing around shushing her other guests that she never noticed the patient had flown the coop. She claims to have peeked every half hour or so, but I expect we'll find Edna resorted to the old pillow trick to fool her."

"What is the world coming to when we can't even rely on a busybody like Ideen to keep track of people?" I asked.

The chief pursed his lips, and I suspected he was fighting the temptation to utter an uncharitable remark about Ideen. Fortunately for his conscience a distraction intervened.

"Meg! Jim! Chief! I've got fantastic news!" We all turned to see Dad bouncing across the parking lot waving a sheaf of papers in one hand, with Grandfather trailing behind him.

"It seems to be quite the morning for good news," Mr. Witherington observed.

"Two of the doctors have already said yes," Dad panted out when he reached us.

"What doctors?" I asked.

"Your father agreed to contact some of the leading orthopedic surgeons who perform Tommy John surgery," Mr. Witherington explained, while Dad got his breath back. "Regardless of how much we deplore

Mrs. Edna Johnson's crime, the fact remains that her son has been badly treated, and deprived of much needed medical care. So even though his injury did not happen from playing in a Summerball program, the league has decided to make a substantial donation toward his surgery."

"And the online campaign we started to pay for the rest has already hit its goal," Dad exclaimed.

"And your cousin Festus has found her a good defense attorney," the chief said. "Not sure what kind of a case she's going to have, but who knows how any of us would react if something similar happened to the young ones entrusted to our care."

"Maybe Dad can find her a good psychiatrist," I suggested. "She could plead insanity. If anyone hurt Josh or Jamie the way Biff hurt her son, I might go around the bend."

"It's possible," the chief said. "And what happened to that boy should never have happened."

"Meanwhile, who's going to take care of the kid while his mother's in jail?" I asked. "And afterward, if needed?"

"He has family," the chief said. "Several aunts and uncles who are already falling all over each other to help out."

"And one way or another, we'll make sure he's okay," Mr. Witherington said.

We all stood looking solemn for a few moments.

"So what's that all about?" Cordelia had appeared, returning from the bleachers, and was pointing at something behind my back. "Randall, I thought you said your men had finished with the field."

I turned to see several Shiffley construction trucks turning into the parking lot.

"Yes, ma'am," Randall said. "The fields are as ready as they're going to be today. I'm just having my men unload some supplies for the next round of fixing up."

"What now?" I said. "Is something else wrong with the field?"

"Nothing that hasn't been wrong with it for years," Randall said. "As soon as today's games are over, we're going to start work."

"On what?" I realized I probably sounded a little combative. "I'm sure whatever you're planning will be fine, but I'm the acting league president at the moment, and I've had more than enough surprises already this week. Just fill me in."

"Take a look." Randall held up a large rolled-up paper and shook it as if in triumph. Then he unrolled it and held it up so I could see. Dad, Grandfather, Cordelia,

Mr. Witherington, and Chief Burke all crowded around to see as well.

It was a ball field. Not our ball field, because it had towering lights and spiffy new dugouts with wooden roofs. Along both sides were new, sturdy-looking bleachers covered with canvas sunshades, and to the right of the field, where the porta-potties now stood, was a building. A big sign saying "Snack Shack" hung over a wide service counter. You could see the suggestion of sinks and refrigerators behind the counter. And on the left and right sides of the building were arrows with the words MEN and WOMEN above them.

"It could take a few weeks to get the shell up," Randall said. "And a few more to get it all built out and pretty. But we're going to make the sinks and toilets our first priority."

"Awesome," I said. "Of course, those improvements won't be free — in fact, by the look of it, they're going to cost a pretty penny. Both in my role as your executive assistant and my new role as acting Summerball league president, I should point out that neither the league nor the Caerphilly government has a whole lot of surplus cash to throw at this."

"I have good news on the financial front," Randall said. "I've had a donor come forward and offer to pay for all the improvements we want to do to the field. Wants us to rename the field, but we were planning to do that anyway."

"As long as Biff isn't the donor," I said.

"Actually, I'm the donor," Grandfather said.

"You've already got a building at the college named after you," Cordelia said. "And now you want the baseball field, too? Getting a little greedy, aren't you?"

"Actually," Grandfather said, "I thought that might be a little over the top, so I was going to have them call it the Cordelia Lee Mason Field."

Cordelia blinked a couple of times, then frowned.

"Why do you want to do a fool thing like that?" she asked.

"You said it yourself," Grandfather said. "I've already got the theater building. And you're the baseball expert, not me."

"I can pay for my own field, thank you very much," Cordelia said. "Randall, you let me know how much you need for the field and I'll write you a check."

"I already wrote him a check, dammit," Grandfather bellowed.

"Folks, if you both want to donate baseball fields, there's also the elementary school field," Randall said. "Needs at least as much work as the county field."

"And if we could get that fixed up and re-configured to Summerball standards, it would certainly make scheduling games and practices a lot easier," I added. "And I know your great-grandsons would enjoy having a nice field to play on at school."

Grandfather and Cordelia glared at each other for a few long moments.

"Suit yourself," Grandfather said finally.

"Randall, you work up an estimate of how much both fields will cost," Cordelia said. "And I'll give you a check for half. We'll talk about this field naming thing later."

"Yes, ma'am," Randall said.

"Mommy! Mommy!" Josh and Jamie came running out. "The game's about to start."

"You go back and watch," I said. "I'll join you in a few minutes."

"No, Mommy," Josh said, frowning and shaking his head. "You have to throw out the first ball."

" 'Cause you're the boss now!" Jamie crowed. "And you get to yell 'Play ball!' "

"Here." Jim Witherington tossed me a brand-new baseball. Luckily, I didn't disgrace myself by dropping it.

"Okay," I said. "You guys want to come

with me and make sure I do it right?"

I tossed the ball to Michael so he could carry it and I could hold hands with both twins as we walked out to the pitcher's mound.

ABOUT THE AUTHOR

Donna Andrews is a winner of the Agatha, Anthony, and Barry awards, a *Romantic Times* Award for best first novel, and three Lefty and two Toby Bromberg awards for funniest mystery. She is a member of MWA, Sisters in Crime, and the Private Investigators and Security Association. Andrews lives in Reston, Virginia.